Contract

Killer

JIMMY DASAINT

and

NICHOLAS BLACK

1

JUL 15

PA

<u>*Author's note:*</u> The events described in this work are fiction. As in, *not real.* Have not happened. Probably won't happen. And, unless you're whacked-out on some powerful drugs, nothing you read could ever happen . . . ever! All the characters are made-up, no more real than fairies and goblins and space aliens. So, seriously, if you should accidentally find a name, person, place, or product that is similar to any *real,* or living person, place, or product, don't start laying lawsuits on us. It's a total and complete coincidence, and your lawyers will laugh at you. This especially applies to ex-girlfriends and former parole officers.

Published by DASAINT ENTERTAINMENT LLC.

Written by JIMMY DASAINT AND NICHOLAS BLACK

Edited by NICHOLAS BLACK

Copyright information:

ISBN: 978-0-9823111-3-4

For More information contact:

Jimmy DaSaint
DASAINT ENTERTAINMENT
Email: info@dasaintent.com
Website: www.dasaintentertainment.com

Nicholas Black
Website: www.Nicholasblackbooks.com

Contract Killer

"The most violent book in America. And I loved every minute of it!"

—*Freeway Ricky Ross, from BET's American Gangster Series.*

"Contract Killer is a modern day western that will be talked about for many years to come. If you are a person that enjoys non-stop action and constant drama, then this is the perfect book."

—*UrbanCelebrityMag.com*

Acknowledgments:

There's no way that this book would have been finished without the constant support and assistance of "Freeway" Ricky Ross. From start to finish he was behind us.

We need to give a special note to our friends in D-2. They got to listen to us argue almost nonstop about which direction the book should take. They even argued with us some times, and the book is better because of it. Specifically: Ryan, Watts, Mel, and Self.

And finally, to our man Hank Day, who helped us get this thing off the ground, proofread, edited, and turned into something that we think will become a classic.

Prologue

HE TOOK SEVERAL breaths, going through the routine that he had gone through so many times before. After a while, it just becomes habit. The sky was filled with dark clouds that seemed low enough to touch. As he relaxed his body he took five breaths, nice and slow. He had to lower his heart rate way   below   one   beat   per   second.

The best trained snipers in the world could lower their heart rate to the same speed as a person who was asleep. Ty Jacobs—Voodoo, as he was called by the few people who actually knew him—could lower his heart rate to 42 beats per minute. Only, he wasn't sleeping . . . he was waiting.

Watching.

He was a messenger.

And the message that he delivered was a mercury-tipped bullet delivered as several thousand feet-per-second.

He was several stories up, watching the small pieces of string he had tied up hours earlier, to see if the wind would affect his shot. The streamers were barely moving, so there was no reason to readjust the scope for windage.

He settled his body flat on the piece of black plastic. It was all about trigger control, now. No reason to rush. He did his homework, so there was no need to cut corners.

Then came the eyes. He blinked, in succession, 10 or 15 times to coat his eyes with liquid. That way, once he settled into the scope, he wouldn't have to blink as often. On either side of the sheet of black plastic were several small bags of rice, wrapped in socks. These would steady his rifle, a *Remington 700*, in .308 caliber.

This rifle was not designed for anything other than killing humans. Just a messenger.

He spread his legs, keeping them straight, his toes facing outwards as his heels dug into the edges of the plastic. His knees, thighs, stomach, and chest were flat on the ground. His right arm was bent, his palm and fingers holding the rifle tight to his right shoulder.

His left hand was folded under the stock of the gun, with one of the rice bags in his hand. With just the slightest pressure from his left hand the back of the rifle would lift, bringing the scope down on his target.

His eyes instantly picked-up the limousine making its way down the street below. Beside his rifle were six gray canisters that looked like coke cans, with key rings hanging from the tops—flash and smoke grenades.

Even the busy New Yorkers took a second to glance at the stretched, white Lincoln Limo. The kind of ride that makes a statement. His right eye was looking through a 4 ½ by 14 scope that could see well past 1000 yards. But this was going to be a relatively easy shot. From this distance he could put out Washington's eyes out on a quarter.

As the shiny white limo came to a stop, the doors popped open and several well-armed men in high-dollar suits jumped out of the front and back, clearing the area from the edge of the street to the entrance to the *Tiffany's* Jewelers. People that rode around in limos like that, with bodyguards that sharp, were usually very important, or very powerful.

Voodoo didn't care which.

His finger tightened down on the trigger delicately as the tiny cross-hairs found a beautiful, dark-complected latin woman with shoulder-length black hair. She took her time stepping from the limo. She was wearing tinted *Gucci* sunglasses. She had on a brown leather coat that probably cost as much as most people's cars. She was model thin, with long legs, and wore black pants that might have been sprayed on they were so tight.

Voodoo took several breaths, then slowly let the air escape from his lungs. He released all of the tension in his body. Perfectly in focus, the latin woman turned and reached a hand out to a small boy, probably five or six-years-old.

She led him, with his curly black hair, out to the sidewalk where they were immediately flanked by several bodyguards on each side. Each of the bodyguards had their arms floating near their jackets, where pistols and small machine guns were waiting to be put to use.

Voodoo took one final breath, and then he slowly exhaled half of the air and waited. This was where a sniper was most deadly . . . the half-breath pause.

No movement.

No shaking.

No anxiety.

Nothing other than mathematics. The cross-hairs sat near the woman's head until the child with his mange of hair and his blue sweater turned to look at something in the street.

Without hesitation his left hand tensed ever so slightly, bringing the cross-hairs down to the child, the tiny dot in the middle of the cross-hairs floating near his upper lip. Without guilt or remorse, he added just the slightest extra pull on the trigger.

And then, as he watched through the scope . . . everything seemed to slow down.

The mother started to say something to the little boy.

. . . *the bullet racing down!*

She blinked between words.

. . . *the bullet racing down!*

He turned the side of his mouth into something that might have been a smile.

. . . *Thump!*

The mercury-tipped slug entered just above the small boy's top lip, folding the upper teeth, and everything else in his mouth into the shock wave that folded the bullet through his brain.

Instantaneous kill shot!

And because of the speed of the travelling bullet, his head exploded before anyone on the ground even heard the shot. One second he was a smiling, happy child. The next . . . he was an inanimate piece of flesh and bone, no more alive than the mailbox or a street sign.

The mother, several of the bodyguards, and most of the sidewalk below was painted in a red and gray splatter with bits of white bone and curly black hair. The bodyguards immediately tackled the mother, protecting her, and what was left of the child, gun barrels pointing in every direction.

Voodoo turned away. Still, there was no nervousness, no apprehension. He was as relaxed as if he had just finished watching the weather report. As disinterested as if he's just read the ingredients on the back of a cereal box.

He was just an anonymous guy delivering a message.

With a quick but controlled cadence, he began to strip down the rifle like he had done it a thousand times before. He broke it into several smaller parts that were then wrapped inside of the plastic sheet he had been laying on.

Below him there were screams and horns and alarms echoing between the buildings, but none of that was his concern. His first job was finished. 28 seconds later, the rifle was wrapped in plastic, unrecognizable.

Now he had to affect his escape from the area. That's where the grenades came in. He grabbed the smoke grenades, one after the next, pulling the pins, and throwing them over the right, front, and left sides of the building. They would quickly blanket the area in a thick grey smoke that people would instantly take notice of.

The flash grenades came next, in the same pattern, following the smoke grenades down to the ground where the ear-shattering explosions would surely startle the crowd of unknowing onlookers.

With the buildings being as tightly packed as they were, the ensuing echoes and explosions that they would make would startle most people into a panic. He was, of course, playing off of the hysteria that 9/11 had created.

You even mention bomb in New York and you have yourself a stampede.

And so he pulled the pins and tossed all of the grenades as he counted in his head the seconds until chaos would ensue.

5 . . . 4 . . .

He got to his feet.

3 . . . 2 . . .

He started towards the stairwell.

Boom!

Ba-boom! Boom!

Voodoo wasted no time in making his way into the stairwell and entering the building as the explosions from the flash-bangs were still rattling the air around him. There were already people evacuating, running and screaming, thinking the worst.

With his glasses on, his black leather jacket hanging loosely over a clean white t-shirt, he could have been anybody. Just another scared New Yorker, hoping that jets weren't crashing into the buildings again. With his dark skin and chiseled features, he was just another worried guy, trying to get to safety . . . wherever that might be.

An elderly woman wearing a white jogging suit and tennis shoes bumped into him, causing the rifle parts in the plastic bag to rattle together awkwardly.

"What's going on?" she said, her face twisted with fear.

He shrugged, glancing back over his shoulder, "Al Qaeda, maybe."

The woman's face flushed white as she turned back to the crowd of people going in every direction.

He toggled the cell phone in his jacket pocket that called a pre-programmed set of numbers. Each number was to a different cell phone in the surrounding buildings. And each of those cell phones was wired to the fire alarms in those buildings. With each call a new alarm would go off. Another building thrown into chaos and panic. Thousands of people would be pouring into the smoke- and blood-filled streets.

11

Confusion and disorder . . . the perfect cover.

He would be hidden in plain sight.

Hearing the words "Al Qaeda" come out of his mouth the woman's eyes grew three times larger as she fought her way down the stairs, pulling and clawing past her neighbors. Like a log caught in a rushing river, Voodoo flowed among the terrified mothers and frightened children as they descended to the street. In a situation like this, there was no *right* way to run. So he went left.

He found the alley, and made his way to the third blue dumpster. Without missing a beat he pushed the dumpster aside to reveal an open manhole. He dropped the plastic bag, and all of its parts down into the darkness below, not waiting for a noise.

He then slid the heavily rusted cover back over the manhole and re-positioned the dumpster back over the hole. He began to fast walk down the alley, to another dumpster, where he took off a pair of silicon surgical gloves, wadding them up in a ball, and placing them in an unfinished carton of Sweet-n-sour pork. He tossed the carton back into the dumpster.

Time to play scared, he thought to himself as he exited the alley. New York's finest were skidding around, jumping curbs, and flashing sirens. Firetrucks and ambulances were appearing from every direction. He was three blocks away from the site of the shooting, figuring that in the next few minutes they would send somebody up to the roofs of every building in the area. They would do their dusting and printing, and look for trace evidence.

But there wouldn't be any of that. They would look for a bullet casing, like the one he had dropped down into the manhole. *Good luck with that*, he thought.

As he descended the stairs that led to the subway he looked for a public phone. At the bottom of the stairs, about 10 feet from the turnstile, there was a pay phone. He slid some quarters in and dialed the number that he had committed to memory.

And he waited.

A voice with a thick Russian accent answered, "Hyello?"

"Excuse me," Voodoo said, " . . . may I speak to Ari?"

"No Ari live here," the voice growled.

"My mistake," Voodoo apologized, "I must have miss-dialed."

"Yeah . . . may-bee so," the voice replied. *Click.* And then the line went dead.

Voodoo placed the phone back on the metal hook and headed for a subway car. As he was walking a few policemen had made their way down into the subway station, and they were asking if anyone had seen anything strange in the last few minutes. One of them glanced over at Voodoo and lifted his hands as if to stop him.

"Foreigners," Voodoo snorted to the cop, shaking his head as he walked by. The officer nodded and then turned back to the gathering crowd of frightened onlookers.

37 minutes later he was walking out of an elevator with a large bag full of Chinese food, making his way to the front door of his loft apartment. As he reached forward with the key, his neighbor, Antonio Ferretti—a New York Police officer—backed out of the next door down the hall. He seemed to be in a hurry . . . more so than normal.

Antonio was dressed in his cop's uniform, with a bullet-proof vest half on, dangling from his left arm as he locked the door. He noticed Voodoo.

"Ty!" he said, surprised to see his neighbor. "Total mess out there. Did you hear?"

Voodoo furled his eyebrows curiously, shaking his head.

"Total fuckin' nightmare," Antonio said. "Somebody shot a kid in front of *Tiffany's*. Kid was the son of some El Salvadorian mob boss," he explained, his voice thick with a Brooklyn accent.

"Geez," Voodoo said, his face looking shocked.

"I gotta go do an extra shift. People think it's the end of the world or some shit. Total fuckin' nightmare. I gotta go!" And with that he raced down the hall towards the elevator.

"Hope you catch 'em," Voodoo said as he turned to his door and inserted the key. But it was all a facade.

Voodoo took no pleasure in his work. He felt no pain or sorrow. He didn't get happy or sad or depressed or elated. He was a tool . . . an instrument like any surgeon might use. There was no emotion in how he made his living.

He was just the messenger.

ONE

BRONX, NEW YORK
LATER THAT NIGHT...

AFTER RETURNING HOME from the medical examiner's office, Juan-Carlos walked over to the sofa and sat sadly down as if he was made of lead, his entire body sinking as he did so. An empty look seemed etched into his face.

He still couldn't believe that his only child—six-year-old Juan-Carlos Jr.—had been murdered in broad daylight. What had made it even worse was that it had happened in the heart of downtown Manhattan, in front of a group of well-trained bodyguards and thousands of onlookers. This loss felt even worse than when his wife Maria had died from cancer two-and-a-half years ago.

That was pain.

This was something indescribably worse. There were not words sufficient to describe the torment he was suffering. Juan-Carlos sat back, his head hanging down as four of his top men stood near him in silence.

Sitting in a chair right across from him was his beautiful, 22-year-old bride, Carmen. Her eyes were bloodshot red from crying all day. And the slightest noise made her shake.

After seeing Carlos Jr. die right in front of her, she had been a nervous wreck.

Juan-Carlos was the 42-year-old boss of the El Salvadorian gang known as the 'Matas'. *Killers*. They were a violent gang of men that had migrated from the poorest slums in Central America, to the poor ghettos along the east coast of America. Besides New York, the Matas were in Philadelphia, parts of New Jersey, Baltimore, and Washington DC.

The Matas were involved in everything from selling drugs, to extortion, kidnapping, prostitution, and murder. The mayor of New York had proclaimed them the most violent gang in the city after several murders involving machetes took place out in public. It was the kind of thing that *CNN* and *MSNBC* couldn't even air without blurring the images.

In the past three years the Matas were responsible for the murder of rival drug dealers, three police officers, an assistant District Attorney, and a member of the city council. And that wasn't even the entire list.

Juan-Carlos ran his organization with an iron fist. Either you followed his rules, or you found yourself getting chopped to pieces by one of his enforcers and scattered in the Hudson River. See, the Matas didn't want to hide the bodies of their victims. Every murder was a warning. A statement.

No exceptions.

No gray area.

At just over 5 ½ feet tall he was short compared to all of the people he ruled over. Even his beautiful wife Carmen was a couple inches taller than he was. But what Juan-Carlos lacked in height, he made up for in power and influence. At the snap of a finger someone's life could be snatched away from them.

He had men in his organization that were devoted soldiers. Men who would not hesitate to put their life on the line to save his and to enforce his will on others. If he told them, they would kill someone for no reason at all. Without so much as a curious breath.

They only needed his direction. And the ones who were caught by law enforcement all stood by a code, not only of silence, but of disdain.

Death before dishonor. They'd spit in a detectives face before they would answer a single question. They didn't even have a word for cooperation.

He didn't have snitches in his organization. You worked with the cops, you die. Your family dies. Your kids, your friends, and everything else you ever loved would die.

If you turned on the Matas . . . they would come for you with their sharpened machetes. No words. No expressions on their faces. Just blood in their eyes. And it wouldn't be fast. Death would be measures in hours, not in minutes or seconds.

Juan-Carlos looked up at his best friend and confidant, Caesar. He was a tall, brown-skinned man with a handsome face and short dark hair. At 33-years-old, Caesar was Juan's right hand man. The violent underboss that many considered more dangerous than Juan-Carlos, himself. Caesar was a man that rarely talked. Instead, he chose to let his pistol or machete fill in all the blanks.

"I don't care how long it takes!" Juan-Carlos yelled angrily as he spat, "I want every last one of those niggers dead!" He used his hand to wipe his face. "Dead!"

Caesar approached his hurting friend and said, "Don't worry, Juan, I'm already on it. The Black Royals will get everything that's coming. Those pinches pendejos van a saber!"

17

His words were solid and reassuring. And the message was clear: Those *fucking idiots are going to find out!*

Juan-Carlos stood up from the sofa and looked up into Caesar's dark eyes. "Ellos han matado mi hijo!"

They have killed my son.

" . . . and now, I have to bury him next to his mother. What kind of father has to bury his son . . . next to his wife? Today . . . part of me has died along with him, and the only way for me to feel any relief is to know that every last Black Royal has been killed. Caesar, you're going to make that happen."

"I will. No te molestes. I will," Caesar said without hesitation.

Juan-Carlos leaned forward and kissed Caesar on both sides of his face, a customary gesture of deep respect. Juan-Carlos then stood up and walked over to his sobbing young wife. He placed his hand delicately on her shoulder, "Carmen, are you . . . are you okay?"

"I'll be fine," she said, using her hands to wipe away the tears. Juan-Carlos watched as Carmen stood up slowly and turned to him. "I need some air. Today has been one of the worst days of my life. I just . . . I can't breathe."

Juan-Carlos reached out and took Carmen's trembling hands. "Don't worry, my love. The people responsible will pay."

Carmen stared into her husband's eyes, "I know they will. But that still won't bring back my step-son." She reached down on the chair and grabbed her car keys and purse. "I really need some air, and time to gather my thoughts. Today has been," she wiped her eyes again as the tears rolled down her cheeks.

She swallowed, "I'm going for a drive."

Juan-Carlos looked nervous, "I don't know if that's a good idea with everything that happened. Do you want some of my men to follow you?"

"No," Carmen said, "I'll be fine. If those monsters had wanted to kill me, they would have already. I just need to go and clear my head. I'll meet you back at the house in a few hours."

"I won't be here," Juan-Carlos said. "Caesar and I have to make a trip down to Philadelphia. I won't be back home until tomorrow afternoon."

Carmen leaned forward and kissed the mob boss softly on the lips, and as she backed away her hands gently stroked his cheek. "When you return from Philly, I'll be at home waiting for you. And don't worry, I'll be just fine."

Juan-Carlos watched as Carmen turned and walked away. When she had left the house, he looked over at a couple of his men and nodded, "Follow her and make sure she is safe."

"Si, Jeffe," the two men said as they turned and walked out the front door with purpose in their steps.

From a window Juan-Carlos watched the two soldiers climb inside a black *Cadillac Escalade*. As they rolled off, Carmen was already halfway down the street.

Inside her all-white *Mercedes Benz*, she glanced in the rearview mirror before making a sharp left turn at the corner. She knew that Juan-Carlos would always send a few of his men to watch and follow her. He was over-protective and extremely jealous. Even though Carmen had never given him any reason to feel that way . . . he was only human.

Seeing the black truck following her, she stepped on the gas pedal and maneuvered the *Mercedes* quickly through the slower moving traffic. Putting more and more cars between them, she finally glanced back, in the rearview mirror. Pretty soon the *Escalade* was nowhere to be found.

Tonight, Carmen didn't want to be followed, she needed a break and some time to clear her mind.

SOUTH BRONX, NEW YORK
INSIDE A HOUSE ON 138ᵀᴴ AND WILLIS AVENUE . . .

Reggie King looked over at his younger brother, Ronnie, and smiled. They were the two bosses of the Black Royals drug organization. And the number one enemy of the Matas. For three years both sides had been killing each other over drugs, prostitution, and territory. Both King brothers were tall, with athletic physiques, and dark complexions.

Reggie was 32-years-old, four years older than his brother Ronnie. The Black Royals had over 75 made members in their organization. Reggie was considered the brains, and Ronnie was the muscle and heart. Each month the Black Royals were bringing in millions of dollars from all of their illegal activities.

But with the sudden rise of the Matas, they had seen their money and territory slowly dwindling. With each lost inch, their war with the Matas had escalated.

"The hit on Juan's son was exactly what we needed," Reggie said as he nodded. "The message is pretty fucking clear. Now he knows this shit ain't no game!"

He took a few steps, peering at his brother, "There's no rules in war, and kids are not excluded. Being five don't give you a pass. We'll turn this bitch into Bagdad on their punk asses!"

"Fuck all them fake-ass Mexicans!" Ronnie added. "That was payback for what they did to Leroy with that machete."

He was breathing hard, his fists clenched as his jaw tightened. He took some time to regain his composure.

Ronnie then sighed and looked down at his gold *Rolex* watch, "I have to make a run somewhere."

Reggie smiled and said, "Take one of the men with you. From now on, there are no rules. We have to be extra safe. You know they'll be gunning for us."

"I'm not worried about them. They should be worried about me!"

"They're not stupid," Reggie warned. "They'll put this together in no time. They might be planning right now."

Just as Ronnie was about to say something his cell phone started ringing. He quickly answered it, listening to the muffled voice. He nodded a couple times and said, "I'll be there shortly."

He closed the phone and turned to his brother, "I don't need nobody to watch me tonight, I'll be fine." And a large grin crept across Ronnie's statuesque face.

"I'll see you later?" Reggie asked.

"Probably not. Tonight is kinda special," Ronnie said, grabbing his jacked and heading towards the front door. "Don't wait up," he yelled back as he shut the door behind him.

TWO

VOODOO STEPPED OUT of the shower, his feet leaving wet prints on the granite tiles as he walked. He studied his face in the mirror as the steam circled around the bathroom behind him.

His face that nobody knew.

His eyes and nose and chin that looked as if they were cut from the same granite that the floor tiles were. His body was a machine; a finely honed device. He splashed some cold water on his face, and raised his head as his eyes slowly opened. As the droplets of water fell from his eyebrows and rolled off of his nose, he took a deep breath, wondering if this was normal.

Why didn't it bother him that he could do the things he could do?

Why didn't it hurt him to kill people?

Why didn't he feel a single, tiny, echo of emotion? His mind was like a copy of a copy, too far removed to feel anything real. There was no substance, to his emotions. No flavor.

22

The money was nice . . . but that wasn't it, either.

He raised a dark blue towel and blotted his face, then wrapped the towel around his waist as he turned away from the mirror. There were no answers in his reflection. There were no solutions to be found by staring at himself. He just . . . *was.*

He left the bathroom wearing only the dark blue towel around his waist. He walked quietly across the thick gray carpet in the bedroom. He could hear some anchorman's words as he broke down the catastrophe that had occurred in Manhattan.

" . . . *I'm saying, simply, that there are no more rules in a gang war,*" the voice said caustically. "*No matter who you are, if you get in between these types of people, you're dead. They don't care about the value of life. They might as well be extremist terrorists. They don't care about . . .* "

He walked through his bedroom, and then out into the living room where the flat screen plasma television was fixed to the wall like a painting. He walked past a white leather couch, grabbing the television's remote, and stood in the center of the living room.

With the remote hanging at his wrist, he muted the screen, standing there in the middle of silence, the images of the killing repeated over and over. They had some grainy footage from a security camera that captured the little boy's head exploding.

Over and over.

There was only so much footage that the news agencies had of the event, so they would run it over and over, until every New Yorker could dream about it in real-time.

A copy of a copy of a copy.

On the couch behind him, something moved. Voodoo didn't turn around. He knew she was sitting there. Waiting for him.

"If you turn the sound down, you can't hear what they're saying," the soft voice said. She unfolded her legs and stood, slowly approaching him from behind. He still didn't answer her. He might have been a statue for all she knew.

Angie was just over five feet tall, with smooth light skin, and a perfectly proportioned body. "There's a lot to be learned from the news," she said as she closed to within inches of his back."

He turned his head sideways, not enough to see her, really, just to catch her in his peripheral vision. And right at the point where he was about to say something, he turned back to the television, lifted the remote, and the screen went black. He tossed the remote over onto the sofa as he turned around to look at her.

Her eyes were a light hazel color, wide and liquidly. She didn't wear a lot of makeup because she had a natural beauty that left little room for improvement. And, barely hidden beneath the *Victoria's Secret* nightgown, her breasts were full and perky.

His eyes studied the black fabric that was barely covering her body, raised near her nipples. She had her belly button pierced with a small green stone fit in silver.

Her lips were slightly open as she studied him, trying to figure out what was going on in there. "What are you thinking about?"

He stared at her, his eyes resting on a part of her body, then slowly moving on to another, and another.

Slowly, she placed her hands on his shoulders, quietly tracing the muscles in his chest. Inch by inch, they continued making their way across his washboard stomach, until they were just above the towel.

With a slow, delicate touch she ran her fingers around his waist, feeling both his skin and the soft towel beneath her fingertips. "Sometimes," she whispered, "I think you're a robot."

He didn't answer with words, but she could tell that he was listening to her . . . feeling her touch.

Her hand slowly crept down beneath the towel, stroking the inside of his thigh, purposely torturing him. Her hand climbed higher as she pressed her chest against his. "You're a mute," she said as she kissed him on the neck. "That's it. You can't talk because you're a mute."

The towel dropped to the floor between them.

He used his fingers to slide off the thin strings of black silk that held her nightgown on. Seconds later, the black fabric fell between their bodies, gathering at their feet on top of the towel.

He reached down to her waist, spinning her around so that he was behind her.

She turned her head to the side not really looking *at* him, but in the general direction. "Oh, so now you want to fuck me? Not a word, huh?" She smiled, waiting for a response.

"You shouldn't talk so much," he said as his hands reached slowly around her waist, stroking her wetness gently.

She swallowed, feeling him hard behind her as her heart rate soared. "You . . . you can talk," she said as she swallowed. Her eyes closed as his fingers rubbed her into a state of near frenzy.

Her body started to writhe in anticipation. "Why do you like me?"

25

He didn't answer as he continued to stimulate her, causing her to twist and arch.

"Of all the girls you could call, you keep calling me," she said, her words sporadic and slurred as she started to feel the electricity pulse through her body. She knew she would be moaning soon.

"I like you," he said, as he picked her up and carried her towards the bedroom, " . . . because you don't talk too much."

THE HILTON HOTEL, MANHATTAN
45 MINUTES LATER . . .

Carmen stepped off of the elevator on the eighth floor, then nervously looked around as the door swept closed behind her. The hallway was completely empty, but still, she knew that it was better to be safe than sorry. She walked slowly down the hall and stopped at room #805.

After inserting her card-key into the door, it clicked open and she stepped quickly inside. The large elegant suite was dimly lit, and the smooth, soulful voice of Jill Scott was filling the air.

Carmen laid her purse down on a small glass table near the entrance. Then, with a big smile of anticipation forming on her face, she walked back towards the master bedroom.

After turning the knob, the door opened to the exquisitely furnished bedroom. Everything was first-class.

She paused to admire the tall, dark, ruggedly handsome man that was laying across the bed, completely naked. Every muscle in his body was cut and defined as if he'd been created by a sculptor.

"What took you so long?" Ronnie said, folding his arms behind his head, the gentle flutter of a candle reflecting off of his glistening body.

She approached him slowly, "I had to lose the guys that were following me. And the traffic was a little more heavy than normal."

Ronnie nodded his head and watched as Carmen started to undress. After kicking off her $400 *Gucci* heels, she started to take off the matching black *Gucci* dress. Her skin was honey brown, and flawless.

Ronnie watched with pleasure as Carmen slid the dress down her curvaceous body. And just like all of the times they had secretly met before, Carmen wasn't wearing any underwear.

Her body was a work of Spanish art. She could fill the cover of any magazine and not look out of place. She had the type of body that made men look twice. Carmen stepped out of her dress and joined her black lover in bed.

She cuddled up beside him and looked deep into his brown eyes. "They couldn't wait until I got into the store before they shot that spoiled little brat? His blood splattered all over my new jacket." She almost hissed. "You know . . . all of those clothes are ruined."

Ronnie had a wry smile on his face as he spoke, "I told you before that I have no say in any of that. Just trust me, you'll never be harmed."

Carmen studied him for a moment, her eyes narrow and skeptical. Slowly she leaned forward, her face softening. She kissed him on the lips, backing just inches away, "I trust you. Just don't fuck with me . . . *fuck* me."

As Ronnie started to rub his hand along her hips, he said, "Still not ready to give me the scoop?"

27

Carmen sat up on the bed and looked deep into Ronnie's eyes, "I told you before . . . what goes on between you and my husband is between you two, only. I will not tell you any of his secrets. Not that he ever tells me anything, anyway."

She shook her head slowly, "I'm not your spy. And even though I enjoy being with you, the Matas are still my people."

Carmen took a deep breath, studying Ronnie's eyes, "Please, don't ask me questions that you know I won't ever answer. Leave me out of your little war." Her tone was serious.

Ronnie grinned as he sat up on the bed next to her, "You're right. Let us men handle things the way we do." Delicately he laid her back on the bed and climbed his dark naked body on top of her. They started passionately kissing, tongues twisting inside each other's mouths like slithering snakes.

As he kissed and sucked around her neck, he used his legs to spread hers apart. Everything was smooth, as if he'd done it so many times before. They had their own cadence. This could be a well rehearsed dance between them.

"You ready?" he whispered softly into her ear as he kissed the side of her neck and shoulder.

"Yes, Papi," she said, positioning herself and wrapping her arms around his muscular body. "I'm ready."

After sucking on her erect nipples he raised his body, his hips coming close to hers. Both of their eyes were filled with wanting lust.

Ronnie placed both of Carmen's legs on top of his broad shoulders. Then he looked into her beautiful face and just smiled. In one smooth motion, he slid his hard black dick deep into her hot, wet pussy. As he started stroking, in and out, he watched as Carmen began to moan out in ecstasy.

With every thrust he pushed harder inside of her, and each time he did so Carmen dug her manicured nails deeper into his back.

"Yes, Papi! Oooohh! Yessss, Papi!" she cried out in explosions of pure bliss, her body shaking with each thrust of his hips.

For the last six months, Ronnie had been giving Carmen the best sex she had ever experienced. Enough to keep her sneaking off, two and sometimes three times a week. She was sexually hooked, as if what he gave her was a forbidden drug . . . but then, so was he.

Ronnie was determined to one day break her, and get Carmen to tell him all about her husband's organization. But all in good time.

The best things in life come to those who wait.

In the tranquility of their private hotel suite, Carmen was pinned down on the bed, moaning out in pleasure as her body quivered. She was receiving the fucking of her life, from her husband's number one enemy, and loving every single moment of it.

And even though she knew she was risking her life . . . she had no choice. She needed what only Ronnie could give her. And she needed it a lot.

THREE

ON THE CORNER of 178th Street the tinted black van was parked, and two of the Matas' most violent street enforcers were patiently waiting inside. Their names were Pepe and Felipe, and violence was all that they knew. They had an advanced education in torture.

Both men had dark black curly hair and darkish brown complexions that looked as if they had been living on beaches for their entire lives.

Pepe was the shorter of the two, standing just an inch over five feet. His partner in crime, murder, and torture was Felipe; standing taller at nearly six feet. It was their job to protect all the drug territories owned by the Matas.

They were also involved with kidnapping, extortion, and murder. Tattooed across both of their chests in bold black letters, were the words,

Matadores Por Vida

Killers for life.

And the men both swore and lived by those words.

Pepe and Felipe sat back in their seats, patiently waiting. They had been there for over an hour. Loaded 9mm pistols were resting in their hands. But the pistols weren't their weapons of choice. Not for the type of pain that these two liked to inflict. Guns were more of a convenience.

Instead, they preferred the two sharpened machetes that were inside of a long black leather bag, waiting inches below Pepe's seat.

They watched as the front door of an apartment building suddenly opened and a tall, light-skinned man walked out of the house. Standing right behind him was an attractive Spanish woman. The man and woman kissed passionately before she turned and walked back into the apartment, closing the door behind her.

The man stood on the porch for a moment, looking up and down the street. It was in his nature to be skeptical and paranoid. Not only was this mainly a Spanish section ruled by the Matas, but an assassination had just taken place.

He stepped down and made his way across the walkway towards his parked red, *Dodge Magnum*. The man's name was Calvin King. He was the younger cousin of Reggie and Ronnie King, and one of their top street lieutenants. He knew his way around the game . . . or so he thought.

Calvin had just finished enjoying a wonderful night of sex with a woman named Maria, who he had met a few days earlier at a bar in Harlem. Now he was on his way back home, at the Forest Projects, to take a shower and get some sleep.

The sky was dark and the street was completely empty and calm. When Calvin reached his car he noticed the tinted black van parked right behind it. Before he could reach the handle, the doors of the tinted van flew open.

Pepe and Felipe rushed out suddenly, pointing their weapons at Calvin's head. He was caught completely off guard, and all that he could do was throw up his hands as he ducked his head. You know when you're outnumbered.

"Get in the van or die where you stand!" Pepe told him in his Spanish-accented English.

"Fuck!" Calvin muttered to himself. He knew that he had no other choice but to obey the man's order. As he looked at the two gunmen, the thing that stuck with him was their eyes. They were cold and vacant. It didn't take a genius to realize that doing anything other than what they said would get him ventilated.

Maybe it's just a robbery-kidnapping, he thought to himself. Perhaps they just wanted a nice ransom before letting him go? *Maybe?* That's what he kept telling himself as they led him to the van.

It had happened many times before. Low-life street thugs robbing and kidnapping drug dealers for some cash. This was probably just a quick score. *No worries,* he kept telling himself. *Just be cool. Do what they say.*

As the doors to the van slid closed, Felipe glanced back with a sinister smile and then started the engine. The van made its way down the dark street, disappearing into the night.

Calvin was handcuffed and sitting on the back seat. Pepe was sitting across from him, leaning against the wall of the van, his eyes barely open. The 9mm in his right hand was laying across his lap, pointing at Calvin's stomach. Any attempt to escape would be bloody and futile.

32

Calvin watched nervously as Pepe placed the pistol inside his belt, behind his back, and reached for the black leather bag.

Pepe's face slowly became more animated as if some button had been pressed. His eyes became vibrant and alive, a devilish grin starting to form.

Something inside of Calvin, that voice that had been telling him to relax, was now quiet and nervous. This wasn't a simple robbery-kidnapping. These weren't simple street thugs looking for a come-up. In this van of total silence, Calvin closed his eyes and began to pray. He began to see all of the things in his life that he truly cared about. All of those precious memories that might soon disappear.

}}}

VOODOO'S APARTMENT...

"Here," Voodoo said as he tossed Angie her clothes. She had been milling around for a couple of minutes, barely awake, and still worn out.

"Is that your way of telling a lady she needs to leave?" she said sarcastically as she used her fingers to comb her hair behind her ears.

Voodoo walked out of the bedroom, already wearing a pair of faded jeans and a black, hooded sweatshirt.

Angie watched him from the bed as she unfolded her clothes and found $300 in crisp 20-dollar bills. She looked around the bedroom at all of the artwork—various black and white sketches of different buildings. She watched as he walked back and forth from the living room to the kitchen.

"What are you doing?" she asked softly.

33

With no answer, she started to slip back-on the *Victoria's Secret* nightgown, and then her dark green blouse and skirt. Her eyes glanced around for her heels, which were still out by the white couch in the living room.

As she made her way quietly across the threshold, he surprised her with a glass of cold orange juice and a banana. She just couldn't figure him out.

"Is this . . . breakfast?" She laughed, "Who eats bananas?"

"Potassium and vitamin C," he said as he picked up his cell phone and dialed a number, " . . . it's good for you."

"Are *you* good for me?" she said as she sat at the couch, drinking her juice as she wiggled her toes into her black heels.

He smiled briefly, kind of laughing to himself, as he placed the cell phone to his ear.

The phone rang twice before the familiar Russian voice picked-up.

"Da?"

"It's me," Voodoo said.

"We need to . . . ah . . . talk, ti pani-mayish?" the voice said.

"Yeah," Voodoo said glancing across the room at a small clock. "Where?"

"You know my favorite place to eat," the Russian said.

"Yeah."

"Sorak-pyat minuti," the voice instructed.

45 minutes.

"Okay," Voodoo answered as the line went dead.

He glanced over at Angie, watching her place the large glass of orange juice to her mouth like a small child. So simple. So full of innocence.

"Tell me, again, why you like me," Angie said as she lowered the glass, still not having eaten even a bit of the banana.

"I like you because you don't eat too much," he said, making her giggle.

She walked forward until they were just inches apart. She was looking up into his dark eyes. He was looking down at her.

" . . . now burn off," he said as he reached around and slapped her on the ass.

She narrowed her eyes playfully at him, took about half a step, and then leaned in quickly, giving him a kiss on the cheek. He tilted his head to the side like a curious dog, trying to figure her out.

"I'm going to understand you, one of these days," Angie said as she headed towards the door. On her way she left the empty glass and untouched banana on his kitchen counter.

"You'll see . . . " her voice trailed off as the door opened and closed.

And again, there was silence in the apartment.

He sat there for a moment, as the wetness from her kiss slowly evaporated from his cheek. *Odd girl*, he thought as he grabbed the banana for himself.

He then gathered up his wallet and two *Spyderco* knives, placing one in his pants, and the other on the inside of his left boot. Glancing around the apartment one last time he nodded, and then headed out the front door.

It was time to go and see his old friend, Victor.

}}}

VICE AVENUE

Inside a house on Vice Avenue, Pepe, Felipe, and their victim Calvin were all down inside the large humid basement. Calvin's naked body was completely covered in a thick red mat of liquid, tied down to a long wooden table that was stained brown and black from the half-dried blood.

His mouth was gagged with thick silver duct tape, and blood and mucus had stained both the tape, and his face and neck. He looked like he had gotten into a car accident.

For two long hours, Calvin had been systematically beaten and tortured. Dark red and bluish bruises were all over his swollen face. He looked more like the elephant man, than the man on his driver's license.

Blood was dripping slowly from his flattened nose and busted lips that were swollen to the size of hotdogs they were so puffed out. Calvin stared out, in a daze, way past fear. Pepe and Felipe stood over him. Both of them were holding long machetes, hand-sharpened on both sides of the blade.

"Nigger," Pepe said, placing the blade of the machete against Calvin's neck, "we know who you are. And you're gonna get it just like your friend . . . Lee-roy." His eyebrows fluttered up and down, "You remember Lee-roy, don't you?"

"Hold on!" a voice ordered from behind.

When Pepe and Felipe turned, they saw Maria standing at the bottom of the steps with a big smile on her face. Clutched tightly inside her right hand was a sharp, 12-inch kitchen knife. She walked over towards them, and when Calvin's eyes focused through his swollen cheeks and eye sockets he recognized her.

Trying to swallow the blood that continued to gather in his throat he mumbled some unrecognizable words as a tear managed to roll down his boulder of a face.

He had been set-up.

Played like the fool of fools.

Maria looked into Calvin's trembling eyes and said, "Your dick has gotten you in a whole lot of trouble, tonight."

Then Calvin watched as Maria grabbed a handful of her long, black hair and lifted it up. As she slowly turned her body around he saw the small tattoo on the back of her neck.

Matadores Por Vida.

Killers For Life.

Pepe tapped the frightened man on the chest with the tip of his machete, each time leaving a small slice in his dark skin that started to bleed.

"Hey, puta," he said with ice in his words, "you need to tell me who the fuck killed Juan-Carlos' kid."

He took a step back and smiled, "I'm hoping that you don't answer me at first. See, all of this," Pepe said as he sliced across Calvin's stomach, " . . . all of this is for me, mother-fucker. We haven't even begun the questions, yet, because this is like . . . our little fun. So when I finally *do* ask you a question, you need to know that I'm gonna skin you for each wrong answer."

Then Pepe leaned in and spit on Calvin's stomach, where the fresh cut was starting to bleed. "And like I said, I hope you hold out for a little while longer."

Felipe shrugged, as if he had no control over Pepe. "Hey, seriously man, he's not fucking kidding. He pulls this shit all the time. Like he's fucked-up in the head or something. Make it easy on yourself. You saw what he did to Leroy? That shit was like nothing compared to this."

37

Pepe smiled, "This ain't about how long you're going to live, it's about how slowly you're going to die. And I really don't have shit to do for the next couple of days."

Pepe turned to Felipe, "You have somewhere to be?"

Felipe shrugged, "No . . . nothing comes to mind."

Pepe nodded, "You see, you have our undivided attentions, puta."

And with that Pepe began cutting as Felipe and Maria headed back up the stairs. What Pepe was about to do was too disgusting for even them to watch.

And he was just getting started.

FOUR

VOODOO WAS WEARING red-tinted, small, circular glasses as he entered the small diner. It didn't take him more than a second to spot Victor Pavlovich, sitting quietly in the back corner, a cigarette hanging off of his lip while he studied the paper for scores from last night's games. Victor booked bets on the side when business was slow.

The Russian looked up as Voodoo approached, a smile sending curls of bluish-grey smoke swirling upwards. The diner had that *burnt-everything* smell. Eggs and bacon and toast and coffee and cancer.

The Russian liked smoking European cigarettes that would probably kill the average man in one puff. But, despite the cigarettes and coffee, Victor's teeth were pearly white, and miraculously straight. On the sides of his mouth, the teeth got sharper and more jagged, like a shark.

His eyes were a cold baby blue, with snow around the edges, and he glanced around every few seconds to see who was watching him. You wouldn't call him *paranoid*, well . . . not to his face, anyway. His skin was so pale that you would

39

think he would burst into flames if he touched sunlight for even a second.

"Kak dila, moy druk?" Victor said through the smoke.

How's it going, my friend?

He was wearing a blue *Adidas* Track suit, with gold chains dangling from his thin neck. He was the stereotypical gangster. He liked the image. He wanted people to know what he was, even if they didn't know exactly who.

One of Victor's mottos was, 'Anything from bullets to battleships . . . if the money's right, I'll get it for you.'

And he wasn't kidding.

Voodoo slid into the other side of the booth, wafting the smoke out of his face.

"Ti hochesh cafe?" Victor asked as he pushed his plate of eggs to the side.

You want coffee?

"Money, Victor," Voodoo said behind his glasses.

"You look like . . . rock-star," Victor said as he pulled out his *iPhone* and typed in some numbers on the screen. Satisfied, glancing up at Voodoo and back to the phone several times, he turned the phone around and slid it across the green plastic table top.

Voodoo took the phone and entered a series of numbers and passwords to access his account information at *Atlantic International Bank of Belize*. He waited a couple of seconds before his account information came up.

True to his word, there was a recent deposit of $150,000 in non-traceable US Dollars. Satisfied, Voodoo exited the screen and slid the phone back to Victor.

"Rock-star is happy?" Victor said, each word a struggle. He had lived in the United States for over 20 years and he still hated speaking English. He thought the language was ugly and uncultured.

Voodoo's mouth curved on the edges, almost a smile. Victor had been like an uncle to him. And even though they never said it, they loved each other like family. "Rockstars make more money than this."

Victor leaned back, laughing, "Yeah, but . . . rock-star must be work lot longer hours than you. Your job much better, trust me."

Voodoo rolled his eyes as a waitress came over to their table. She looked like her skin had been replaced with old dried-out leather, her eyes changed for glass marbles.

"Can I get you fellas something?"

Before Voodoo could answer, Victor spoke, "Get coffee and slice of . . . ah . . . ap-ple pie."

She looked down at Voodoo for approval. He nodded, and she turned and stalked off as if she has somewhere better to be.

Victor stared at Voodoo for a moment and then leaned forward. "I got a rush job for you." He let the words linger for a moment.

" . . . what you think?"

Voodoo crossed his arms, "When?"

"Zaftra, na zaftra," Victor answered quietly.

Tomorrow, in the morning.

"Tools?"

"Da, pyat-dyesit," the Russian said with a wink.

Yes, fifty-caliber.

Voodoo sat back, considering the task. He knew, just from hearing the weapon, that this was an important job. Slowly he nodded.

Victor reached into his shiny blue sweat top and grabbed a large envelope. He placed it on the table, under his newspaper and slid it forward, as if this was some kind of ritual they had shared before.

Victor watched as Voodoo slid the paper off the table, his eyes and emotions still hidden behind the red lenses, and placed the envelope inside his jacket without giving it so much as a glance.

"Don't you want to know who is target?" Victor asked as he stubbed out what was left of his cigarette.

Voodoo shrugged, "Makes no difference to me. I just deliver messages."

"Better than Fe-de-ral Express," Victor said as he laughed to himself.

} } }

ONE DAY LATER . . .

The clouds were thick and low in the sky over the cemetery. The line of black limousines, *Cadillacs*, and *Mercedes* stretched so far into the mist and fog that you couldn't see the end.

Gathered around the burial site were Juan-Carlos, his wife Carmen, and several other members of their immediate family. All of them were standing in a circle around the dark wet hole that the small casket would soon be lowered into.

The rain had stopped an hour earlier, allowing the hundreds of people in attendance to lower their umbrellas and

42

mourn together in relative silence. All the women were dressed in black, with wide-brimmed hats and dark netting over their faces.

The men were dressed in black suits with white ties—a trademark of the Matas. Among the *family* members were Caesar, the second-in-command; Hector, Caesar's closest lieutenant; and several other of the Matas' high-ranking members.

The casket was covered in red and black roses, with a large crucifix on the top bearing the depiction of Jesus on the cross. It was so quiet they could hear the rain drops drip off of the casket and fall to the mud below.

Nobody spoke.

Not a word.

The catholic priests were there, but had been told to make their blessings in silence. The only person who was going to speak was going to be Juan-Carlos.

Beyond the immediate family and Matas members, there were more than 25 gang members spread throughout the cemetery just hoping that some of the Black Royals would make a move. Through the white mist, that floated eerily around them, they only had about 20 yards of visibility.

But nobody was insane enough to try anything on a day like this. There were over 40 heavily armed Matas members driving around the streets outside the cemetery. In all, the count was well over 70 men. A small army was protecting a general as he buried his fallen son.

Needless to say, there were a lot of itching trigger fingers in every direction, as far as the eye could see . . . farther, even.

Already, they were on the verge of an all out war. And even though Juan-Carlos didn't have any proof that the King brothers were responsible . . . he knew. He felt it in every ounce of his heart. He knew it in the way that animals *know* when they're being hunted.

The Black Royals will all have to pay for the death of his son.

Nobody will be spared.

But he needed evidence in order to issue the green light. One of the policemen on his payroll was a New York Homicide Detective. When they had finally pieced all of this together, Juan-Carlos would know exactly where the killing should start.

Juan-Carlos took a step forward on the damp grass, beads of water slowly rolling down his face. He cleared his throat as he took a moment to look at each and every face in the crowd. He wanted to connect with them. To let them know he felt their pain, and to share his.

The tears in his eyes mixed with the humidity and rain drops as they fell down his neck, and along his body. In his wounded soul, those cold, salty drops were like blood draining from his heart, trickling slowly down his chest.

He leaned forward, bringing his right hand to his mouth, kissing his fingers, and then gently placing his hand on the casket. And with his eyes closed firmly, his hand still on the casket, he started to speak.

"Mi hijo. My child of God. You have left me, now . . . forever. But it is I who have failed you. I did not protect you from the monsters that call this city their home."

He stood slowly, backing away from the brushed silver box that would be the eternal resting place for his child's shattered body.

He took a deep breath as he turned towards the gathering of crying grief-stricken family members. He swallowed difficultly, forcing down the pain and sorrow like jagged pieces of metal.

"... I want to promise you all that I will give the proper response for this horrible act."

He locked eyes with Caesar, who nodded through clenched teeth, quietly assuring his boss that blood would be spilt for this.

Juan-Carlos turned back, facing the casket as he raised his voice, "I give you my word that I will . . . " he lowered his head, his eyes lifting to see the catholic priests as he spoke, " . . . that I will avenge the death of my son! I will unleash upon those who did this a fury that they cannot imagine!"

His voice was growing steadily louder and stronger, thundering through the cemetery so that all could hear his warning.

"... I swear to God, and may He strike me down if—"

And in the space between two words, Juan-Carlos lurched suddenly forward, falling face-first onto his son's coffin as a fine mist of red liquid covered everyone nearby.

Caesar started to take a step forward when he heard the thunderous noise!

Ka-boooom!

Everyone started to scream and scatter as Caesar dove forward only to find a hole the size of a basketball in Juan-Carlos' chest! The bullet-proof vest he had been wearing had done nothing to protect him.

Caesar already had his pistol out, looking through the gaps in the fog and low clouds where somebody might have taken the shot. He quickly yelled orders to Hector to get the family members back to their vehicles, and away from the cemetery as fast as possible.

Looking back down at Juan-Carlos' body, or what was left of it, he realized that he was covered in blood and fragments of bone, and organs, and death. His right hand was holding a pistol as he crouched. His left hand was pressed against bits of human matter mixed with mud and grass.

One second his boss had been vowing for revenge . . . and a split-second later, Caesar was looking at a corpse laying across the casket of another corpse.

A dead father laying atop his dead son.

A copy of a copy.

It was no longer just a cemetery, where people come to grieve their lost loved ones . . . it was now a graveyard, where death and ghosts and horror are lurking with their every step.

} } }

2 MINUTES EARLIER . . .

Voodoo sat behind the scope of the *Barret Light* .50 caliber sniper rifle. It could take down targets at a range of over a mile-and-a-half. Some trained soldiers had claimed to use it accurately at over 2 miles. But Voodoo was barely a mile away, on top of a parked 18-wheeler. This was an easy shot for him.

Little more than well-paid target practice.

Again he slowed his breathing as his eyes fought for a picture between the thick sheets of fog that seemed to intermittently roll by. The air was dense so he compensated accordingly, knowing that with as many bodyguards as there were he would only get one clean shot.

The thick mist worked against him, and also for him. It would make his shot slightly more difficult to calculate, but also mask his location. Nature's camouflage.

He had only one target, and he could only see him every few seconds as the puffs of white and grey moisture crossed by.

His cheek pressed against the stock of the rifle, steadying it even more. He realized that his window for taking the shot was narrow. His finger delicately hung on the end of the trigger, waiting for the perfect moment. The bullet he was using was composed of depleted Uranium—a highly dangerous military round.

The effect would be . . . dramatic.

His eyes began to settle into the cross-hairs as the fog thinned for a moment.

His finger tightened.

This was it.

He steadied his body as all of the people circled around the burial site came into focus. It was time to deliver the message.

His scope was so powerful that he could count the beads of sweat on the back of the target's neck. One might ask what a person feels when he is looking through the scope at a man, surrounded by his family, as they all cry, mourning the loss of a small innocent child?

What did Voodoo feel at a time like this?

Recoil!

The bullet exploded out of the barrel at several thousand feet per second, creating a perfect line between sniper and target.

And after watching the body spill forward, a large cavity of emptiness opening where the man's torso used to be, Voodoo quickly began the process of stripping the weapon down, rolling it up in an old blanket, and making his way off of the 18-wheeler.

He was too far away to hear the screaming and crying and panic that must have ensued. He was too far away to see the looks of fear and utter terror that his single shot had created.

And in his mind, he was too far away to care.

The rifle, a one-time-use item, was quickly deposited in the dumpster of a small hotel a block away. It would be carried off to a dump, or discovered by police. Either way it didn't matter. The rifle had been sprayed down with ammonia to destroy any trace evidence or DNA that might have been left there.

And like a ghost that suddenly disappears when the lights are turned on . . . he was gone.

Just a messenger.

An echo in the wind.

FIVE

SPECIAL AGENT DAN Gonzalez glanced at the file in front of him as he waited to see the prisoner. Looking around he noticed the oatmeal colored walls, the stale fluorescent lights, and cameras that accented the Attorney/client Visiting Room at ADX Florence, Colorado.

This was a maximum security facility where only the worst and most dangerous prisoners in the United States came to stay. Usually they would be placed here to live out the rest of their lives without any human contact . . . *ever*.

Referred to as a 'Super-max' the facility had residents that included convicted Al Qaeda terrorists that had been responsible for the planning of the 9/11 attacks. There were serial killers that had somehow avoided the death penalty so that they could be studied like laboratory animals. And there were even spies, like Robert Hanson and Aldrich Ames, who had turned on their country, selling secrets to the Russian KGB during the Cold War.

Most of these men were serving '*all day*', a term which is used to signify a sentence of natural life, without the possibility of parole.

But there were other inmates being held here that were less well known. Less popular to the public. These were the political prisoners. Men who had done things that the United States Government determined were *too dangerous* to allow to be free; even if the alleged crimes had been committed outside the United States' *legal* jurisdiction. Men like this did not get their day in court. They didn't have lawyers or get to go before judges.

Likely, they were kidnapped from wherever in the world they were, in the dead of night, and put on a plane that would land at some military base in the dark hours of the morning. Before they could figure out what was happening to them, they were being gagged and shackled, on their way to a place like ADX Florence. And this would be their new home, maybe forever.

And Alex Karsh was one such prisoner. His cell had only a small foam mattress on a concrete slab. There were no windows, nor was he allowed any human contact. If he got mail he'd have to read it on a black-and-white monitor. But then, he didn't get mail because nobody knew where he was, or even that he was still alive.

No radio.

No sunlight.

His only reading materials consisted of a King James version of the bible. He had no pens, no pencils, nothing. His toilet paper was checked by an X-ray machine to make sure he was not smuggling anything out of the prison, nor anything in.

He was being held at the request of the former president, George W. Bush. Current president Barack Obama did not even know he existed. And the reason was simple . . . he was an assassin.

Considered so deadly in and around Africa that the governments of South Africa, Gambia, Namibia, and Senegal had all come together to hunt him down. In the end, only the power and might of the United States could catch him. And it was only a lucky accident that they did.

A storm had forced Karsh's plane to land, and US. customs agents had been routinely inspecting baggage found a peculiar bag with three different passports. An hour later Alex Karsh was in US. Custody, being held as a combatant, and not afforded a lawyer, nor any access to the legal system.

Dan Gonzalez was a Special Agent with CID (Criminal Investigation Division) inside the Treasury Department. He had been assigned to an anti-gang task force that had been set up with the New York Police after many foreign drug cartels suddenly started to sprout up on the east coast.

Alex Karsh wasn't being investigated by the task force, but he had knowledge that Dan needed. His name had been whispered to Dan by a *friend* at the Pentagon, as somebody who might be able to shed a little light on the recent killings that had taken place in New York, Philadelphia, and New Jersey. And Dan had run out of leads . . . so why not?

Over the intercom, a muffled scratchy voice rattled, "Inmate to enter the Visiting Area . . . stand-by please."

Seconds later, a series of loud thumps and clicks vibrated through the room as a thick steel door creaked open electrically. Wearing a yellow jumpsuit, blue slippers, his hands and feet shackled to his body, he half-stepped his way into the visiting area, and towards the table where Dan was sitting.

51

The thing the agent noticed right off was that Mr. Karsh immediately locked eyes with him, sizing him up. Once the prisoner didn't feel worried, his eyes darted around looking at each and every part of the room. It was obvious that he'd never been here before. No attorneys were fighting for his cause, whatever that was.

There was no system of justice for guys like this. Too dangerous to be free; too clever to be caught, legally.

Four guards, dressed in blue polo shirts with black combat fatigues marched him, waiting with clubs in their hands, just hoping they'd get to take a shot at him.

"Special Agent Gonzales," one of the guards said, "here's your inmate. I suggest you—"

"Take his shackles off," Dan interrupted.

"What?" the guard shot back, unsure if this fed knew what he was asking.

"You can leave his cuffs on his wrists, but all of that other shit has to go," Dan said clearly, nodding at Karsh as he tried to establish some rapport. "Now, officer . . . now."

Hesitantly, the guards began taking off the ankle shackles, and the large chain circled around the prisoner's waist.

"Your funeral," the guard mumbled as he backed away.

"You guys can leave, now," Dan said. Slowly, the guards backed away, heading past the electric door. More clicks, more buzzing, and they were gone.

For a moment Dan and Alex just sat there quietly, sizing each other up. The South African, former special forces man, was short and wiry, with deep green calculating eyes, light brown skin, and the hint of red hair of his recently shaved head. His body was thin, but muscled as if he was composed of steel and cable underneath his skin.

He looked dangerous. And his file seemed to agree.

Dan smiled, "You want some coffee?"

"Coffee here is shit," the man said in a thick, South African accent.

Dan grinned, "Yeah, you're probably right. Besides, they might piss in it at this point."

The man laughed, sat back, and rolled his head in a long, slow circle, stretching before he looked back. He took a deep breath through his nose and his eyebrows raised. "So . . . what can you do for me?"

"My name is Special Agent Dan Gonzalez. I work with the Treasury Department. And I'm in a bit of a pickle."

"You?" the man said as he extended his cuffed wrists. "Please sing me your sad fucking story." And even though his words were coarse, he wasn't angry. Just stating the obvious.

"Mr. Karsh—"

"You can call me Alex."

Dan nodded, "Alex . . . I was given your name by a friend of mine in D.C. He told me that you were a mercenary in Africa, and that you were one of the most highly-trained assassins on the planet."

Alex didn't respond.

Dan continued, "He tells me, and I read a little about it, that you used to be a police officer in Joberg, South Africa. That must have been tough work."

"Dan . . . if you have questions, just ask questions. I don't need you to blow smoke up my ass. Your government is holding me illegally, against the Geneva convention. I've been here, I don't know . . . maybe five years. It's all one long fucking coma of a day, so I don't know. And, I don't really feel like cooperating with you and your illegal government. I hope those Muslims kill every one of you fucking assholes."

Dan knew that Alex was trying to get a rise out of him, get him out of his game. He took a moment, sighed slowly, and continued. "I may be able to help you, if you can help me."

There was no response from Alex.

"I've been investigating a series of killings on the east coast, and I think that they are more . . . I don't know, skillful. They aren't gang-style hits. Whoever is doing the killings seems to be very proficient."

Dan leaned forward, sliding several crime scene photographs in front of Alex.

"So what?"

"So . . . " Dan pressed, "these were done from several hundred yards away. This one . . . " he pointed to the grainy image of Juan-Carlos' body, spilled over the top of a small casket. "That happened from at least a thousand meters . . . maybe more."

The agent tapped his finger lightly on the corner of the photo, "That's a *professional* hit." He leaned back, "My first thought was military sniper, but . . . I don't know. There's something curious about all of this. He's part of a gang war. I don't know. I thought maybe you could help."

"Help what?" Alex said. "You know as much as I do. You have your pictures and your ballistics. What can I do?"

Dan placed his hand down on Alex's file. "You participated in several Political assassinations, right?"

Alex crossed his arms, studying the agent. "Allegedly," he said through clenched teeth, his eyes narrowing as he wondered if this was some elaborate ruse set up to get him linked to a new crime. Something they could use to put him away for life.

54

"Yeah," Dan said, "well, assuming you were good enough to do stuff like that—"

"Trying to appeal to my vanity, Special Agent, is a sad and rather disappointing tactic," Alex said as he shook his head.

"Well, no," Dan backpedaled, "I didn't mean to assume."

"You have my file, the one that the government cooked-up about me, right in front of your face. Does it say I'm 'good enough'? Do you have any idea who I am? Your file there . . . it's way too thin to be completely accurate."

Dan didn't say a word. It was time to let the artist brag. All geniuses needed to be appreciated. Alex Karsh was a genius at making war, and killing.

"I have *allegedly* taken juman targets at three thousand, two hundred meters. Two of your fucking miles, Dan. That was before I went into Lebanon in the early eighties. I was just a youngster, then. I've done things you people can't even imagine."

Alex leaned forward, holding Dan's gaze, "But . . . I was never caught for anything that I *supposedly* did. *Never*. Not once." He waved his finger, "Your government cheats when it can't win. And I am only one man."

Dan nodded, "And that's why I need your help. Because maybe you can help me catch a guy like you. An assassin. A contract killer who I think is working the eastern seaboard, right now."

"I can't track anyone from in here. And looking at pictures won't help you. I would have to leave this place."

"If you were in my shoes, how would you catch this guy?"

Alex kind of half laughed, and half sighed, "Buy a lot of caskets." He shrugged, "Hope that he gets food poisoning or in some random car accident. You'll never catch him if he a real operator."

"You got caught," Dan said delicately.

"The facts of my custody and arrest are still very curious. A freak of nature," Alex said as he leaned back. "But I wouldn't expect lightning to strike twice."

Dan played with the corner of the file folder, his thumb going back and forth over it. "But if you had to be me, what would you do?"

Alex closed his eyes, his head hanging lazily back on the chair, and then he swallowed and sat slowly forward. He opened his eyes, "I would hunt him, in the same way that I would hunt a lion."

Dan scooted forward, "A lion?"

"I would find out what he likes to eat, where he sleeps, what makes him tick. I would become his shadow, and his nightmare. Because, guys like us are only ever worried about *other* guys like us. I'd find out who his targets are, and work it backwards. Try to get him to come to me."

"That sounds like a risk," Dan said folding his hands in front of him.

Alex laughed to himself, "Crossing the street is a risk."

Dan leaned back, considering this man's words. A man considered the most dangerous hired gun in Africa. A man who had killed three different presidents, two of them women. Nightmare was certainly a fitting term.

"Look," Alex said, "I know that you can't get this guy on your own. And I also know that you don't have enough influence to get me out of here. More or less you're a foot soldier, just like me."

"I mean, I have—"

"But," Alex continued, " . . . you *could* get me transferred. That's within your power. If I could see some grass. Feel the sun. I'd probably be a lot more willing to help."

Dan gave it some thought, "I don't know . . . " He stood slowly up, gathering the photographs. And then he looked down on Alex, wondering how one single man, who seems pleasant enough, could be so dangerous.

He turned around and walked about 10 feet before he turned back, "I'll see what I can do, Alex. No promises. But I'll see."

"Take your time, Special Agent. Every day is another body."

Dan nodded, turned, and headed to the glass window where the guards were waiting.

SIX

AFTER THE MURDER of Juan-Carlos, Caesar was appointed the boss of the Matas. A day earlier, Caesar watched as his former boss and close friend was buried in the same Cemetery where he had been shot and killed. And it had all happened right next to his wife and the gravestone of his six-year-old son, Juan-Carlos Jr.

Caesar had made a promise to himself that he would kill everyone who was even remotely involved with the murder of Juan-Carlos. Though he felt that the Black Royals were responsible in the killings, deep down he knew that there was something more to all of this.

The hits on Juan-Carlos and his son were too professional.

Too perfect.

And Caesar knew that there was no way that Juan-Carlos could have been shot and killed, surrounded the whole time by his top bodyguards, unless the hit was done by a professional hitman. Somebody practiced in the art of assassination.

Inside a house on Daley Avenue, Caesar and his new right-hand man, Hector Fernandez, sat at a table talking. Caesar looked over at Hector and said, "Noticias nuevas?"

New news?

"Nada, just the things we already know. The boss was hit with a fifty-caliber bullet, and the cops say that the shot came from nearly a mile away, maybe more. Whoever did this had to be a pro. This wasn't a killing, it was a *hit*. There's no other way to put it."

Caesar shook his head in disgust, his soul burning for revenge. "Those niggers hired a professional hitman to kill Juan-Carlos! That's the only way they could get him and get away with it. Now, even drug dealers are outsourcing."

Hector, behind his dark brown eyes and thick black hair, said, "Why don't we do the same thing?"

Caesar shrugged frustrated, "I don't know any hitmen in this country. And I doubt that any of our people back in El Salvador could get here any time soon. You know any assassins?" He took a sip of red wine and leaned back, considering their options.

Hector thought for a second, "Not personally . . . but, our Russian friend, Victor."

"Victor . . . who is this?"

"The guy we buy all the guns from," Hector reminded. "He told me, once, that he knew a few people in that line of work. Like, I don't know, old soldiers or something. Maybe he can help us?"

Caesar stood up from his chair and pondered the thought as he shook the glass slowly in his hand making the red wine slosh around. "Maybe that's what we need to do. The King brothers have been too hard for us to get, but . . . what is hard for us might be simple for a professional assassin."

"Exactly!" Hector said with an evil grin. He stood up from the table and added, "If you want me to contact Victor immediately and get things set-up I could—"

"The sooner the better," Caesar interrupted. "You do that, Hector. Two can play this dangerous game that the Black Royals seem so insistent on playing. But still, I want to find out who's the man that killed our boss. I want him to pay just like the niggers who hired him. Maybe we'll get our hitman to kill theirs. That would be a poetic end to this game."

"Don't worry, Caesar. We'll find them and kill them all." Hector nodded to his friend and boss, "I assure you of that."

Caesar took another sip of wine. "Where's Pepe and Felipe?" he asked, changing the subject.

"I sent them over to the Melbrook Projects to pick up some money and drop off some more product," Hector explained as they walked toward the front door.

When they stepped out of the house, six of their men were standing around, armed and waiting for an order.

Hector straightened his jacket, "I'm going to set up a meeting with Victor, now. I'll call you as soon as I hear something." He then leaned forward and kissed Caesar on both sides of the face.

Caesar stood back, watching as Hector and three of his men climbed into an all-black *Lincoln Navigator*. When they drove off he walked over to a grey *Lexus* and slowly opened the door as the clouds above him rumbled.

He stared up at the sky and it was like he was back at the cemetery, waiting for a bullet to come from some place he couldn't see. He got quickly into the car and shut the door, glancing in the rearview mirror as his men got into their *Escalade*.

Slowly he pulled off down the street with his men closely behind. His mind was deep in thought, and his heart was still wounded from the death of his closest friend, Juan-Carlos.

And it was a strange thing, but he was having a hard time picturing the man alive. All he had now was the image of his former boss with a giant hole in his body, slumped over a small silver casket as the rain and blood poured down from above.

} } }

NEAR 241ST STREET...

Inside a Jamaican restaurant, near 241st Street, Reggie and Ronnie King were in a small back room discussing business. The restaurant was just one of their many legitimate establishments that they owned. The King brothers had businesses situated all throughout New York city.

They had hair salons and barber shops in Harlem. A clothing store in Manhattan. There were pool halls, grocery stores, and even restaurants in Queens, and in the Bronx. They were getting bigger and bigger by the day.

There was a knock on the door and Reggie stopped talking to his brother and said, "Who is it?"

"It's me . . . Ruthless," a scratchy voice rumbled from the other side of the door.

"Ruthless, come in, man," Reggie told him.

When the door opened, a huge dark-skinned man stepped inside. He was wearing a black *Boss* suit, with a crisp red shirt underneath. He shut the door behind him, and walked forward. He stood about 6'4", 285 pounds of solid muscle, with long black dread-locks hanging down past his shoulders.

It looked as if his muscles were going to rip through his suit at any second. His name was Ruthless, and he was everything his name said . . . and more.

Ruthless was a cold-blooded killer. He was a man that didn't demand respect, he demanded fear. Since his release from the Clinton maximum Security Prison, in upstate New York, Ruthless had been the King brothers' number one street enforcer.

Out of the nine people that he had already killed, four of them had died from injuries he had inflicted with his bare hands. And he liked to get messy.

"What's up, Ruthless? We were discussing some important business," Reggie said.

Ruthless stood there with a blank look on his face. He was carrying a brown leather sports bag. "I have some good news and some bad news," he said. "The good news is," he jiggled the bag around, " . . . this is the three-hundred thousand that I picked-up this morning from our workers over at the Patterson and Mitchell housing projects." Ruthless walked over and passed the bag to Reggie.

"So, what's the bad news?" Ronnie asked curiously.

After a long sigh, Ruthless looked at both men and said, "The Matas got to Calvin. His head and one of his arms were found in the Hudson River, over in City Island."

Reggie's face tightened, "What?"

Ruthless continued, "That ain't all. They found his legs in a trash dumpster over there by One-Fifty-eighth. The rest of Calvin's body ain't been found. But . . . you know." He shrugged, "It was in today's' New York Post."

Reggie and Ronnie both stood there with disbelief painted on their faces. They knew that something was wrong when Calvin had suddenly disappeared. Now they knew what it was. He had been caught and killed by the Matas. And, he had been given the same horrible death that Leroy had suffered.

"Fuck!" Ronnie spat. Calvin had been his favorite younger cousin, and now he was dead. They had expected reprisals from the Matas, but not so close to home.

"There's something else," Ruthless said, almost hesitantly.

"What is it?" Reggie snapped.

"On the night that Calvin disappeared, he told me that he was going to see some new Spanish bitch named Maria. Something keep telling me that this bitch had something to do with it. I should of said something at the time, but, you know . . . . you can't tell Calvin nothin'."

"You think she's one of the Matas?" Ronnie wondered out loud.

"Most likely she is. Or, at least, she runs with 'em. She probably set Calvin up and got him chopped to pieces. Them Spanish bitches is shiesty!" Ruthless barked.

Reggie walked up to Ruthless and said, "Make sure you find this bitch? And you know what to do when you do," he added, his voice low and serious.

Ruthless grinned, "You ain't gotta worry about that. That bitch will get what she's got coming." Then he turned and started to say something, shook his head, and walked out of the room without another word.

When Reggie looked over at Ronnie he noticed his eyes welling up. "Save your tears, man. That ain't gonna bring Calvin back. What we gotta do now is make sure that every one of those Matas are dead for what they did."

With the leather bag strapped over his shoulder, Reggie turned and walked out of the room, leaving Ronnie alone with his thoughts. He felt an emptiness that he couldn't describe.

The loss of his younger cousin Calvin was weighing heavily on his soul.

What was worse: After the hits on Juan-Carlos and his son, Reggie should have expected this. They were foolish to think that the Matas wouldn't respond so quickly.

SEVEN

Candice Jacobs ran with the baby wrapped in a green blanket, tears rolling down her cheeks as her feet sunk into the soft mud near the creek where Ms. Josephine lived. It was dark out, luckily, so that nobody would pay her too much attention.

Ms. Josephine would know what to do. She was into Voodoo, and Black Magic, and Sangria. And she would be able to help. She had to, because Candice had nowhere else to turn.

As she made her way down the path, passing by the wind chimes made of different animal bones and the strange piles of different colored rocks, she found Ms. Josephine's place. It was an old Victorian house that had last seen paint in the late days of the Civil War. In the front window was a cluster of black and red candles that had been burning for a long time.

As she ran, as quick as her legs could possibly move, she didn't notice that her child wasn't making any noise.

No crying.

Not a peep.

"Ms. Josephine! Ms. Josephine!" she yelled as she made her way up the porch, rapping her knuckles against the old

65

wooden door. There were strange symbols painted around the porch. They warded off the evil spirits, or so Ms. Josephine said.

"Ms. Josephine!" Candice cried as she pounded the door.

Suddenly the door opened, "My word, child . . . what is it?" Ms. Josephine said, her big green eyes studying the young girl. Ms. Josephine was a big woman, with dark maple skin, and a big heart filled with compassion. Even though she was into things that most people didn't necessarily believe in, people trusted her judgment. She was one of those people who could *see* things that others couldn't.

"The baby, Ms. Josephine . . . he was born early. I think he's evil," Candice cried as she handed the baby across the threshold.

"Well, hold on, now," Ms. Josephine said as she took the tiny child. "Let's have us a look and see." And as she opened the blanket she took a deep, quick breath. "He's . . . " she looked up at Candice. "His eyes."

"They different, Ms. Josephine. He's wrong. He's evil. I'm sure of it. I can't raise no evil child. I don't know what—"

"When's the last time you talked to yo mother?" Ms. Josephine asked. Candice was one of those free spirits that ran the streets all the time, only spending a couple of nights in any one place.

"She don't know about him, she can't . . . you know why," Candice answered as she continued to shake.

Ms. Josephine did know why. Candice had been raped, and even though she had never said who had done it, Ms. Josephine had her suspicions. And if the truth ever came out, it would cause more trouble in their community than they could afford.

So Ms. Josephine had agreed to keep her suspicions a secret. Candice had never gotten big enough during her pregnancy for anyone to even notice. And with the baby coming a month early, well . . . nobody would ever have to know.

"So, what do you want me to do, child?" Ms. Josephine asked as she started to sense something in this child's eyes that she had never seen before. Something dark and haunting . . . but pure.

"I can't . . . I just can't," Candice said, and then she reached out her hand, touching the child delicately, and then turned and ran away as fast as she could out into the darkness of the night.

The wind seemed to pick up as the chimes started to play their chilling songs. Ms. Josephine looked out into the darkness that the trees around her provided. She hugged the baby to her chest, and backed into the house, closing the old creaky door.

Once inside, she carefully laid the child down on an old brown sofa and got some warm water from the kitchen. She cleaned him, found him some cotton sheets that she cut into diapers, and made him a place to sleep next to her bed in the back of the house.

That old house was filled with creaks and groans as the wind pressed against the old boards. The smell of incense wafted through the house as she began to prepare a life for him. She knew that she was the only person who could raise this strange child.

With eyes that could *see* things.

With a black glow around him.

He was special, alright . . . different. And, if anyone else raised this child, well . . . there might be problems. He needed spiritual guidance, not just an upbringing. And so, on that dark night, with the warm Louisiana air blowing off of the creek behind her house, she made the decision to raise Ty—named after her first son who had died in Vietnam.

Her little Voodoo Child.

} } }

Angie laid quietly beside Voodoo, curled up like a cat, slowly stroking his chest as he slept. She wondered what could be going on behind the invisible wall he put up. She knew him as Ty Jacobs, a fairly successful insurance salesman. He always left his job pretty vague, never discussing his work.

The few times he mentioned the insurance business to her, he made is sound completely dull. But then, he didn't like to talk much. Their relationship, if that's what you would call it, was one of intense sex, and then solitude.

He was very clean, almost obsessively. And he was careful about everything he did. He never rushed into a room without looking around. He would always check to make sure the stove was turned off, or the refrigerator door was closed. She figured that people who were always working around actuarial tables and insurance claims were probably obsessively careful in their own lives.

Towels were always folded, sheets pressed, and he never, ever, left the toilet seat up. Ty was meticulous in every detail, including his body which, to Angie, was like a work of art. Like a Greek statue.

As her fingers slowly slid over a small circular scar on his chest, she gazed at his closed eyes, and wondered what he was dreaming about.

Did he even have dreams?

Slowly, Voodoo awoke, his eyes blinking several times as he turned towards Angie. She leaned over, crawling on top of him, her hips straddling his.

"What were you dreaming about?" she whispered as she leaned down and hissed his chest.

In the darkness, he could see the silhouette of her naked body. Without a word, his hands slowly climbed her legs, sliding along her stomach until he was gently cupping her breasts.

She continued kissing his chest, lowering her body. Kissing his stomach, she continued lower and lower. Soft little nibbles from her lips as her hands massaged the insides of his thighs. Inch by inch, she lowered her mouth to his rock-hard stomach.

She took him into her mouth, and as she did she could hear him sigh, his body warm with pleasure.

} } }

Hector walked casually, looking for the Chinese restaurant where Victor was supposed to meet him. He had only met the Russian on a couple of occasions, and thought him to be a fairly trustworthy guy . . . for a Russian.

Hector passed through the metal detectors, having nothing on him, and that was probably the reason why Victor liked meeting at the Airport in the first place. Always paranoid, those Russians.

As he entered the restaurant, he saw a booth that was either on fire, or the guy was smoking about 20 cigarettes at once. Hector smiled as he slid into the booth with the pale Russian, "I don't think you're even allowed to smoke in here."

"What they gonna do . . . arrest me? It's free country, no?" Victor said as a cigarette sat in his left hand. "Now, my friend . . . what can Victor do for you?"

Hector leaned in, not that anyone else was watching them, but more out of habit. "I need a favor."

"Favor, huh?" Victor blew out a huge puff of smoke and then crushed the cigarette onto the side of his fried rice bowl, the ashes falling into the uneaten food. "Maybe I can make favor for you, my friend. But my favors cost money. I'm like . . . ah, King of favors."

Hector nodded, his face tight and serious, "You've heard about what happened with a friend of mine . . . and his son? The killings?"

Victor took a spoonful of fried rice, ash and all, and poured it into his mouth. Still chewing, he answered, "Yeah . . . I read about this in Post. Terrible, terrible things." He continued chewing. "It be sound like Afghanistan. Terrible."

"One time you told me that you knew some people," Hector whispered. "Maybe some of your people . . . professionals?"

Victor shrugged as he chewed, "I know lots of people. Victor know everybody. I be like *celebrity* or something."

"I would like to hire your services," Hector said under his breath.

Victor swallowed, placed the spoon down and locked eyes with the El Salvadorian, "My people, I mean . . . if I even knew somebody for that kind of work, they be very expensive. I don't know if you can—"

"Money is not a concern, Victor," Hector pressed as he leaned forward.

Victor's face slowly morphed into a smile, "In that case, I think that Victor can help you. We deal just like for other things. Half money up front, no refundable. After job be finished, other half. Immediate wire transfer. No questions asked. Ever."

"Just tell me where and when," Hector said as he pulled out his cell phone.

Victor held up his hands, "First we eat, okay. You look like you could use some beef and broccoli."

EIGHT

*ADX FLORENCE, SUPER-MAXIMUM SECURITY PRISON, COLORADO .
. .*

CASE MANAGER, PHIL Mitchell couldn't understand it.
He hung up the phone and checked the computer. Slowly
scratching his head he sat back in his chair. His bald head
was sweating, not because of the heat, but because of what
they were about to do with one of the inmates in his case
load.

"Unfucking believable!" he said to himself as he closed
his eyes. He sighed through his nose, his mind doing back
flips.

There was a single knock on his office door and then it
swung open. Without waiting for Phil to acknowledge him,
Warden Hank Day started talking, "I feel like I'm the last guy
to learn things in this place. Why do you think that is, Phil?"

Phil raised his hands in defense. "I had nothing to do
with this. It was that Treasury Agent," he said as she slid
folders and papers aside until he got down to the notepad buried under a mountain of unfinished paperwork.

He read, "A . . . *Special Agent Daniel Gonzalez* had it sent through Washington, and then Region signed-off on it. It was out of our hands."

"The don't put transfer requests through that quickly. Especially without getting our opinion on the inmate. I don't know how this happened," Warden Day growled, his pale white skin turning pinkish red as he thought about it. He walked around the room, his arms crossed tightly over his chest, breathing deeply through his nose.

"I guess they have other concerns. I mean, how important is this Alex Karsh, anyway? I never even saw his indictment." Phil placed his hands flat on the messy desk, tapping his fingers.

"I know that he was supposedly considered a danger to society," Warden Day stammered. "How did it go, ' . . . *so dangerous that he must not be given any human contact, of any kind. No reading materials. No cleaning chemicals. He has an understanding of chemistry and high-explosives . . .* ' and on and on."

" . . . and then, and I heard this directly from the guys at the State Department who grabbed him, '*that he's never to be left alone with any less than four guards, and shackled at all times.*' So . . . on the one hand, he's the most dangerous guy ever. And then they say, '*Oh, everything is better, now. Go ahead and stick him on the chain for the Transfer Center.*'"

"I read Mr. Karsh's file over and over," Phil said as he opened the large blue folder. But there were only a few pages. Some pictures, some medical notes, and a basic psychological assessment. Beyond that, all there was were security procedures that basically stripped him of any constitutional rights he might have had, were he *actually* here.

Which, *officially*, he isn't.

"There's nothing here, Hank," Phil said as he lifted the file for the Warden to inspect.

Warden Day waved it off. "What really fucks with me, really burns my ass, is that I wonder, late at night sometimes, why in the hell half of these guys are in here. If they're *so* dangerous, why aren't they riding the lightning? And if they aren't, why are we keeping them down here in this dungeon?"

"If they're here," Phil said as he dropped the file back down on his messy desk, " . . . then they did something to get here. Our, well, your job is to keep the house locked, and mine is to keep them alive long enough to serve their debt to society."

"Forever?" the Warden said as he looked at some pictures on the wall of Phil's family in Phoenix.

"Well, not for us. Shit, I retire in seventeen months. If they want to redesignate some South African whacko," Phil said as he tapped his teeth together lightly, "so what? Let them. That's all semantics for people way over my pay grade."

"That Treasury Agent must have had some pull," the Warden said, "because in my nine years here, I've never seen one leave under his circumstances . . . except in a body bag."

Two stairways, five hallways, eleven electric doors, and one glass wall away, sitting on a foam bed, Alex Karsh was laying on his back, his eyes closed, with a big grin on his face. It looked like Special Agent Dan had come through, after all.

There just might be hope for this country, he joked to himself. Lewisburg Penitentiary, here comes inmate 00241-002, otherwise known as '*The Wolf*.'

}}}
74

Victor straightened his tie. He didn't normally wear anything as formal as a suit, but this was a different kind of meeting.

He glanced briefly at himself in the mirror on the inside of the elevator. Beside him were two large Russian men—Sergei and Igor. They had known Victor for a long time, and even though they probably thought that the *Glava* (Boss) gave him too much freedom, they still respected him. Both men were tall and muscular, with necks as thick as paint cans . . . and twice as dense.

"Kak dila, Victor," Sergei said, breaking the uncomfortable silence in the elevator.

How's it going, Victor.

Victor twisted his head, "Ya ne mogu eta, fucking tie!"

I hate this fucking tie!

Sergei and Igor started to chuckle, and as they did their eyes bulged a bit. *Probably the steroids*, Victor thought, but it would have been unwise to mention. So he just nodded with a half grin on his face.

"Eta harasho zdyes," Igor growled.

It's nice here.

Victor half shrugged, rolling his eyes as he nervously fumbled a silver *Zippo* lighter.

Click-snap.

Click-snap.

The elevator slowed and within seconds the door slid to the side with a whoosh sound, as if they were aboard some spaceship. Uncomfortably, Victor left the elevator and met several more guards.

In accented English a giant guard said, "I must be search you, Victor. No dis-re-spect, okay."

Victor nodded, his eyes telling everyone that this whole ordeal was a major headache for him. His place was in the streets, not up here in some fancy office building. But then, when the Glava of the Russian Syndicate asks to speak with you . . . you don't refuse.

Click-snap. Victor held up the lighter, "Mozhit beet ti hochesh eta?"

Perhaps you want this?

The large guard smiled, showing a line of yellowed, jagged teeth. "Nyet, Victor. Nyet. Mui idyom."

No, Victor. No. Let's go.

And so they walked slowly across several very expensive carpets, past a bunch of priceless artwork and sculptures. Past a group of beautiful Russian girls—probably prostitutes fresh from Moscow.

Past a vault door that looked like it could guard nuclear weapons, they walked quietly. They made their way down a yellow-lit hallway to a large wooden door, where four more guards were posted. They seemed a little less relaxed, holding *AK-47* Machine-pistols in their hands.

"Victor!" one of the guards said with a smile, his hand still flirting with the trigger of his machine gun. "How fucking you are?"

Victor shook his head, "How the fuck *are* you? Practice your English, Vladimir. You don't want to be a fucking door-guy your whole life."

The guard looked uncomprehendingly at him, kind of nodded, and then used his free hand to knock twice at the door before toggling his radio. He spoke rapid-fire Russian into the microphone and then smiled. "Harasho, Victor."

With that, he opened the door slowly and Victor was allowed to walk in alone. As the door was closing behind him, the words, "Dobre din, Gaspadin Chyorni," echoed out into the hall.

Good day, Mr. Chyorni.

Click-snap.

And then, "Siditsa, moi druk. Sluchat."

Sit, my friend. Listen.

And the door closed.

NINE

THE SPOTLIGHT BAR was a popular spot in the South Bronx, where many of the Black Royals hung out. The large bar was another of the King brother's legal establishments. As the sound of hard-core rap music blasted from the speakers, people were moving around, drinking and conversing, while others were in the middle of the bar getting their groove-on. The dance floor was small, but it only made for a more intimate setting.

Four Black Royals' members were standing out in front of the door, pat searching people before they were allowed to enter the bar. Security procedures at all of their establishments had escalated since the violence between the Black Royals and the Matas had increased.

Two other members were chilling inside parked cars, keeping an eye on everything and everyone that entered, exited, or even drove by the bar. With loaded *AK-47s* laid across their laps, they were prepared for any sudden attack made by the Matas.

Unbeknownst to all of the Black Royals inside the bar, and the ones who protected it from the outside, one of the Matas most deadly members was sitting on a stool at the bar enjoying herself.

Wearing a skin-tight grey dress that clung to each and every curve on her body, Maria sat on the bar stool sipping a cold *Corona.* Once again, she had come alone.

She was searching for her next victim.

Maria was Pepe's and Felipe's beautiful secret weapon. She was their number one asset when it came to kidnapping and setting people up. Few men could resist her charm and sexuality.

In the last month she had been two for two, setting up two top members of the Black Royals—Leroy and Calvin. Both of them had been easy, and now she was working on her third.

As she sat there scanning through the boisterous crowd, she noticed a large, dark man staring back at her. She smiled and then winked, motioning him over with her eyes.

He's perfect, she thought when the man started walking towards her. As he neared, she smiled and slowly got off of the stool, extending her legs deliberately to focus his attention. She could follow his eyes as they moved up and down her firm hourglass figure. Her long, black hair was tied-up into a ponytail, hanging down to the center of her back.

Without a doubt, she was the finest woman in the bar . . . and certainly, the most deadly.

"How you doing, Ma?" he said as he gazed into her eyes.

"Fine, now," Maria flirted back.

He edged closer, looking down at her breasts briefly before his eyes rose to meet hers. "My name is Ruthless," he said, extending his hand.

"Ma . . . Silvia," she said, catching herself in mid-word.

He smiled, "How 'bout we grab a few drinks and go sit at one of the small tables in the back? There we can talk and have a little privacy."

"Sounds fine with me, handsome," Maria said, licking her lips slowly, as her eyes filled with lust.

After Ruthless had gotten a few beers from the bar, Maria followed him through the crowd, heading towards the small tables in the back. With Maria close behind him, Ruthless had a satisfied grin plastered on his face. And it was only growing with his anticipation.

He knew exactly who she was: Maria, one of the Matas' beautiful female spies. And the same person that was responsible for Calvin's death. Ruthless had discovered everything he needed to know about her.

Now, ironically, the black widow had fallen into a snake pit.

$$ \} \} \} $$

"Angie!" the shrill voice yelled out. "Angie, one of your regulars is asking if you're free for tonight?"

Angie, wearing a pair of grey sweat pants and a pink shirt, took her earphones out and set down her MP-3 player. She turned towards the hallway. "Who is it?" she yelled back, her voice echoing down the hall, out across a large living area where several attractive girls were relaxing.

Myrna, a large, bald woman with heavy gold loops that drug her ears down to her shoulder shook her head. She rolled her egg-shaped eyes, "It's Sam . . . from Manhattan . . . "

Joy—Angie's closest friend at the escort agency—leaned in to her room, her eyes narrow and curious. She turned her head towards Myrna, their dispatcher. "You gonna go?"

Angie's eyes slowly met Joy's, "I don't think so . . . I'm worn-out, tonight."

Joy nodded her head, turned slightly, and yelled, "Give it to somebody else, Myrna. Angie's too tired to go on another date."

Angie looked down, "I was thinking he might call."

Joy walked into the room, sitting down on Angie's bed. She was wearing short green shorts with a grey sweater. Her hair was dark brown, cut shoulder-length, with curls at the edges. Her body was thin and curvy, like an underwear model.

Joy leaned forward, "Angie, are you startin' to fall for this guy?"

Angie folded her hands near her waist. "I don't think so . . ."

Joy's head tilted curiously, not accepting her friend's answer. Her green eyes locked with Angie's.

"I don't know . . . " Angie relented. "Maybe."

Joy looked up, taking a large deliberate breath, "Oh, no. Girl, you can't fall for no john."

"He's different, Joy. There's more to it than just sex," she tried to explain.

"Does he invite you out for dinner?"

Angie didn't answer.

"Has he ever asked you to meet his friends? See a movie?" Joy pressed.

Still, no answer. Angie's eyes lowered at her shoulders slumped downwards.

"Does he tell you about himself . . . anything personal?"

"I get your point," Angie surrendered. "But—"

"But nothing," Joy interrupted. She leaned forward, her hands resting on Angie's knees as if she was here to save her. "Look, every now and then, in this job, you're going to meet some guy who just does things that you like. You two accidentally fit. And you're going to read into it, something that ain't there. But there ain't nothing. He just hiring your body."

"He's different," Angie said carefully. "He's not like that. You don't know him."

"Girl," Joy said with a sad laugh, "I know all of them. Once you've fucked ten men, you know them all. This is a physical business we're in. There ain't no *Pretty Woman*, happy ending, shit going on here. The only happy ending is that we make a thousand dollars a day sleeping with rich guys that can't get laid at home."

Joy shook Angie's legs playfully, "We're just dessert."

Angie didn't respond. There was nothing to say. Joy didn't understand. Nobody did. But there was something different about Ty. Something that she couldn't explain. It was like there was this thing between them that neither of them would mention.

She knew, in the way that women just *know* things, that they shared . . . something.

And even though he kept calling her at odd hours, paying her in crisp 100-dollar bills, and saying little or nothing to her. There was a delicate side of him that she glimpsed every now and then, if only for a fleeting moment. A part of him that made her long to see him more than anything else in the world.

}}}

Ruthless and Maria had sat around talking, laughing, and drinking. They had even gotten up once to dance to one of Ludacris' latest songs. The bar was filled to capacity. Half drunk men and women were searching around for potential one-night stands. Sex was on everybody's mind.

Maria was cuddled up under Ruthless' strong, massive arms. Under the table, she had reached her left hand down, unbuttoned and unzipped his pants, and had pulled his dick out, rubbing slowly as she talked to him. With every word, her stroking was faster and faster.

Feeling himself on the verge of coming, Ruthless leaned over and whispered into her hear, "Let's get up out of here, we can go over to my place. It's just a few blocks away from here."

"Sounds good to me," Maria said as she removed her hand. Her eyes glanced down at the table, "I'll let you deal with that."

He reached down and forced himself back into his pants. He nodded, "I hope not."

When they walked out the front of the bar, Ruthless walked over to one of his men and whispered something into his ear.

"Okay, I'll take care of everything," the man said with a devilish grin. The man, and three others nearby, were paying close attention as Ruthless and Maria left the bar. They climbed into his white *Ford Expedition*. As soon as the truck pulled out of the parking lot and started down the street, they rushed into a red *Dodge Magnum* and sped off.

Ruthless pulled up and parked his truck in front of a house on Cypress Avenue. He and Maria traded small talk as they got out of the truck and walked up to the front door. Ruthless used his key to open the door and they both stepped inside, kissing at the threshold.

Maria looked around the lavishly decorated home and smiled, "Nice."

"Just wait till you see the bedroom," Ruthless replied.

"Can I use your bathroom?" she asked as she steadied her purse.

"Yeah, it's upstairs. First door on the left," he pointed.

"I'll be right back," Maria said, turning and making her way up the stairs. *He has no idea what he's gotten himself into*, she thought as she walked towards the bathroom.

Ruthless walked over to the window and looked between a part in the curtain. He watched as the red *Dodge Magnum* rolled to a quiet stop a few houses down. Then he walked back to the front door and unlocked it. *This bitch has no idea*, he thought to himself.

Inside the bathroom, Maria was sitting on the toilet holding her cell phone to her ear.

"Pick up, pick up," she whispered to herself.

She was calling Pepe's cell phone to let him know where she was, and who she was with. After 10 rings with no answer, she angrily disconnected the call.

"Where the hell are y'all?" she said under her breath. Her eyes searched nervously around the bathroom. She then dialed Felipe's phone. Again, it rang without answer.

She stood, turning to a mirror over the sink, and fixed herself up. Satisfied, she turned and reached for the doorknob, slowly opening the door.

When she saw Ruthless and three other black men standing there pointing their guns at her, her eyes widened. She couldn't breathe as she searched for words.

"What's the problem? Can't get in touch with your people . . . Maria?" Ruthless said with a slight grin.

Maria stood there in complete and utter silence, her throat choked . . . paralyzed with fear. The color washed from her face until she looked pale and ghostly.

"Bitch," Ruthless shouted, "we know you set-up Leroy and Calvin!"

"Please . . . I, I don't . . . know . . . what—"

Thwaap!

Out of nowhere, Ruthless punched her so hard that she was unconscious before she fell to the floor. He kneeled down beside her, using his foot to roll her over, and lifted up her long, black ponytail. On the back of Maria's neck were the words,

Matadores Por Vida

"Shiesty, fucking bitch!" he hissed as he stood up with a handful of her hair in his clenched fist.

The three men watched as Ruthless drug Maria's unconscious body down the hallway. They all eagerly followed them into the bedroom, almost salivating as if there was about to be a meal served. After the door was shut . . . the party began.

Ruthless was in no rush to kill her. Not yet. First he and his three friends were going to make a playground out of her ass. They were going to explore every possible inch of this dangerous woman's body.

And there were no rules . . . no boundaries.

TEN

SATURDAY MORNING...

AS THE SUN slowly lifted, the sky turned from black to a light purple, then eventually to blue. Birds started chirping in the trees, as the first noises of the day started to echo throughout the neighborhood. The street, still dark between the houses, was empty except for two things.

About three houses down from the corner, thousands of flies had gathered around an inhuman pile of lifeless tissue. And as they buzzed around, laying their eggs, warm steam lifted off of the body as the cold morning air mixed with blood and skin and horror.

The corpse was naked, curled into the fetal position, beaten and bruised in every place. Ribs were broken in her frail chest, threatening to break through the skin at unnatural angles. Her wrists were black and swollen, as were here ankles and neck.

Clotted blood was smeared between her legs, painted like a red dress all over her stomach and thighs. Most of her fingers were broken, bent backwards towards her blood-crusted elbows.

Her black hair was askew and sticky, with bits of clotted and still-wet blood everywhere.

And from behind, it was clear that somebody, or several people, had entered her violently with sharp, wide things. It no longer looked human, this pile of flesh and hair. To a passing car, it might have been a stray dog that got hit by a car.

But it wasn't.

A small hole at the base of her skull opened into a large exit wound that turned her face into nothing more than salty hamburger meat, unrecognizable at a glance. And below that tiny hole on her neck, was a long patch of missing skin, exposing muscle and flesh, where the words, 'Matadores Por Vida' used to be tattooed.

$$\} \} \}$$

ONE HOUR AND 13 MINUTES LATER . . .

After the screaming and the sirens and the yellow tape came the Crime Scene Investigators and the Detectives asking their questions.

But then there was the frightening silence that fell over the crowd of onlookers. A scared, wordless quiet, as people stared at the bloodstained concrete, etched with chalk lines and small orange cones that the cops had used to identify evidence.

People said nothing.

Only thoughts. This was a Spanish neighborhood. These kinds of things didn't happen down here. The Matas made sure of that. At least . . . they used to.

Hector stood just outside the yellow tape, his cell phone pressed to his ear as he talked softly. Pepe and Felipe stood speechless beside him, their eyes full of rage.

Hector was nodding as he listened to the voice on the phone. "Si, Jeffe, pero . . . yo no se. Ellos estaban esperando."

Yes, Boss, but . . . I don't know. They were waiting.

He did a lot of nodding, as he glanced over to Felipe. "Si, si. You voy a hacer lo."

Yes, yes. I'm going to do it.

He dropped the phone back into his jacket pocket, biting the inside of his lip.

"Hay que vengarla, inmediatamente," Hector said coldly.

We have to avenge her, immediately.

"Por supuesto, Hector," Pepe said, almost without his mouth moving.

Of course, Hector.

} } }

KENNEDY AIRPORT, INTERNATIONAL AIR-CARGO RECEIVING OFFICE . . .

Victor, zipped up in his black *Adidas* track suit, hiding most of his gold necklaces, looked around. He removed his diamond-encrusted *Cartier* watch and placed it in his pocket, doing the best he could to not look like a mobster . . . while still looking just the part.

He walked into the office, past a tinted glass door, and headed to the wide counter where international packages and cargo would be received and released after Customs agents had inspected them.

A young white woman with blond hair and light blue eyes smiled politely as he strutted to the counter. "Can I help you, sir?"

"You're beautiful, like Baywatch girls," Victor said as he smiled at her.

The girl half giggled and half blushed from his words. "Umm, thank you, sir. Can I help you, though?"

And just as Victor was about to drop another line on her, a short, stocky white guy, who carried all his weight in his upper body, came out from behind a side door, "Victor . . . come-on, man. She's way to nice for a guy like you."

Victor winked at the girl, "Sorry, Baywatch . . . maybe another time," and then he blew her a cheesy little air-kiss. She started laughing as he walked towards his airport friend.

Paul Scanetti was a 3rd generation Italian-American who had a good union job at JFK International Airport. He was one of the two men responsible for bringing piggy-backed cargo off of international flights and having them sent through Customs before being cleared to their final destinations. Paul, Victor's airport friend, had been *"losing"*— dodging Customs inspection—packages for the Russian for many years, and had been making quite a lucrative side business out of it.

Each month he would lose one or two boxes. Sometimes they were tiny envelopes, sometimes they were as big as walk-in cargo boxes. Paul didn't know what was in the shipments, and he didn't care to know. All he was sure of was that Customs could only check about 5% of the shipments that arrived per day. And that meant that he was paid thousands of dollars that the Russian would place in his hands with each shipment.

Victor had been expecting a *special* box from Moscow, by way of Canada. It had some supplies and materials that he needed for a new job that Hector had already paid a substantial sum of money for.

"Cute, huh?" Paul said, nodding his head back at the main office as they walked towards an hanger a few hundred feet away.

"Cute, yeah. I like blond girls," Victor said. "They be look like they ready for beach. Beach bunnies."

Paul laughed, slapping Victor on the back. "So, my comrade, I have three boxes for you. But they're fuckin' heavy. Whatever you got, I don't wanna know, but you'll need a truck to drive them out of here."

Victor smiled with his lips, his teeth still resting on the tip of his tongue, "I rent truck, already. So," he nodded, "I ready to pick up."

As they got inside the hanger, Paul walked him over to a cluster of boxes covered by an olive-green, musty, old tarp. "Here you go, my man."

Victor pulled out a wad of 50-dollar bills. "Okay," he said as he handed the wad to Paul, who didn't even stop to count it.

Paul smiled, "Victor, you're a hell of a business man."

"I be entrepreneur," Victor said with a shrug as he slapped his hand down on top of the tarp, sending dust into the air. "America the beautiful . . . land of the free," he snorted.

ELEVEN

INSIDE HER LAVISH home, Carmen walked around dimming all of the soft white lights until they were a gentle yellow glow. Fresh scented candles were situated all throughout the house, and the sound of Alicia Keys' voice was flowing out of the speakers.

When she heard the sound of a car pulling up in front of her house, she walked over to the window and peeped out of the blue silk curtains. Ronnie was right on time, just like he had been every day since the murder of her husband, Juan-Carlos.

Carmen watched as her secret black lover stepped out of his gloss-black *Mercedes Benz,* and walked toward the front door. She was dressed in a thin pink teddy, with nothing on underneath. Her body was yearning for Ronnie's powerful sexual healing. He could do things with his body that she had never experienced before, and she was addicted to it. No matter how dangerous her forbidden fruit was.

Carmen opened the front door and let Ronnie inside the house. As soon as she closed the door they started to kiss. She felt like she was melting into his arms. There was something hypnotic about Ronnie that she just couldn't put into words. A quality that she couldn't resist.

And, even if she knew what that special *something* actually was, she still wouldn't gave it up. Carmen was strung-out, and enjoying every second of it.

After their long, passionate kiss, Ronnie lifted Carmen into his arms, slowly carrying her up the stairs.

All she could do was watch and smile as he carried her step-by-step, towards gratification. He turned right and carried her straight into the master bedroom. The room was elegant and tranquil. A large king-sized bed was situated in the middle of the room, sitting on a cushion of soft tan carpet. The entire ceiling was covered in a large mirror, and Carmen looked up to watch herself floating in Ronnie's arms.

She watched herself being gently laid down on the bed. "Take that off," he said.

Carmen slid out of her teddy and tossed it to the floor. Then she laid back on one of the soft silk pillows and said, "Okay, it's your turn."

Ronnie looked at Carmen's beautiful naked body and just shook his head. He had been with lots of attractive women in his life, but there was something about Carmen that brought out the very best in him. His performances were epic.

Carmen watched with lustful eyes as Ronnie started to undress. First he took off his black *Polo* shirt. Then he kicked off his *Timberland* boots and slid down his jeans. When he finally slipped out of his boxers, letting them fall to his feet, Carmen looked frozen, her mouth slightly open. Her eyes were wide and hungry as she gazed in awe of his physique.

Damn, she thought.

93

Ronnie was tall, dark-skinned, and attractive, with a dick twice the size of her late husband. And she wanted it . . . needed it all.

Ronnie walked slowly over and joined her in bed. After climbing on top of her toned, exotic body, they started to kiss slowly. And the kisses became more vibrant and passionate as they continued.

He kissed and sucked all around her neck, his tongue making its way to her shoulders and breasts. Each nipple was given special attention, as the heat grew between them. Warm chills were starting to travel throughout her entire body, causing her back to arch as she fought back tiny moans.

After he worked his way to the inside of her thighs, licking gently all the way down, he spread open her legs and dove his long, powerful tongue into her wetness.

Carmen laid back with both of her eyes shut, moaning out from the wonderful feelings that were spreading throughout her body like lightning bolts. She clawed into the silk sheets as Ronnie massaged her pussy with his lips and tongue.

"Ahhhhh!" she moaned out as a powerful orgasm swept through her trembling body. She was writhing in pleasure, her legs shaking, sweat forming across her body.

Ronnie sucked her juices into his mouth, then slowly made his way on top of her quivering body. He looked down at her perfect body, appreciating it like a piece of exquisite art. After placing her legs on top of his broad shoulders, he grabbed onto her hips, bringing her closer.

For a few seconds they just stared into each other's eyes. Both of them filled with desire and ecstasy. They were hungry and ravenous like wild animals.

"Tell me you're my bitch, now!" he whispered.

Carmen smiled and said, "I'm yours."

"My what . . . " he pressed.

"I'm your bitch!" she said, meaning every word.

In one smooth motion, Ronnie entered his rock hard dick deep inside of her.

Her hands clawed into the soft bed sheets, as she moaned out in both pain and pleasure. A perfect hurting deep inside of her. Dying a little, and being reborn a bit with each thrust of his hips, she tried to breath. But it was difficult. It was too good to control.

She lifted her arms, grasping him around the back, digging her manicured fingernails deep into him. For Ronnie, there was no better joy than fucking Juan-Carlos' widow inside of their own home.

}}}

VOODOO'S APARTMENT . . .

Voodoo had on a pair of faded jeans and a white t-shirt as he closed the refrigerator with a jug of milk in his hand. He heard the knocking on the door.

"It's open," he said as he took a glass out from a cabinet and filled it. He was expecting Angie at any moment. Normally she called him on his cell phone just before she entered the building, but she had been coming over for so long now, and . . . you know women.

"Ty," his neighbor Anthony Ferretti said, "where you at?"

Ty turned and leaned out of the kitchen area, "Kitchen . . . what's up Anthony?"

He was only half surprised to hear his neighbor. He would often come over with a couple of beers to talk about how hectic life on the force was, or how his daughter was growing up way too fast and he was missing it. Most times the conversations ended up with his bitch ex-wife. If you believe Anthony, she came straight from Hell, born from Satan's seed.

It was almost like Voodoo lived out the missing parts of his life through the broken parts of everyone else around him. He was living vicariously through others. But it was like a television program because he could turn it off.

When Anthony left, no more trouble.

When Angie left, no more intimacy.

All of the good stuff, with one of the bad . . . that lasting pain he could just turn off with the closing of a door.

Anthony walked in wearing a pair of blue sweat pants with *NYPD* plastered in cracking yellow silk-screen on each side. He had a mess of papers in his hands, and a frustrated clueless expression on his face, like a brick-layer trying to explain an atom bomb.

"It's this fuckin' life insurance policy. I hate to make you work on a Saturday, but could you take a look and make sure their not giving it to me up the ass . . . know what I mean?"

Voodoo took a sip of milk, reaching out his other hand as he took the papers. He told people that he was an insurance agent. If people pressed him further, he would tell them that it was 'Personal Risk Insurance.' And really, he wasn't that far off.

And, if you're generally quiet, and just let other people do most of the talking, they'll buy just about any story you tell them. People's minds will fill in the gaps. Voodoo liked to listen, and people liked to talk. A good fit for everyone.

"Is this your personal policy?"

"It's me, yeah," Anthony said as he pulled up a stool.

"No," Voodoo responded, "I mean, is this a private policy, or is this the policy that you got through the Police Department?"

"Oh," Anthony said, his face relaxing, "that's the department policy."

Voodoo nodded as his eyes danced across the pages, "Do your union reps still govern this stuff?" As he studied the documents he had an look of expertise on his face, as if he'd done this a thousand times. But really, he's caused a lot of other people to review policies like this . . . for his targets.

Anthony shrugged, "You know how those guys are, real hard-ons for a while, but it's all just sellin' wolf tickets. I don't know if I'm getting' snowed here, or what." He crossed his thick forearms, one of them being dotted with small cuts and scrapes surrounded by clouds of black and blue bruises.

Voodoo glanced at Anthony's arms momentarily, "Union organizers?"

Anthony looked down at his arms, "No, no. some fuckin' guy tries to jump into the Hudson, and as soon as we talk the guy off the ledge, he goes bat-shit nuts and runs at the negotiator." He grins for a second, "Had to tackle his junkie ass on the bridge and stomp a mud-hole in his teeth to get him to calm down."

Voodoo nodded, "Tell you what, let me take a look at these tonight, and we'll get together tomorrow if you've got some time."

"Yeah," Anthony said, nodding as his whole chest raised up, "that would be great. I'll bring over some beer and a couple of franks." He looked around the apartment like all people who investigate for a living instinctively do. He smiled out the side of his mouth, "That cute little thing you been seein', she's comin' over, yeah?"

97

"That obvious?" Voodoo said, glancing around. The place was hospital clean, without even a single couch pillow, or blade of carpet out of place.

"Oh, that bachelor life . . . don't take it for granted, my friend," Anthony said as he turned and headed back for the door, "It'll never be as good after your second divorce."

As the cop's voice trailed off, he said, " . . . have your fun, Ty. Have your fun." And then he heard the door close.

Voodoo smiled, then finished the glass of milk. As he reached for the milk jug again, he noticed his phone vibrating across a glass kitchen table near the living room. This works out well for everyone. And, even though he knew that it was Angie calling him before she hit the elevator, he didn't want it *not* to be her.

He was comfortable around her. She didn't bust his chops too much about his personal life. And yet . . . somehow, she had become a part of it. Well . . . at 300-500 dollars-a-pop, anyway.

Like a sexy little fungus, she just kept growing on him.

A good fit for everyone.

TWELVE

THE SPOTLIGHT BAR was packed to capacity. The parking lot was completely full, with cars circling the outer edges, looking for places to park. People were walking in and out of the bar, laughing and smiling, hoping the night would end as good as it had started. Everyone was having a good time.

Lights were flashing.

Music was pumping.

And two vans crept their way up to the corner two blocks away, the drivers nodding to each other as the stoplight turned yellow for the crossing traffic.

Inside each of the recently stolen vans, the drivers yelled, "Ponte listo!"

Get yourself ready!

And with that, these quiet men checked to make sure that their *AK-47s*, their *Mossberg* .12 gauge shotguns, and *H&K USP 9mm* pistols were loaded and ready.

In each van a quiet tension churned its way between thumbs flicking off the safety levers, and eyes bent on revenge. There were no more words that needed to be said. A statement needed to be made to the Black Royals.

The message: *Fuck with the Matas . . . and you die.*

Simple.

Clear as crystal.

The vans lurched forward as the light changed to green, picking up speed. As the first van got to the corner of the Spotlight Bar's parking lot, it turned right, heading for the side entrance.

The second van headed across the front of the parking lot, turning carefully into the lot so that none of the shooters were out of position.

Doors were unlocked, and prayers whispered as the barrels of these cold weapons made the sign of the cross quickly, angry hands unwilling to release their grip, even for the blessing of god.

Each van had a driver and four men, with one single task. Shoot as many people as possible before the police arrive. The more the merrier. The lead van, approaching on a heading for the front door of the bar, accelerated as it neared the middle of the parking lot, gathering speed as the headlights were extinguished.

The driver pressed the pedal farther to the floor as the van gained more speed.

The van that had entered the side of the parking lot was creeping from the side, its doors already slightly open, just waiting for the right signal to unload.

And everyone was still having a great time.

And couples walked across the parking lot, not really paying attention to what was going on.

The lead van was only about 20 yards from the front entrance when the two Black Royals—who were parked in a car, with their machine guns across their laps—finally noticed them. But by the time that they brought up their weapons and started to yell . . . the four door guys were already being crushed under the weight of the van.

As it crashed halfway through the entrance, sparks and shards of glass exploded in every direction. Like a fire slowly catching in a dry forest, suddenly people started to scream.

Pouring out of the back of the lead van, the four gunmen, their faces covered in black ski masks, spread out around what was left of the front door. There were bodies and wood, and pieces of twisted metal hanging and bent around them as they picked out their targets.

The two Black Royals on the outside of the bar immediately sprang into action, bringing up their weapons as they ran towards the destruction that was the front door. Two of the Matas opened fire on the two rushing Black Royals, taking one of them off his feet as spits of blood exploded out the back of his body.

The second Black Royal dropped to the ground as he held down the trigger on his *AK-47* machine-pistol.

The screams in and around the bar seemed to fade as the loud cracks and pops from the different weapons tore through the night. Firing wildly, the two Matas ran around the other side of the exposed van, vying for cover. Behind them, inside the bar, shots started to whiz by their heads, occasionally bouncing off the wrecked, stolen van.

The rapid fire of a machine gun from inside the bar backed the five Matas against the side of their van, searching for targets to shoot. Their orders were to kill as many Black Royals as possible, but to try to keep the civilians out of it. Try.

101

Dragging himself around the side of a *Cadillac*, one of the Black Royal gunmen flattened himself near the front tire, using the vehicle for cover as he scooted around the edge of the tire, his elbows and stomach on the cold, wet pavement, aiming at the van.

He could see several pairs of legs scrambling around between the side of the crashed van and the front wall of the Spotlight Bar. He closed one eye, steadying the machine-pistol the best he could, and squeezed the trigger.

The weapon bounced around in his arms, its magazine scraping across the pavement with each shot.

Behind the van, two Matas felt the hot tearing pain of the 7.62 rounds ripping through their feet and ankles. They dropped immediately, their hands grasping at what used to be their legs. There was blood everywhere.

As the Black Royal behind the *Cadillac* stood to see if he'd hit anyone, a burst across the parking lot caught him by surprise, tearing at his chest and neck. He was dead before he hit the ground, the machine-pistol sliding across the cold concrete.

The second van accelerated as several Matas ran next to it, using it for cover, and looking for more Black Royals to kill. And really, any black man who was wearing black or gold . . . he was in real trouble.

Within seconds a shootout erupted near the front door of the bar, backing the Matas from the first van into the parking lot as the second van came to support them. They weren't returning fire because they were dragging two wounded men, trails of blood painting the walkway in front of the bar.

"Vaya, vaya!" they yelled.

Go, go!

Inside the bar, several Black Royals, including Ruthless, had used what cover they could fine, and made their way to the front of the bar. From inside they could see the shattered front headlights and grill of the van, stuck halfway inside and outside of the bar.

"Kill any fucking thing that look Mexican!" Ruthless screamed as he crouched with a chrome-plated .45 pistol in each hand, hovering at the front of the van. Beside him were three other men with revolvers, shotguns, and pistols. All of them were searching for brown skin to fire at.

Ruthless motioned with his head to the others, and they burst out, past the right side of the van, hoping to surprise the Matas. They were almost successful.

From the second van, one of the Matas fired several rounds with a 12-gauge shotgun, yelling, "La isquierda, la is-quierda, mira!"

The left, the left, look!

Ruthless watched as a friend of his was doubled over by the blast, instantly falling to the ground, his hands holding what was left of his stomach. Ruthless fired several shots with both pistols and then ducked back behind the van. He crouched down as lead and debris exploded around him, doing his best to drag his friend back to safety . . . but he was only dragging a corpse.

A machine gun opened up from outside the bar, turning up bits of dust and metal everywhere.

"Back in the fucking bar!" Ruthless yelled, as he crawled back inside, a bullet ricocheting off of the van and cutting deep into his shoulder. As he turned from the shot, he saw one of his partners run out with a shotgun in each of his hands, floating at hip level.

Boom, boom, boom!

103

Ruthless couldn't hear what the Matas were screaming, but it seemed like somebody had been hit. Good. *Fuck 'em all,* he thought.

And then the sound of sirens added to the gunfire. Seconds seemed like hours as the shooting continued.

Ruthless crawled across the floor, pistols in each hand, blood spreading through the fabric of his *Sean John* sweat suit. He glanced across the bar, seeing scared and crying faces ducked and hiding in every nook and corner, under tables, and laid flat near the booths. "Don't nobody worry . . . I got this shit. Ain't nobody comin' in here," Ruthless assured them all.

Sitting there, bleeding, smoke all around him, he reloaded the .45s and turned his head, his back leaning against the shattered grill of the van.

He lifted a pistol in each direction, but he could hear the gunfight outside changing. Now they weren't firing at the bar, or at the Black Royals, they were mixing it up with the cops.

Ruthless smiled to himself, speaking under his breath, "Never thought I'd be happy to hear cops."

} } }

The seven of them who were still alive were alternating between firing at the cops, and dragging their dead and wounded into the second van.

Of the original eight shooters, and two drivers, three were dead, and another two wounded. One of them—the driver from the first van—was probably going to die. Somebody had nearly torn his shoulder off with a blast from a shotgun, and there was way more blood than a human should be able to hold, leaking out all over the concrete.

104

The man and the three Matas who carried him were covered in warm red blood.

"Tira los pinche coches!" the other driver yelled as he slammed his door shut."

Shoot the fucking cars!

The idea was that if the cops couldn't follow them, they might still have a chance. So, shot after shot, they aimed at the cars, turning blue- and white-painted metal and fiberglass into scrap metal as the cops backed away from their cars. They were getting cover farther back in the parking lot.

"Vamos, vamos, vamos!" the driver yelled as they all packed themselves in the van.

Let's go, let's go, let's go!

The van was so loaded down with dead weight that the tires didn't even squeal when the driver hit the gas. He made as tight a circle as was possible, hitting the rear-end of a black *AMG 65 Mercedes*, ripping off its bumper as the van headed for the side exit of the parking lot.

The bumper of the *Mercedes* skidded across the pavement, trapped in the undercarriage of the van for several meters, sending sparks out the left side of the van. As they turned out of the parking lot, the *Mercedes* bumper fell free, screeching across the pavement where it finally stopped. And then there were no more shots.

The van raced off into the darkness of some side street.

Two more of New York's finest skidded into the parking lot with lights and sirens blazing.

And almost as quickly as it had started, it was over. All that was left were smoke, and blood, and metal, and fear . . . and bodies. Seven Black Royals were dead.

THIRTEEN

BOTH OF THE King Brothers, Ruthless, and five of their top street Lieutenants were gathered inside of a small house. They were discussing the Matas' surprise attack at the Spotlight Bar. Seven of their men had been shot and killed, along with three of the Matas.

The shootout at the bar had become the talk of the town. It was all over the television and radio, and had made the front page of the *New York Post*. People were interested in this, and it wasn't just the gangsters involved.

Inside the living room everyone sat around watching as Reggie paced the floor. He was furious, and couldn't believe that the Matas had planned and orchestrated such a bold attack at his bar. At a Black Royal establishment! That kind of thing was unheard of. But then, these El Salvadorians were a different breed.

Inside the heart of the Black Royals was a fire growing out of control. It had to be contained or it could destroy them all. Reggie stopped pacing and turned to Ronnie and Ruthless. They were sitting next to each other at one end of a large, dark oak table.

"We have to kill Caesar and Hector! They are the two men who are in control, now. And once the heads are gone, the body will surely fall."

Ronnie stood up from his chair and said, "Reggie, the only way to win this war is to kill every fucking Mata there is! After Juan-Carlos was killed, we thought that things would change . . . but they didn't. They will always have someone else to step into the boss's shoes. Unless we kill 'em all, and there are no more feet left . . . we are going to have the same shit keep happening."

"I agree," Ruthless said as he stood up. His left shoulder was bandaged from getting grazed by one of the Matas' bullets. "This war with the Matas . . . it's been going on for years, and the way things are going, well, it don't look as if it will stop any time soon."

"I have an idea," one of the men said.

"What's that, Nino?" Reggie asked.

"Why don't we call a meeting with the Matas? Think about it . . . if we keep killing each other, then none of us will make any money. And this thing is about makin' money, right? If we wanted a fucking war, we'd join the army. This shit with the Matas is hurting our money. Everyone getting shot ain't helping the drug game."

"Fuck dat shit!" Ruthless yelled out in frustration.

Reggie's eyes narrowed, "Hold up. Just hold up one minute. Nino might be right." He closed his eyes as if the list of options were written on the inside of his eyelids. "Maybe if we had a sit-down with the Matas, we could end this war."

"We could never trust the Matas!" Ronnie said. "After what happened to Juan-Carlos and his son, they'll never trust us. And we can't trust them, neither. Never."

Reggie went back to pacing the floor. His mind was filled with thoughts, possibilities, options, and tricks.

After contemplating the idea of a meeting with the Matas, he stopped and looked over at Ronnie and Ruthless. The room, all the obedient faces, they were all watching . . . completely silent. They were all waiting for the boss's decision.

Reggie's decision.

"Nino is right," Reggie said carefully, his hands crossed behind his head as if he needed more air. "We need to put a stop to this war is we plan to continue to make money. And," he said as his eyes went from face to face, silently reassuring them, " . . . this is about money. We're all here to get rich. "War if for dummies."

Reggie locked eyes with Ruthless, "I want you to let the Matas know that we are willing to sit down and have a peace talk. As soon as possible. If they disagree," he shrugged, "well, then fuck 'em. We won't stop until we kill them all."

"But," Ruthless interjected, "they'll think we're soft. Especially after the shootout at the bar. They'll think we're scared. That they got to us after the attack."

"I don't think so, Ruthless. No one wants a war. Especially a war that can't be won."

"Fine," Ruthless said as he turned and angrily stalked towards the door.

"Ruthless," Reggie said.

Ruthless stopped, slowly turning back around.

"Do we have a problem?" Reggie asked flatly.

Ruthless took a deep breath, his muscled body inflating, and slowly he let the air out, "Nah, Reggie," he nodded. "We good."

}}}

Vladimir squinted as he walked out into the sunlight, heading to the side of the heated pool where their boss—their *Glava*, Nikolai Chyorni—was wading around in the water. Vladimir had a copy of the *New York Post* folded under his arm, on the opposite side of his shoulder holster.

His pale skin was not used to the sunlight. And even though the temperature was in the mid-50s, it seemed far too hot. This would be the middle of the summer in Moscow.

"Gaspadin, Chyorni," Vladimir said politely as he passed several stocky bodyguards.

Mr. Chyorni swam in a little circle, a large cigar still in his mouth as he padded slowly. Mr. Chyorni's dark black eyes blinked several times as Vladimir approached, "Da, da. Ooh vas yest, journal?"

Yes, yes. You have the newspaper?

"Da," Vladimir said, and then tried his English, "I have paper of gang . . . ah . . . silnee, violence, da, violence."

"Very good, Vladimir," Mr. Chyorni, perhaps the most dangerous Russian in the United States, said with a nod as he crossed his arms on the edge of the pool. His English was accented, but very clear. He was not some hood from the street. It was clear that this gangster had been university educated.

Vladimir unfolded the paper, laying it in front of his boss, pointing to the pictures on the front page of the paper. *Violence in the Cemetery* was the title of the article.

"Killing, killing, killing." Vladimir said leaning hard on the *i's*.

Mr. Chyorni's dark eyes glanced at the pictures, and then read a few lines from the news copy. "It's very interesting, Vladi. The blacks are at war with the El Salvadorians."

He laughed to himself, switching the cigar to the other side of his mouth. The thing was big enough to be a hotdog, and had a distinctly Cuban smell. Expensive smoke drifted out of his nostrils as he read.

Vladimir was kneeling, waiting for an opportunity to get back inside before he burst into flames.

Mr. Chyorni could tell that Vladimir was uncomfortable, and he smiled as he looked up from the grainy pictures of death. "Vladimir, do yo like Victor?"

"Da," Vladimir shrugged. "Konyechna. On tak moi brat."

Of course. He's like my brother.

Mr. Chyorni nodded as he chewed on the end of his cigar. The guards around them were waiting for any hint that the Glava might be getting out. Then they would rush over and hand him his robe, shielding him from any possible aggression, not that anyone would be giving them grief on the roof of a 38-story building.

"I will tell you why I like Victor," Mr. Chyorni said slowly, so that Vladimir could understand the words. "I like him because he is a real criminal. Nye prestupnik . . . blat."

Not a petty criminal . . . one with respect.

" . . . he doesn't pretend to be a criminal. It is in his blood. Krov ulitsa."

Street blood.

"Victor is sur-vi-vor. Like spetznats," Vladimir said as he switched from kneeling with his left leg to his right.

110

"Blatata," Mr. Chyorni said slowly.

Real gangster.

"One day," Vladimir said, his eyes glancing up at the gleaming tall buildings and skyscrapers that surrounded them, "I think that we be have all of this. Mozhit beet, Novi Moscva!"

Maybe, New Moscow!

Mr. Chyorni was kind of smiling, but kind of not. As if his face was happy, but his mind was indecisive. It was hard to tell. He took another big puff of his smuggled Cuban, "Mozhit beet, da, Vladimir. Mozhit beet, da."

Maybe so, Vladimir. Maybe so.

FOURTEEN

QUEENS, NEW YORK
TWO DAYS LATER . . .

VOODOO SAT QUIETLY, looking through the binoculars out across the parking lot, into the fitness club. There was a cute little thing jogging on the second running machine to the left of the check-in counter. Compared to the dark night, the *24-Hour Fitness* was a glowing mecca of energy with its blue and red and green neon, floor-to-ceiling vanity mirrors, and wall windows.

Voodoo was chewing on a stick of some gum that claimed to have 'new and improved' flavor. Whatever that means. But it made the time sitting in the dark a little easier. You have to do things to take your mind off of the boredom, and concentrate on the job at hand. Things to keep you sharp, but not so much on the edge that you burn out.

He had to pay attention to the message that he was delivering.

The task at hand.

He glanced away from the binoculars, his eyes rolling over the picture in his lap. Everybody had something unique about them. Something different in their design that a skilled

112

assassin could use to pick them out of a crowd, even when they're wearing disguises.

A giveaway.

It might be their nose.

Their eyes.

A kind of limp, or a commonly used facial expression. A gesture, even. Teeth, or ears, or scars, or something. Everybody has one of these '*tells*.'

Voodoo found that his current target had very distinctive eyes. The brow, the little 'v' on the outside edges of her eyes, and the way the brow came sloping down. All of these things created a *tell* that no amount of makeup was going to obscure.

He'd been waiting for just over an hour, having been notified by Victor as to the mark's most current location. On some jobs, Victor and Voodoo would do a phone relay, back and forth, as a mark moved around the city, getting closer and closer with each call. In this instance, the mark was last seen heading into *24-Hour Fitness*.

Still chewing, he made sure his gear was in order, sitting in the passenger seat. One duffel bag, two towels, three pairs of silicon gloves, a small spray bottle of ammonia solution, and two precision-silenced *.22 Rugers*. The silencers had been specially designed and crafted so that you could fire them in a crowded room, and nobody would hear a thing. You could shoot them in church. No louder than lightly snapping your fingers.

And there she goes, her workout finished. Slowly, her jog became a walk, and then the machine's belt came to a stop. She was wearing a pair of pink sweat pants, with a white *Nike* sports bra. Her hair was long and black, stopping well past her shoulders.

She was thin and fit, her skin an unnatural brown, probably from spending hours a day at a tanning salon. Her finger nails were perfectly manicured, white and glossy. Her skin was clear and smooth. Her lips and nose were model perfect. Symmetrical, as if they had been designed by some ad agency. She was an attractive woman, probably in her mid to late 30s.

Behind the binoculars, he followed her as she headed to the locker room to get her clothes. He wasn't sure if she would take a shower there, or not. Most high-maintenance women don't like taking showers in public places. A minute later she came strutting out of the locker room, heading for the front door.

She waved to a few people, and said a few too many words to some guy wearing a 'Certified Personal Trainer' shirt. Voodoo wondered how much money she was paying for the *lessons* he was teaching her.

Seconds later she was pushing through the glass door, walking down some wide steps, and heading across the parking lot to her champagne-grey *Aston Martin*.

Voodoo, wearing a blue tank-top, and black workout sweats, put down the binoculars and picked up his duffel bag.

As Laura thumbed her keypad, making the car's alarm chirp as it disarmed, Voodoo rounded the row of cars behind hers.

She opened the car door, and tossed in her bag. She carefully sat down, checking her face in the rear-view mirror before closing the door. And then she heard his voice.

"Laura? Is that you?"

The woman turned to see him walking up with a towel in his hand, a gym bag over his shoulder. He was tall and well built, with a pair of small, tinted, oval-shaped glasses. *He's cute*, she thought.

She smiled, "Me?"

Voodoo put on a pleasant smile as he approached her, "Laura, you look great. Absolutely wonderful."

She found herself blushing, used to compliments, but flattered none the less. She squinted, "I don't recognize you. Where do we know each other from?" She had met so many men in the last few years, that it was difficult to keep track.

Voodoo walked to her door, edging his left leg far enough forward that she wouldn't be able to slam the door shut. "It's me," he said as he kneeled down. Her eyes appraised him.

As his body lowered he pulled one of the silenced pistols out of the duffel bag so quick that her mind couldn't make sense of it. He fired three quick, nearly silent bursts.

Psst-psst-psst!

Her face was instantly contorted, as if her uncomprehending mind froze somewhere between fear and surprise. The first two rounds entered her upper chest. Her eyes drained of color when the third shot entered the left side of her head, just below the eye.

At that range, with the rounds loaded down as they were, the bullet that entered her head didn't have enough power to exit the other side of her skull. It just spiralled around inside of her head, like those motorcycle stuntmen do at the circus, just ripping through brain tissue. The two body shots found a home in her upper lungs.

Very little blood.

Very little mess.

No noise.

Her body slowly doubled over as a hushed moan gurgled out of her mouth. Just before her head landed on the steering wheel, Voodoo used the towel to push her over towards the passenger side.

Wasting no time, he used the towel to close the driver's side door and in a matter of moments he was gone.

A ghost.

Two minutes later he was driving across a bridge, toggling one of the throw-away cell phones that were in his duffel bag.

Victor answered the pay phone quickly, "Da?"

"Is this Melinda's Donuts?"

"Nyet. You might be try one-forty-three, seven-seven-two. It's near the steak restaurant."

"Thanks," Voodoo said as he scratched the numbers down on a sheet of paper. Victor was giving him all of the information he would need for his second job of the night.

"Good luck," Victor said before the line went dead.

Voodoo lowered the passenger window, and tossed the cell phone out over the handrail of the bridge, falling quickly into the black abyss, known as the Hudson. That was the one and only call that phone would ever make.

The first message had been delivered.

} } }

43 MINUTES LATER . . .

This was one of the stranger jobs he had been given in a while. Rarely did Victor contract him for two jobs in one night, just minutes apart. And this was even more *connected* than that.

Mob connected.

116

Both of the targets, Laura being the first, and now Jackie *'Whispers'*, were part of the waste management industry. An industry predominately run by the Italians. They were both Italian. They were both mob connected. Laura and Jackie 'Whispers' had a long history. But all that was over, now.

Voodoo drove around the back of the parking lot which led to the small strip of restaurants. One of them, a 'family' owned joint by the name of *Two Guys from Italy* was the current location of Jackie Whispers and his insatiable appetite for Fettuccine Alfredo. The numbers that Victor had given him earlier, when he was confirming the first hit, were the street address of the restaurant.

Voodoo knew that Jackie drove a black *Lincoln Towncar*. Everything was black. Windows, interior, high-gloss paint. Word on the street was that Jackie was a bagman for three of the five families, hence the name Whispers. And a guy like Jackie, he was always surrounded by mobsters.

After parking, Voodoo grabbed a different bag, a small brown paper bag that was under his seat, and slipped it in his jacket as he got out of the car.

As he walked, he pulled the second throw-away cell phone from his jacket, and pressed in some numbers. He made his way to the parking lot of the restaurant, and with only a quick glance his eyes found the glossy black *Lincoln*. It looked like it had just rolled off the showroom floor. As luck would have it, it was parked between two SUVs.

Voodoo made his way to the car, and knelt down slapping the small brown bag to the undercarriage of the Lincoln, near the rear axle. A strong magnet inside the bag, held it to the car's metal frame, with a *Thunk!* sound.

Back on his feet again, he pressed the *Send* button on his phone, calling the bar.

"Two Guys from Italy," a low voice hissed, " . . . how can I help you?"

"Yeah, this is Frankie. You gotta guy in there named Jackie Scarcelli? Cause somebody just tried to break into the trunk of his car, out in the parkin' lot," Voodoo said, giving it his best Brooklyn accent.

"No shit? Hold on . . . " a muffled voice was yelling across the restaurant. "Tell 'Whispers' that somebody tried to fuck wit his car . . . "

The man got back on line, "Yeah, that's Frankie, he's gonna go check it out right now."

"Just lookin' out," Voodoo said as he disconnected the call.

As he backed himself near a dumpster, he quickly dialled another number, but didn't press the *Send* button . . . yet.

About 10 seconds later a short, chubby guy with jet black hair and *Popeye* arms fast-walked out towards his car, with one of his hands tucked inside his leather jacket. Most likely he was carrying a piece with him.

Voodoo waited in the shadows with his thumb on the button.

Jackie went right to the trunk of his car and opened it with the remote on his key-chain.

Jackie's tell was that he walked funny. He also had two different colored eyes—one of them green, the other brown. But the walk was immediately identifiable.

Voodoo pressed *Send*. Well, after the signal had been sent to the 4 pounds of military grade C-4 plastic explosive, Jackie 'Whispers' Scarcelli's eyes were red.

The car exploded straight up into the air, sending a tidal wave of flames and metal in every direction. His burning, mutilated body flew about 20 feet before it crashed like a rag doll into the restaurant's front wall.

Jackie, and the two SUVs that had been parked near his *Lincoln*, were turned into melting twisted scrap. About a hundred car alarms began to sound as people started running out of the restaurants nearby.

Voodoo was back in his car, dialing the cell phone one last time, as the flames were still illuminating the brick wall to his left.

"Da," Victor answered pensively.

"Is this Johnny's Pastries?"

"No. Wrong number. Your phone having problems?"

"No, my phone's fine," Voodoo said, confirming the job. "My fault."

"Whatever," Victor said as he ended the call.

Second message delivered.

$$\} \} \}$$

SEVERAL DAYS BEFORE THE HITS...

Victor looked both ways as he crossed the street, an unlit cigarette dancing around between his lips. As always he was wearing one of his blue *Adidas* track suits. He sauntered over to the black *Lincoln Towncar* and rapped his knuckles several times on the tinted window. It lowered a couple of inches, and a chubby face studied him.

"You Victor?" the man whispered.

"Of course, I Victor. Who else I be?" Victor said, almost offended that everyone didn't know who he was.

"Yeah, get in," Jackie '*Whispers*' Scarcelli said in a hushed tone.

119

Victor got in and closed the door. It had that new car leather smell, mixed with *Marlboro Lights*, coffee, and cheap prostitutes. *Mobsters are so predictable,* Victor laughed to himself. They make all of this money just so they can surround themselves in cheap crap.

"New car . . . very nice," Victor said, trying to calm the guy down. And he didn't really even like the car, it just seemed the nice thing to say.

Jackie's eyes darted around nervously, "Listen, Victor . . . you come highly recommended. I need this thing done in the next few days, if you can. That cheating cunt is giving me a bad name around here."

"Why you don't have *your* people do her?" Victor said as his teeth ground lightly together.

Jackie leaned across the seats, uncomfortably close to Victor. "Her brother is a *made* man. Donnie '*Stub Nose*' Campezi."

Victor shrugged, "I don't know this guy."

"Anyway, I can't handle it in-house, it'd cause too much trouble," Jackie whispered. "I need you to handle it. People say you're the best."

"Why not try a divorce?" Victor offered.

Whispers cocked his head to the side, " . . . you kidding me?" His tone made it sound like it might be easier to find a cure for cancer, or end world hunger. "No . . . that fuckin' bitch needs to take a dirt nap. She's like Satan's fuckin' sister or somethin'."

Victor studied the man for a moment, then said, "Okay . . . one-hundred up front, another fifty when job complete."

"Done."

Victor slid him a small yellow piece of paper with an account number on it. "Now, please."

Jackie half smiled as he grabbed his phone and started dialing. His whore wife would be out of his life soon enough.

} } }

Two trains and one cab ride later . . .

"I want that motha-fucka to suffer. Can you blow that sorry son-of-a-bitch up or something . . . is that possible?" Laura Scarcelli said to Victor as they stood across a cheap hotel room away from each other.

"It's no problem. But not cheap for you."

"How much?" she pressed, the blood almost boiling in her veins. She wasn't so pretty when she was mad like this.

"Have you considered getting divorce?" Victor tried for the second time this evening. He could imagine these two on Jerry Springer. Laura running at Jackie with a wooden stool in her hand, swinging to brain the guy.

"Are you fucking serious?" Laura squeaked as if her nose was being held shut, one of her eyebrows raised in disbelief. " . . . that limped-dick piece of shit?" White trash in Italian skin.

Victor scratched his head. He would need to get enough up front to make up for the back-end money he was never going to get from either of them. He clicked his teeth together as he counted in his head. "Okay . . . two-hundred up front. Fifty when finished."

"And you can blow him up?" she said, her eyes widening eerily.

Victor opened his arms, almost offended. "Of course. He blow up like space shuttle."

121

Her eyes narrowed as she imagined her sack-of-shit husband, Jackie 'Whispers' being blown to bits!

What a tangled web we weave.

FIFTEEN

LOTS OF RUSTED metal. Lots of fractured, cracking concrete. The smell of bleach so heavy that it burned your nose. White, glossy tile, with that marbleized pattern that screams 'old government facility'. That was what would stick with a man as he entered the High-security Federal Prison in Lewisburg, Pennsylvania.

White or off-white walls.

Egg shell moldings and frames on the windows that hadn't seen cleaning since Reagan had been in office.

It was a giant testament to bland government spending . . . all of it surrounded by walls of concrete and razor wire. This is where the bad guys end up. Not the *super*-bad guys. No, they end up where Alex Karsh just came from.

But to Alex, this place was a heaven on earth. He could see the sun, even if only for an hour a day, as it trickled down through layers of cage and fencing. But he could see it.

He could smell nature all around him. He could hear cars off in the distance. He got to talk to people, even though they were other dangerous criminals who were doing long sentences. But it was a far cry from no-human-contact; that kind of living makes people into mumbling zombies.

And while the other inmates he came into contact with were angry, violent, bitter, and beaten . . . Alex had a new-found sense of life. He was freer now than he had been in many years. And with each new day at this institution, he would become freer and freer.

Back in the jungles of the Congo, where Alex had been leading groups of mercenaries to perform assassinations, or take shipments of blood-diamonds, he had often been presented with impossible scenarios. But each and every time that he and his highly-trained thugs ran into seemingly insurmountable odds . . . they found a way.

Alex would say, "There's no such thing as a box you can't open, or a puzzle you can't solve."

Where other people saw finality, he saw beginnings. Where others resigned themselves to be captive or dead, he sculpted freedom and life. Men like him, with no rules to live by . . . well, they can be very capable.

Very dangerous.

He liked to think of himself much as his nickname, The Wolf. And anyone will tell you, you can't cage a wolf forever. He'll find a way.

Yes, Alex Karsh liked his new living conditions at Lewisburg just fine. Wearing his tan khaki pants, with his worn-out white t-shirt, doing his push-ups and sit-ups in a cage that the Humane Society would picket against if it was used to house animals, he took mental notes.

"Karsh!" one of the guards barked. "You got a legal visit . . . let's go."

Without an answer, he hopped to his feet, backed slowly towards the cage door, and slid his hands through a rectangular hole in the fence so that he could be cuffed. He then entered a smaller cage and had his feet shackled.

The guard—a large, muscular white man with a round pink face—looked down at the scruffy South African. "They still killin' blacks in your country?" It was kind of a question, and kind of a statement.

"No, sir," Alex said politely. "Mandella changed all that. Now the country is democratic . . . just like here in the United States."

The guard started to chuckle to himself, "Democracy, huh? That shit ain't worked too good here, neither."

} } }

4 MINUTES, 3 HALLWAYS, 2 BODY CAVITY SEARCHES, AND 1 METAL DETECTOR LATER . . .

Different visiting room, same rugged plastic furniture. Different guards, same attitude. As Alex was marched into the visiting area, Special Agent Dan Gonzalez stood up, his face looking tired and puffy. Gravity was getting the best of him.

"Leave the cuffs on," Dan instructed, " . . . but get rid of the shackles."

"Your funeral," a short, stuffy little guard said as he shifted the chewing tobacco from one side of his mouth to the other.

Dan laughed to himself, "I hear that a lot around here."

When they were finally alone, only the sound of the air-conditioning humming in the background, Dan placed his hands on a manila folder. "What do you think about your new accommodations?"

Alex almost smiled, just for a brief second. He looked around the room, "I saw the sun yesterday, for the first time in, I don't know how long." He nodded. "Thank you."

Dan eyed him, trying to figure the guy out. What was his story? Everyone has a story. Most of our stories aren't filled with political assassination and worldwide chaos, but we've all got one. Alex's was interesting.

"I wonder," Dan said, "If you wouldn't mind brainstorming with me a little bit." He tapped his hands down on the folder. "Take a look at these, tell me what you think."

Alex leaned forward as Dan poured out the glossy crime-scene photographs. They were full color, in your face, crystal clear death. 10 or 15 photos in all.

Dan laid them out, very slowly and carefully. "This isn't being recorded. I'm not going to make any notes, unless you give me permission."

Alex's eyes glanced up at Dan's, then back down to the photos. He slowly raised his cuffed wrists and slid one of the pictures to the right. Then another, and another. He made two piles of photos. "There you are."

Dan looked down at the piles, having a slight grin pass across his face, and asked, "So . . . what's your favorite stack?"

"These on the right," Alex said. "They're your gangland-style murders. No real magic. Anybody with a desire to kill, could pull them off."

Dan bit the inside of his lip, "And the other pile?"

Alex leaned back, yawned, and took a deep slow breath. "You might have some trouble putting your hands on this guy."

Dan grabbed the second pile of photos and spread them out, again. There were eight of them in all. And he had known that Alex would pick them out from the others.

"So these would be . . . what?"

"Professional," Alex said, completing the thought. "They were done by a person who makes death his life's work. Like an artist, maybe."

Dan's eyebrows bent, as his curiosity was piqued, "Elaborate."

"Well, look at the hits." Alex moved his cuffed wrists around as if he was playing with a Ouija board, summoning the dead to speak. "This . . . this is a cemetery, right?"

They both stared down on the picture of Juan-Carlos, nearly cut in half, his insides falling out, dripping over a small silver coffin. It could have been fake, something from a movie set. Something too horrible to be real.

"This was a statement killing," Alex explained. "Whoever did this, was ordered to do this for effect. Like, an exclamation point. I see this kind of job among oil and mining companies in Africa. It starts with agreements that turn into contracts that get violated. It's like a daisy-chain that escalates until executives are getting dumped like this guy." He studied Dan's face, "Was he an executive?"

"Kind of," Dan said. "Organized crime."

"Same thing," Alex said, nodding.

"Yeah," Dan said. "You're right." He paused for a moment, a thought running its course through his mind. "Anything else look odd?"

"Who killed the kid?" Alex asked softly.

"I didn't say anything about a kid," Dan backpedaled.

Alex tapped his fingers delicately on the coffin, as if he might get blood on his hands. "It's an old trick . . . goes back centuries. The ninja had a target that they couldn't get to. Maybe the guy was always inside, secluded behind a fortress or something. So, they killed one of his family members.

"Well . . . everyone goes to the funeral. And then, at the ceremony, when everyone's crying and their heads are looking down," Alex suddenly slapped his hands down on the photograph.

"Bam!" He smiled, "That's when they get you."

"Somebody hit the kid a few days earlier," Dan said, sliding the other photo in front of Alex. "On the sidewalk. They did it with a . . . "

"Three-oh-eight," Alex answered for him. "Everyone's favorite sniper round. Practically designed for killing humans."

"We think that the shot came from a nearby building, several stories up. Could have been as far as four-hundred meters."

Alex laughed.

"What?"

"Four-hundred meters," Alex said as if it left a bad taste in his mouth. "That's like a child's shot. A blind, fucking idiot could make that shot. No windage to worry about. No real light issues. Only a minor angular adjustment. That's an easy shot for a trained trigger."

"But it was a kid," Dan countered, almost disgusted.

Alex shrugged, "Do you think that makes any difference, Dan? A child, a mother, a monster, a president. A target is just a target. It's a paycheck. Even for those people who do their killing for ideological reasons . . . they still get a form of payment. It's all just business, mate."

"So," Dan said, "do you think this guy is some mobster, or is he a trained hitman?"

"He's a professional. He usually only fires once," Alex said, sliding his hands over the cemetery picture. "he took this shot . . . " he squinted, lowering his head, " . . . that was a fifty-cal, from," he looked up, "do you have a picture of the bullet fragments that were left?"

Dan shook his head, "Not with me, but you're right. Fifty-cal, from about a mile away, maybe more. And he used a D-U round."

Alex closed his eyes, his arms resting near his chest, "Now that's odd. You wouldn't need to use Depleted Uranium for this kind of job. That's an armor-piercing round. Radioactive, very dangerous . . . even for the sniper to handle. You can get radiation poisoning from handling those things too often. It's a military round."

Alex sighed and cleared his throat, "You have bigger problems on your hands." The violent memories in his mind weren't far from the surface. You can try to forget what you've done for a lifetime, and it only takes a tiny mention of your past to bring it all right back.

"Problems like what?" Dan asked.

"*Russians*," Alex said, almost letting the words fall out of his mouth letter by letter.

Dan nodded, "He used flash and smoke grenades to cover his escape when he hit the kid."

"These are gang hits?" Alex asked as he looked over the photos of people shot in their cars, hit from afar, and taken apart by large caliber bullets. Some of them were black. Some of them Hispanic.

"Different gangs, feuding against each other," Dan said.

"Well, I think it's the same assassin," Alex said cautiously. "And I think I would keep my head down if I was asking questions about him. He's probably pretty well connected. With lots of resources. Tread lightly, special agent."

"Yeah," Dan said as he sat back, the air almost knocked out of him, " . . . and carry a big stick."

After their visit had ended, Dan made his way out of the Lewisburg facility and out into his rental car. He sat down, closing the door behind him, and dialed the number he knew by heart, and then placed the cell phone to his ear.

A pleasant female voice answered, "You've reached the Central Intelligence Agency, how may I direct your call, please?"

"I need Shane Abbot, at the Russian Desk."

" . . . hold for one moment while I transfer you . . . " and then, "This is Cindy, you are speaking on a non-secure line, how can I help you?"

"Hi, Cindy, this is Dan Gonzalez," Dan said as he rubbed between his eyes with his free hand, "I need to speak with Shane. Is he in?" He waited a few more seconds until he heard the familiar growl.

A low pitched voice answered, "Danny boy . . . what's the word?"

"I may have a Russian Problem," Dan said.

$$ \} \} \} $$

NEW YORK
VOODOO'S APARTMENT . . .

Voodoo was sitting back on his clean white sofa while Victor paced around the living room playing with his *Zippo* lighter.

Click-snap, click, snap.

"One-hundred and seventy-five for last two jobs," Victor said.

Voodoo was staring down at Victor's iPhone, checking his account at *Atlantic International*. Everything was in order, as usual. "Nice."

Victor—all skin and bones and gold jewelry, and more dangerous than a sack full of rattle-snakes—said, "I have new job for you . . . if you be want the work."

Voodoo tossed Victor his phone back. "Work's what keeps me sane."

Victor smiled as he pulled out a newspaper clipping with a photograph of Reggie King. "You know this man?"

Voodoo took the photograph, studying it as if it was a map. Every curve meaning something. "Gangbanger. He's got a brother and a . . . bunch of clubs." He shrugged.

"He's very dangerous guy . . . lots of bodyguards, lots of guns. Everybody want excuse to shoot. What you think?"

Voodoo placed the picture in his pocket and reached for a *National Geographic*. "Good money?"

"Your cut, two-hundred," Victor said, seeing if Voodoo's posture changed even a little bit.

"When?"

"Three, maybe four days," the Russian answered. "You have to do your prep, so . . . week at the most."

Voodoo shrugged disinterestedly.

"You sure you not scared?"

Voodoo laughed to himself as his eyes rolled, "That's what I like about you, Victor . . . you've got a sense of humor."

"What you have to drink in this place?" Victor said, opening his mouth as if he had walked through the desert to get there.

"There's Gatorade in the refrigerator."

"You're like communist dictator," Victor said as he walked to the kitchen, " . . . I want *real* drink. Like wodka."

"You should drink something healthy for a change. You look like a vampire."

"Maybe I be vampire, who knows?" Victor said as he stuck his head into the cold mist of the refrigerator, pushing cartons of low-fat milk and fruit to the side.

Behind him he could hear Voodoo's phone vibrating its way across the glass table.

Voodoo answered, "Yeah?"

"Am I speaking to Ty Jacobs?"

"Who is this?"

"My name is Paul Singleton, I'm with Humanity First. I was given this number to call in the event that we had any problems with Miss Josephine Taylor."

Victor was starting to say something as he approached, but Voodoo held up his hand, nodding as the voice on the phone explained the situation.

Victor watched, drinking milk straight from the carton, as Voodoo seemed to take the news badly. His face tense as he listened to the call.

"Okay, I'll . . . I'll be there," Voodoo glanced at his watch, "I'll catch the first flight out." He nodded some more. "Alright, thank you, Paul." And then he lowered his arm, the phone hanging at his side.

"Voodoo, you don't look so good," Victor said. "What be problem?"

"She's sick, Victor. Ms. Josephine's sick. And they don't give her more than a couple of weeks, tops." He placed the phone on the glass table and crossed his arms. "I have to go to New Orleans for a couple of days."

"Okay," Victor said as he put down the milk carton. "We make trip to deep south."

"You don't have to come, Victor."

"Hey, Voodoo," Victor said, his fingers warning his friend, "we all family. If we be have family problem . . . we solve problem. Together. Family be first."

And in a rare gesture, Voodoo smiled, nodding, "Thanks, Victor."

"You make bags, I be get tickets from *Priceline*," Victor said seriously, "Captain Kirk get me best deals available."

Voodoo headed off towards the bedroom to pack a bag. Ms. Josephine, the closest thing he'd ever had to a mother, was sick.

There were things between them that needed to be said.

Things more important than money.

More important than a paycheck.

SIXTEEN

INSIDE A HOUSE on Daley Avenue, the top members of the Matas were down in the basement talking. The house was just one of many that the Matas used to have their secret meetings. A place where they could talk without prying eyes, or curious ears.

A few hours earlier, Hector had received a message that the Black Royals were willing to sit down and discuss the possibility of a cease-fire.

Diplomacy for the greater good.

Peace talks.

"Fuck da Royals!" Pepe hissed. "They killed Maria, and the boss, and his son. We could never trust those pinche negras."

Caesar, Hector, and Felipe stood back watching as Pepe vented out his frustration and hatred he had built-up inside of him for the Black Royals. And even though they didn't say it, most of them shared his feelings. But business and feelings are two different things, entirely.

134

Since their war had begun, Pepe had personally killed six Black Royals. But blood was on all of their hands, even if they didn't personally pull a trigger, or swing a machete.

"Maybe we should listen to what they have to say," Caesar said. "This war . . . with the Black Royals," he sighed, " . . . it has been slowing down a lot of our money."

"Fuck those niggers!" Hector fumed coldly. "I already had a talk with our Russian friend, and he said that everything will be taken care of. Soon."

Caesar walked over and sat down in a wide, brown leather chair. "I want to have the meeting with the Black Royals. So let them know that we agree to a sit-down."

Hector's mouth stood open, the veins in his head throbbing. "No disrespect to you, Jeffe," he said as he walked towards Caesar, "but I think that maybe you should reconsider. Juan-Carlos would never have agreed to anything like this. Never!"

Caesar stood up and studied his friend. "I'm not Juan-Carlos. And I don't want to keep watching my men die over a war that's been going on way too long. It's so old we don't even know what we're fighting for. My hatred of the Black Royals will never change, but if they are willing to talk, then I'm willing to listen. This is a business decision, nothing more."

"They are just scared!" Pepe shouted. "After we killed seven of their men, now they are ready to talk about peace. Fuck that. When you have somebody down on the ground, you can't let them up . . . you step on their neck." He slammed his food down onto the concrete floor. And nobody had a hard time imagining Pepe stomping the life out of someone.

Felipe stood back, leaning against the wall with his arms crossed. He was much less animated than the others. He buried his emotions, not ever wanting to show his hand . . . even among friends. Slowly, a tired smile started to form on his face as he watched Pepe rant.

Pepe was buzzing around the room like a bumble-bee on speed, "We can't trust them. Niggers are only good for three things: Basketball, rap music, and dying! And look . . . I can't play basketball, and I don't know how to rap . . . but I don't mind helping them to die."

Caesar let them vent; get it out of their systems. Better now, than in front of a bunch of men, hell-bent on violence. He raised his hands, calming the group, "We will have the meeting. This is no longer open for discussion. I understand how we all feel, and I'm not ignoring that. But we have to rise above our anger and hatred."

He nodded to Hector, "Set it up."

Everyone looked at Caesar and saw the serious expression on his face. Rules were rules. The decision had been made.

"What about the hit on Reggie?" Hector asked quietly. "Do you want me to contact my Russian friend and call it off?"

Caesar considered it for a moment. "No . . . not yet. First, let's just see what happens at this meeting. If all goes well, then you can tell your friend to call it off." He crossed his arms behind his head, "When do they want to have the meeting?"

"Sunday," Hector said. "Somewhere neutral like Manhattan," he added.

"Make sure everything is prepared. Take every precaution." As Caesar looked around the room, he sensed the apprehension in their faces. "We'll be ready for anything, amigos. If this is a trick . . . they will have started the beginning of the end."

"Caesar, please . . . "

"My mind is made up, Pepe. Now leave it alone," he said before Pepe could get out another word.

Pepe put his head down, his teeth clenched together, his jaw tight. Anger was boiling deep inside of him, and only a machete and a pile of bodies would satisfy his hunger for revenge.

Caesar cleared his throat, stood up, and stretched his neck, "I need time to think. I'll talk to you all later." He watched as Hector, Pepe, and Felipe marched frustrated out of the basement.

Caesar sat back in deep thought, knowing that the meeting with the Black Royals was just another chess move in the brutal game of survival. Only, in this game, one wrong move and you died . . . no exceptions.

What he didn't tell his men was that he wanted revenge more than all of them combined. It was taking every ounce of his self-control not to succumb to the thirst for payback. But that was the mindset of a soldier . . . not a leader. He was wearing a different hat now, and could not be driven by his emotions.

Pepe and Felipe both watched as Hector got into a cream-colored *Jaguar* and drove off down the street.

When they climbed inside their tinted black *Dodge Caravan,* Pepe looked over at Felipe and said, "I dont' care what Caesar says, I will always be at war with the Royals. They killed Maria and Juan-Carlos. I will never forget that. Never."

Felipe started up the van and slowly pulled away from the curb, heading down the street. He glanced over at Pepe, "I think they're scared, too. We got 'em good at that bar and now they're afraid of us. But Caesar is the new boss, so we have to follow his orders . . . even if we don't agree. He knows things that we don't. He sees the bigger picture."

Pepe sat back with his arms crossed and a strained look on his face. "When is this meeting set for?"

"Sunday," Felipe said as he stopped the van at a stop sign, checking in every direction.

"Cool. Let's drive over to the Edenwals and see if we can catch us a nigger," Pepe said with an evil grin on his face, nothing but teeth. "Besides, this meeting ain't till Sunday, so we still got a few days to use our machetes."

"Fine with me," Felipe said, making a quick U-turn and heading towards the Edenwals Housing Projects.

Diplomacy for the greater good.

$$\} \} \}$$

169TH Street . . .

Inside Ruthless' Bronx apartment, on 169th Street, between Washington and Park Avenue, he and Nino sat on the couch watching as the attractive woman stood in front of them, stripping away her clothes.

Her name was Joy Adams, and a few times a week she made her own private appointments. A little extra cash on the side. For almost a year, Joy had been the Black Royals' number one call girl. And in time she had established good friendships with some of their top members.

Joy unsnapped her pink lace bra and tossed it over to Nino. Then she slid out of her black thong panties and tossed

138

them over to Ruthless, who caught them in mid-air with a 6-year-old's smile on his face.

"Are y'all boys ready?" she asked seductively, the air around her smelling like flowers and sugar and sex.

"Been ready," Ruthless answered as he and Nino stood up from the couch. Both men were completely naked, with lust and hunger in their eyes.

Joy walked up to Ruthless and looked up at his face as her hands gently caressed the sides of his bare legs. "Will I be staying all night, again?"

"Yeah," Ruthless said, staring into her beautiful green eyes. "And you'll be taken care of," he assured her.

Ruthless watched as Joy kneeled down, grabbing the backs of both of both of his legs as she took his long, hard dick into her mouth. Her soft, warm lips traveled further and further, as his hands rested on her shoulders.

While she was sucking every inch of Ruthless, Nino walked around and placed his hands on her hips, slowly lifting her until his hips were directly behind hers. His hands played with her for a few seconds until he was ready. And then he thrust deep inside her hot, wetness until his hips pressed against her ass.

Moments later the moans and heavy breaths of ravenous sex filled the air.

This wasn't love making. It was fucking.

This wasn't beautiful and tender. It was hard and wet.

Dirty. Pain and sex and money all rolled together like a ball of mating snakes. They used her as if she was an appliance. Something you plugged in, turned on, and wore out. And whether it was the money, the sexual gratification, or just the attention . . . she enjoyed every second of it.

Here, among these men, she felt needed.

Wanted.

Nino, pushing himself as deep inside her as he possibly could, felt his legs begin to quiver and shake.

Ruthless, pulling her mouth around him while she licked and sucked as deeply as she could, closed his eyes to savor the moment.

And there was Joy in the middle—little more than a piece of functional meat to feed their desires.

SEVENTEEN

AFTER A THREE-hour long shopping spree at some of Manhattan's most elegant and luxurious stores, Carmen watched as a young man put all of her shopping bags into the trunk of her car. It was a mountain of bulging plastic and colorful paper. When she gave him the crisp 100-dollar tip, his face lit up with a smile bigger than the mountain of bags.

"Thank you, Ma'am," he said before turning away and going back into the *Louis Vuitton* store. Carmen walked around her *Mercedes* and got inside, the smell of fresh leather and perfume surrounding her.

When she started the engine, it purred to life as the electronic dashboard came to life. Now she might have been inside the cockpit of some private jet. Instantly, the mellow voice of Mary J. Blige flowed out of the speakers as if Mary was sitting in the back seat, playing a live performance.

Making a show if it, she slowly placed her tinted *Gucci* shades on, and pulled off down the street. No rush. She wanted everyone to see her. To have their mouths drop at her success. To envy her.

141

Today was one of the happiest days of her life. The four million dollar life insurance check for her husband's untimely death had finally cleared.

He had also been wise enough, when he was alive, to make sure it covered *acts of* violence, paying out somewhere in the neighborhood of two-and-a-half-million dollars for the passing of Juan-Carlos Jr. But that was taking some time for the investigators to clear. Though, it was just a matter of time. That was her money. They could curse her all they wanted, but they had better pay-up.

With over $75,000 worth of shoes, bags, and other expensive accessories that she certainly didn't need, she felt like the luckiest woman alive.

Minutes later she pulled to a stop in front of a condominium apartment building on Madison Avenue. She parked and got out. With the press of a button, the trunk opened as the bags pushed the trunk upwards.

She took one of the bags out, and headed up the walkway where two doormen greeted her. They were all smiles and nods, their heads lowering as if she was the princess of some oil-producing country.

She entered the lobby, impressed as always by its beauty and elegance. Money makes money. And this place screamed money.

A few men were admiring her as she walked, one foot in front of the other as if she was on the runway at a fashion show. Seconds later she had disappeared into one of the waiting elevators.

Looking more like a model from the cover of Vogue, than a gangster's widow, it was obvious to all that this Spanish beauty was out of everyone's league.

Unobtainable.

The elevator stopped at the third floor and Carmen stepped off, holding a single bag at her side. She walked down the empty hall and stopped at door 3-C. She used her key card and entered into the gorgeous 3000 sq.ft. condo, as the smell of vanilla- and cinnamon-scented candles wafted past her.

The condo had a built-in fireplace, over-sized windows, marble baths, 10 foot ceilings, and a private balcony, all of it set on an oak-planked floor that was so polished it looked wet. This place—her new condo—wasn't completely furnished yet . . . but she smiled, never-the-less.

It was the kind of place where people respected your privacy. Where they treated you like royalty, no matter what you were wearing. If you lived here, you were worth millions, and were treated accordingly. She closed her eyes and smiled.

For her—a girl from the slums of New Jersey who had used her undeniable beauty to climb the ladder—this was the top. She had smiled, and winked, and fucked her way to the bigtime. She had earned this. Every over-priced square foot. Every piece of abstract art. Every *Versace* throw pillow and *Gucci* comforter. The diamonds, the platinum, the gold-plated water faucets. All of it. She had worked hard, using what tools she had.

Tanned perfect skin.

Round sensual eyes.

Curves, sculpted by God.

Juan-Carlos had been her meal ticket. Her chip in the big game. And now that her former husband and his only heir were dead, Carmen was ready to live her life to the fullest. With Juan-Carlos' over-protectiveness, she had lived a limited and sheltered existence. But now that he was gone—stitched

143

crudely back together like some stuffed dear, and sitting in a casket next to his son—there was nothing that could hold her back.

Her inner freak had been dying to be released, and there was only one man who could control it. Who could feed her hunger.

After inhaling the scent of the burning candles, she walked towards the master bedroom. When she turned the doorknob and walked into the large bedroom, her handsome black lover was laying across the king-sized bed.

Ronnie King was completely naked, laying on his back, only a soft pillow covering his waist. With his hands behind his head, he said, "What's in the bag?"

Her eyes studied his body as she walked closer, "some stuff I bought for you." She sat the bag down and started to undress, really giving every motion a slow deliberateness.

Putting on a show.

Ronnie watched as she undressed, and then walked over, crawling onto the bed like a cat.

"I'm all yours, now," she said, climbing on top of him.

Alone, inside their cozy bedroom, they started to kiss. The kisses became longer and more passionate with each breath. Their hands wrapped each other up, sliding up and down, in and out, making them both hard and wet, as they slid around each other. And the two of them became as one, rolling around each other, exploring the most sacred parts of each other.

They were doing more than just touching each other. There was an unspoken emotional connection that they had. They were making love.

And yet, it was primal.

}}}

Joy walked out of the high-rise building and looked up the street. She had just finished having sex with one of her wealthy white clients—an older Jewish man that owned one of the largest book publishers in the country.

For months Joy had been his favorite call girl. She did things that were probably illegal for a man who follows the Torah. But then, a man's got to have his outlet.

Joy stood outside watching as the cars and yellow cabs drove up and down the street. She glanced at her gold *Cartier* watch, a gift from her Jewish friend, and she saw that it was half past four. She had to be at another appointment by five o'clock.

When she spotted Angie's dark blue *Lexus* coming down the street, she felt the relief wash through her body. As soon as Angie pulled up in front of the building, Joy rushed over to the door, pulling the door open, jumping inside, and closing it in a single motion.

"Damn girl, what took you so long?" Joy said, as she fastened her seatbelt carefully across her chest.

"Big Tony took longer than usual," she explained as she pulled away from the curb. "I think he used a Viagra."

"Cheater," Joy laughed. "So, did it add any more minutes to the three he already had?"

"A few," Angie smiled. "What about you . . . how was your night with the thugs?"

"Wonderful! You need to stop acting all high and mighty and start making some extra cash on the side. It's easy money. The agency takes more than half of our money, so why

145

not have a little hustle on the side? You have any idea how much money I made last night?" Her eyes widened, and you could almost see dollar signs rolling like a slot machine.

"I'm sure you're gonna tell me," Angie said as she made a right turn down East 52nd Street. She watched as Joy went inside of her leather *Fendi* bag and pulled out a large stack of bills.

"This is twenty-five hundred dollars, Angie. All for less than one day's work. And, besides the money, the sex was amazing!" Joy had an evil grin, "I haven't been fucked like that since I was in junior high. I can't even count how many times I came." Her voice quivered as she thought about it.

"I'm fine," Angie said with a half disapproving laugh. She slowed down and stopped at a red light, taking a breath, her body a little lower than before. "I'll continue to stick to my regulars. At least I know it's safe."

"Girl, you need to stop trippin'. We both know what it really is," Joy said, turning and staring directly at Angie. "You falling in love with that man . . . Ty. That man got you strung out like a crackhead. When are you gonna realize that you're nothing but a piece of expensive ass for him? Nothing else."

Angie looked over at Joy, "Sometimes he makes me feel like it's more." Then she turned back to the road, "I'm not stupid. I know the difference between the job and the real thing . . . and sometimes . . . "

A car honked behind her, bringing Angie back to reality. "It's not just work, with Ty. There's more to it."

Joy couldn't hold in the laughter, and burst out, "Damn, girl! Let me find out that you can't control these tricks. That nigga don't give a fuck about you, girl! All y'all do is fuck.

Did he ever ask you for anything other than to get between your legs? Anything?"

" . . . but," Angie tried.

"But shit!" Joy interrupted. "You're pretty with a nice body and the sex *must* be good or the guy wouldn't call and only ask just for you. But believe me when I tell you that it's all about pussy."

Joy placed both of her hands over her crotch, "Nigga ain't never been shit, so why do you think he'll start now?"

Angie sat back listening to the same advice that had been given to her a hundred times before. To the same advice she would give to any of the other girls she knew.

Still, there was something deep . . . deep inside of her that told her that there was more to Ty. He was different. At least, that's what she hoped and wanted. Even though all they ever did was have sex—powerful, blissful, earth-shaking sex—Ty made her feel special and appreciated.

It had gotten to the point where all she wanted to do was spend time with Ty. Even if they weren't talking. Just to be near him.

Proximity feeding, like a pet.

Every time she was with another paying client, she couldn't help but to think about Ty. Wishing that it was him inside of her, instead of some anonymous john.

As they pulled off down the street, Angie's mind was clouded with thoughts. While Joy continued to lay it all out for her, Angie was in another place and time. Some life far removed from this one.

She was in the arms of a man named, Ty. Who she didn't know at all, but that she was somehow falling in love with.

EIGHTEEN

VOODOO AND VICTOR were laying quietly back, sitting in the first-class section of the plane. Victor had only purchased economy class tickets, but two 100-dollar bills palmed in his hand while he gave a flirtatious handshake to one of the flight attendants, and their seats had been magically upgraded.

Airlines would rather leave those seats empty rather than allow people to move up without paying the extra couple thousand dollars. But flight attendants, Victor explained under his breath, they like tax-free cash under the table. Hard currency. "Just like communist country," Victor had snorted as they had been led to their plush leather seats.

He was nursing his sixth miniature *Stolichnaya* Vodka bottle.

Just minutes earlier, when the beautiful young attendant had brought the first of the small, clear bottles, Voodoo had laughed, and Victor cocked his head back, as if she was kidding.

"What is this for?" he said, a bit confused. "This is child's serving of wodka?" He was still having trouble with his *V*s.

She looked at Voodoo, who shrugged and gave her the *I can't help you* glance. "He's Russian."

"Yeah," Victor said proudly, "I be Russian. And we grows up, from little babies, to drink wodka." He lifted the bottle between his two fingers as if it was a cigarette, dangling lightly. "This is like toy bottle. Maybe for young, attrac-tive girl like you."

Victor folded his arms in front of his chest defiantly, "I be need more."

The attendant smiled, blushing, the way all women somehow did around Victor, and shook her head. "Well . . . " she whispered, "I'm not really supposed to, but I'll get you a few extra."

Victor turned to Voodoo, lifted his eyebrows a couple of times, turned back to the girl, reading her name-tag, and said, "Tammy . . . I think you are wonderful woman. Maybe I be marry you."

She giggled, her cheeks turning pink, as she sauntered off.

"How do you do that?" Voodoo asked as he turned towards the window, his head leaning against the cold clear plastic. Nothing but clouds and blue heaven above and below them. Like, in this place, above it all, there was no wrong in the world. Quiet peace.

Artificial sanctuary.

"What can I say . . . ladies love Victor," he opened his fingers. "I be like sex sym-bol or something."

Slowly, looking out at the curving blue world that surrounded them, Voodoo faded off to sleep. And even in his slumber, there was his friend.

}}}

14 YEARS AGO, ON THE WEST SIDE OF NEW ORLEANS . . .

Voodoo, wrapped in an old green army-surplus jacket, with his whole life packed in a black duffel bag that was slung over his shoulder, wondered if anyone would ever stop.

Would any person in their right mind stop, on this side of Interstate 10, just past the 17th ward?

And . . . would they pick up a young black kid who didn't know anything about the world other than the notion that he had to find out who he was, and where he fit into it?

He must have walked for miles, hours; through rain, mud, and choking blue smoke. And then the dusty old *Cadillac* passed him by, skidded as the brake lights glowed bright red in the night, followed almost immediately by the small white reverse bulbs, as small as Christmas lights. The loose gravel and rocks kicked and popped as the car reversed and stopped near him.

The window whined its way down as a thin, white face, with bulging grey eyes, as cold as a snowman's, peered out at him. "You be need ride, kid?" the man said, his accent strange and unfamiliar.

"Yeah," Voodoo said, still not moving towards the door.

The man shrugged, his gold jewelry jingling around his neck, his left hand tapping on the steering wheel anxiously, "Okay . . . well, you want ride on hood, or inside?"

Voodoo snapped to, opening the door and quickly slipping inside. Two screeches later they were on their way east. Neither of them spoke for several minutes. But strangely, it wasn't uncomfortable. Each of them were lost in their own thoughts.

They had their own problems.

Their own demons to slay.

The inside of the *Cadillac* was littered with candy bar wrappers, soda cans, and small see-through sandwich bags. Hanging from the rearview mirror was a small flag divided into three different colors—red, blue, and white.

Noticing the boy staring at the flag, the man said, "I be from Soviet Union. I be Victor Pavlovich." And, switching a cigarette from his right hand to his left, he extended his hand.

"I'm Ty . . . Ty Jacobs," the boy said, shaking Victor's hand. "People call me Voodoo."

"Why they call you that?" Victor said out of the side of his mouth, his eyes glancing from the road, to Voodoo, and back. "You eat people, or what?"

He didn't sound too worried as he spoke. Victor had an easy confidence about him, as if he could kill you at any moment, but would rather just let the cards fall where they may. He was like one of those old land mines that might blow up at any second, or never at all.

Ty smiled, "No, it ain't nothing like that. My eyes . . . people say they're kind of odd looking." He raised his sunglasses to reveal dark, almost black eyes, with grey around the edges. They could have been polished black pearls from the bottom of the ocean.

Deep black marbles.

Victor looked, nodded to himself, and then placed the unlit cigarette back in his mouth. "Eyes is eyes. I don't think you look so scary. Maybe you have . . . night-vision or something?"

He maneuvered the white stick from one side of his mouth to the other. "You be mind if I smoke?"

"No, sir," Voodoo said.

Victor eyed him, suspiciously, "*Sir . . .* " he smiled, "you be call me 'sir', like in army?"

Victor started to laugh, a real hearty gut-bending laugh. "Coorava matsch, stadi! Just Victor, okay. Victor."

"Victor," Voodoo echoed. "So what do you do?"

Victor's laughing subsided quickly. He studied Voodoo for a few seconds, considering his words. " . . . I in very complicated business. Import-export. You know of this?"

Voodoo shrugged, "Not really."

"Yeah," Victor repeated, a bit more relaxed. "I be import-export guy. America is good for this business. Good for me. This is why I stay."

"You don't miss home?"

"Do you miss your home?" Victor countered, turning the spotlight around.

Voodoo slumped in his seat. "I don't really have a home. I mean . . . I'm not sure where I fit in. To all of this . . . " he said as he stared out of the cold glass window into the darkness that surrounded them like a giant wet blanket.

"How far you want to go?" Victor asked.

"As far as you're willing to take me," Voodoo answered.

Victor smiled, "Voodoo . . . my new American friend. I will take you to a brave new land, where anyone can become rich and powerful if they have desire to succeed. Do you have desire?"

Voodoo laughed, probably for the first time in so many years, all his past just a fading memory in the dust behind them, "I got nothing *but* desire."

Victor leaned back in his seat, relaxing. You could see the pistol hanging from his shoulder holster starting to peek out from his unzipped sweater top.

"The world," the Russian said, "is full of opportunity if you have . . . ah . . . " he thought of the right words, " . . . balls. Balls to take opportunity by the neck, bite off its nose, and laugh."

Voodoo turned towards Victor, not quite sure what he meant by all that, but getting the general idea.

Victor shifted his wet, unlit cigarette, shrugging, "It's Russian proverb. Hard to translate."

Voodoo laughed, and they drove on.

Through Kentucky.

Into Florida.

Up the coast.

Slept through Georgia.

Passed through New Jersey.

And ended up in New York. And then there was the incident. And then Voodoo learned what Victor *really* did for a living. What *import-export* really meant.

And then he saw the money.

And the respect.

And the freedom.

And this strange white man, with his funny Russian accent, and his gold chains, and his unlit cigarettes, and his pale eyes, and his guns . . . he gave Voodoo a life. And Voodoo took it. He grabbed opportunity by the neck and bit off its nose.

And he laughed, just like Victor said he should. He taught Voodoo everything that the Russian army had taught him when he was too young to think any differently. Too innocent to blink.

And he became a weapon, more dangerous than anyone could have ever imagined. And he finally found out who he was, and what his purpose in life was.

He was an executioner.

An assassin.

A messenger.

NINETEEN

A COUPLE OF hours of smooth flight, a few flashing seat-belt signs, and their plane had landed. Victor and Voodoo made their way, like mice in a maze, to the baggage carousel, and collected their bags.

As they exited the New Orleans International Airport, Victor squinted at the bright sky above them. It was the kind of white where the sun was hiding just behind the clouds, threatening to break through. White like a flood light in your face. Like looking directly at an atom bomb explosion.

Or, at least, that's how Victor would tell it.

He watched Voodoo as they both slipped on their sun-glasses, "Do you feel . . . what is word . . . nostalgia?"

"Smells like tar and bug spray and old, stale beer," Voodoo said as they headed towards the rental car office.

"You pretty much summed-up this whole state," Victor said as he lifted his phone, trying to get good reception. That iPhone was like another appendage to Victor. Like an extension of himself. He looked frustrated, "I don't understand."

"What?"

"How fucking I can't get service here in New Orleans. Big city. Bla-bla. You put man on moon. You fly to Mars. And I can't get more than two bar of reception. Suka blat!"

"You won't need that phone, here, Victor," Voodoo said. "We're not going to be here very long."

"Good," Victor said as his hands unzipped and searched through his duffel bag for something.

They got a white *Caprice Classic* from Allstar Automobiles, and headed off.

$$\} \} \}$$

54 MINUTES LATER...

The closer they got to the rundown old Victorian mansion, the quieter everything became. Victor was driving, glancing down at a small, crumpled map that Voodoo had drawn on a napkin.

"I think this be the place."

Voodoo sat up, his eyes collecting information, filling in gaps that his imagination had been glossing-over for nearly 15 years. The house looked so much smaller than he remembered, as they approached down the brown dirt road, pockmarked and gullied throughout.

As they winded to the left, going denser into the tree line, it seemed as if the trees were more crowded . . . almost frantic. And every so often, as they rolled slowly forward, the house came in and out of view, obscured by the thick, hanging branches.

"Looks like trees be sad, here," Victor said softly, more to himself. "This place is, ah . . . strange."

156

"Do you know what Voodoo is, Victor?"

Victor shook his head slightly as he weaved around the large holes in the trail.

Voodoo, also spelled *Voudou*, or *Vodun*, or in French *Vaudou* is an official religion in Haiti. Together with Roman Catholicism. Voodoo is a Creolized religion, forged by descendants of Dahomean, Congo, Yoruba, and other African ethnic groups who had been enslaved and brought to colonial St. Dominique (as Haiti was known then) and Christianized by Roman Catholic missionaries. The word Voodoo means *spirit*, or *deity* in the Fon language of the African kind of Dahomey.

"It's fundamental principle is that everything is a spirit. And that Humans are spirits who inhabit the visible world. The unseen world is populated by the Iwa."

"*Iwa*?"

"Spirits," Voodoo said. "God created the universe, and the spirits to help him govern all of us and the world we inhabit. The natural world."

During religious rights, believers sometimes enter a trance-like state in which the devotee may eat and drink, perform stylized dances, give supernaturally inspired advice to people, perform medical cures, and other special physical feats. It's about restoring balance and energy in relationships between people and the spirits of the unseen worlds.

As Voodoo was explaining this to Victor, you could see the Russian's eyes growing wider, more aware. Less comfortable. In Russia they didn't believe in things like Voodoo and black magic. Life was too cold, too short for all that.

And yet, something stirred inside of him as they drove among the haunting trees. He didn't believe in God, either . . . but he was still scared of him.

"And you believe these things?" Victor said. "These spirits you can't see . . . and ghosts hiding in the trees?"

"Ms. Josephine raised me that way," Voodoo said as his eyes studied the old mansion. "She taught me that the world we see is every bit as real as our dream world. That we have greater purpose in our lives."

Victor brought the *Caprice* to a stop, grayish-brown dust rising around the car. "Ms. Josephine still be live here? This place look like farm house in Siberia."

"It's almost two-hundred years old," Voodoo said as he got out of the car. "Parts would collapse and we'd fix them."

The old place was patches and mending's, and pieces of old wood nailed to other bits of older wood, trying to keep the place from falling in on itself. Hundred-year-old planks were the 'new' supports for pieces of warped birch and oak that were cut by Confederates.

Robert E. Lee might have cut some of the trees that made this groaning place.

The stories it could tell.

The secrets it would never betray.

Voodoo and Victor made their way across the grass, wild and thick because it had never seen a mower, ever. They both glanced at each other nervously as they prepared to walk up onto the warped porch to the front door. It was kind of like drawing straws to see who was going to fall through the unsteady, rotted floor first.

As the wind pushed through the thick mat of trees, several wind chimes made sounds like lost children, all around them. And even though Victor was the kind of guy who would put 20 bullets into a man just on principal, he jumped just a bit when the chimes started their haunting songs.

Victor, who once made a guy swallow a balloon full of the guy's own fingers—that Victor had just taken off with a pair of garden shears. The same guy who probably hasn't cried since the end of the Cold War. Those chimes, they made Victor pause, the hair on the back of his neck standing up, just for a second.

"I don't know about your house," Victor said between clenched teeth. "Maybe I need gun."

In front of them was a large, black door with strange markings in white chalk all over it.

"Voodoo?" Victor asked, already knowing the answer.

"Yeah," Voodoo answered. "Voodoo."

He reached out and knocked several times, not sure if the door would come down when he did, and then he heard her voice. And as dark and dismal and eerie as this place was, her voice was exactly opposite.

"Tell me that's my Voodoo child," her voice beamed. And though it was low and powerful, it had the sweetness of a church choir. The softness of Aretha Franklin.

"Ms. Josephine," Voodoo called out as he reached for the tarnished-green brass doorknob. The door coughed several times as he pushed it open, scraping the floor as it went.

As they walked inside, Voodoo said, "Ms. Josephine, where are you?"

And then, out of the candle-lit darkness, she motioned for him to come into the living room. In contrast to the look on the outside of the house, the inside was antique, and clean. Almost like a museum. This place had been cared for, on the inside, to make up for the lack of care on the outside.

The couches and chairs were covered in deep red felt, the legs and surfaces made of a dark maple. There were only candles burning for light, but as their eyes adjusted, every-thing came into focus.

This old house, it was so much smaller than it had been all those years ago.

Everything Voodoo had known, every piece of furniture, door threshold, and piece of art . . . all of it replaced by small-er versions of the same. This was his memory, only smaller.

A copy of a copy of a copy.

Laying back, under a thick, handmade blanket that cov-ered her entire body except for her face, she smiled at them. Her dark brown skin glowed with the soft flickering of the candles. "Come here, my little Voodoo child. You is some-thin' special."

The years had been kind to Ms. Josephine. Even though her black hair had been replaced with white, her face and skin were smooth and clear, as if she was faking it. As if she could just sit up, stretch, and lift Voodoo into her arms like she had so many times . . . so long ago.

"You don't look sick," Voodoo said, swallowing several times. His mouth suddenly felt dry. His throat ached. He had seen enough death to know when it was closing in. He was pretty sure that if he looked hard enough in the darkest corners of this old house, he'd see the Ferryman waiting for her to cross over.

She smiled, her bright green animated eyes and perfect teeth, relaxing them all. There was a tiredness to her expres-sions, as if the mere act of smiling was difficult to her. "This must be your friend . . . Victor."

Victor—his *Zippo* quietly *click-snapping* in his pocket the whole time—approached her slowly, nodding several times as if he was meeting a national hero. He lowered his head, humbled by her presence. "Hyello, Ms. Josephine. Voodoo is very good boy . . . man. Very honorable man. I be trust him with my life." He nodded, glancing at Voodoo as they sat in antique chairs around the couch. "He say very good things about you."

She reached her hand out to Victor, taking his palm into hers. "You took real good care of him, Victor. You turned my baby into a man." She turned to look at Voodoo as her eyes welled-up, " . . . a good man."

Victor's eyes narrowed suspiciously, that eerie stirring feeling running around in his stomach, "How you be know my name?"

She smiled, "Victor, I've been dreaming of you two for so many years now, that I can't count 'em no more. You look thinner in person."

"Dreams, you know, they add ten pounds," Victor said with a nervous grin.

Victor and Voodoo traded the kind of glances that people usually reserve for seeing ghosts . . . for real.

She patted his hand, "I don't care about none of your business. We all walk our own path through this dream we call livin'. You took care of my precious Voodoo child. And for that . . . I'm grateful."

"I just . . . you know?" Victor said as he shrugged.

She sniffed a bit, and then she started to cough, over and over. And they were those painful, gut-wrenching coughs where everyone in the room feels a little pain.

She turned to Voodoo, extending her hands, "Come close, my Voodoo child . . . there is some things I need to tell you before I go."

"Ms. Josephine," Voodoo contested. "You need to let—"

"Shush, boy!" she said, her voice growing weaker. "I don't have too much time left. That's why I sent all them doctors away. I'm about ready to move on over to that *other* side. But I need to talk to you . . . and you need to listen. It's about your mother. Your *real* mother."

TWENTY

THE LINE OF sports and luxury cars that were waiting for valets to open their doors and trade them their keys for small paper tickets looked like what you might expect to form outside of the Academy Awards. But this wasn't an awards show . . . it was *Cipriani.*

You'll find everyone from chic, rich, sexy Europeans, to the familiar faces that visit your television set every night. Diddy, J.Lo, Naomi Campbell were just a few of the recognizable names that appeared. Frequented by the way-too-rich, the way-too-beautiful, or just the way-too-lucky. Unless you had some major clout, forget about even driving up. Reservations? *Yeah*, right.

The owner, Giuseppe Cipriani, owned a hotel in Venice, among several other high-end restaurants. He was the kind of man who knew what elegance looked like. He knew how to treat his star-studded clientele. And, he knew that when Reggie King call you, personally, and asks to have complete use of the back of your establishment, that you agree.

You nervously bite your lip, asking him how many will be in his party. He tells you, " . . . no more than ten." You swallow, and make the arrangements, telling him that everything will be fine. But when Sunday actually rolls around, and you see the large, well-dressed black gangsters start to arrive, your heart rate jumps up just a little bit. Maybe you have a quick drink at the bar to calm your nerves.

And when the door guys call you on your radio to let you know that five well-dressed El Salvadorian mobsters are having their *Bentleys* and *Mercedes* parked, maybe your pulse gets a little faster. You take another drink, this time a double, and you nervously smile at the beautiful young waitresses, telling them to be quiet, and smile, and please don't do anything to upset these men.

As Caesar, Hector, Felipe, Pepe, and Julio walked by Giuseppe, they nodded. Caesar—dressed in a cream-colored *Dolce & Gabbana* suit—smiled at the owner, "I'm here to meet with a Mister Reggie King, please."

"Si, si, si," Giuseppe said as he led them to the back. High windows with light wood frames, soft lighting, and comfortable chairs gave the place a swank but classy feel. They were led past several movie stars, who seemed to stop chewing their food in mid-bite. The Matas walked by, not paying them a second glance.

As they were ushered into the back, they saw a large table with place settings for at least 10 people. On one side, pushed away from the table as they made small talk, were Reggie and Ronnie King. Beside them were Ruthless, Nino, and Jamal—the man in charge of taking drugs and distributing them to the street dealers. All of them dressed in black suits, with gold jewelry, and silk handkerchiefs flowering out of their breast pockets.

164

No guns had been allowed at this meeting. This sit-down was just a verbal meeting. No blood would be shed here. This area was considered neutral territory, and both sides had agreed to the *no-guns* policy. But then, there were enough knives at the table that a bloodbath could still break out at any moment.

And though there was a no-guns policy in effect inside the restaurant, that didn't mean that on the outside there weren't hoards of soldiers, from both the Black Royals and the Matas, sitting in cars, walking around mingling with the affluent crowd, waiting for any reason to pull out their weapons.

They could easily turn a Sunday in New York into a Sunday in Beirut, in less than a minute.

But, this was about business.

Diplomacy for the greater good.

Nobody makes money if they have to fight a war all the time. And as the Black Royals' upper echelon stood to greet the Matas, there was a strange calm and silence that echoed throughout the restaurant. It was as if the stars and models and lawyers and trust-fund babies had all agreed not to say a word. Not to even breath. As if they could accidentally start some kind of violent chain reaction.

Reggie nodded to Caesar, "Thank you for coming, Caesar."

Caesar nodded, "Well, this craziness has gone on long enough, no?"

The others—Ronnie, Hector, Ruthless, Felipe, Nino, Pepe—all sized each other up. A few of them nodded as they took their seats on the other side of the table.

165

Reggie smiled, as if he was meeting a business client. He lifted up a menu, ignoring the table, "I think we should get something to eat. I can't negotiate on an empty stomach."

Caesar and Hector traded curious glances, and then followed suit by picking up the menus in front of them.

This was the kind of place where there are no prices on the menus. If you have to ask how much something costs, you're probably in the wrong restaurant.

Their waitresses made their way to the table, many of them attractive enough to be runway models . . . not to say that some of them weren't.

Reggie smiled at a tall, thin blond whose hair was pulled back into a ponytail. "I would like several bottles of something white and fresh . . . Italian," he warned with a smile. "Not French."

He looked around the table, both at his men and the Matas. "Gentlemen, the sommelier, here, is wonderful. I let him pick all of my wines, and he never misses."

"We'll try whatever he's having," Caesar said, folding up his menu. The other Matas slowly followed suit.

Reggie lifted his head, watching Caesar carefully, wondering what was going through his mind. Murder? Revenge? Money? Legend?

The blond nodded, smiled, and then backed away quietly.

With the air of a college philosopher, Reggie sat back and asked, "Caesar . . . do you know the history of your name?"

Caesar leaned back in his chair, curious where this was going. "It comes from the Roman ruler."

Reggie nodded slowly, "Yes. You are correct. I studied Caesar, when I was in school. Much the way I have studied you."

Caesar laughed to himself, "This is to know one's enemy, yes?"

"That's right," Reggie said. "Because when we study our enemies, we study ourselves. We are defined by those who we engage in battle. Caesar, he had Pompey. Early on, Julius Caesar identified his strategies carefully, and he only did things that put him in a firm position to measure up to Pompey in battle."

Reggie took a slow sip of water and continued, "When war finally broke out between the two, Caesar was at the peak of his game. He defeated him . . . but the,, and not too long after their war, he realized that he had no more rivals. No more enemies. He lost all sense of perspective. He was way the fuck out-of-touch, even though he was treated as a God. You see, when he destroyed his enemy, the very man who defined him, he destroyed a little of himself."

Caesar smiled, "Your enemies, they give you a sense of reality . . . humility, frailty. A reason to be."

Reggie looked slowly around the table. "Look at all of us. Mortal enemies. There isn't a man here who wouldn't want to see the other side of the table wiped off the face of the planet, in an instant. Revenge!" he said as he lifted his fist into the air.

Then, slowly, he opened his fingers, spreading them as he flipped his hand over, palm open as if he was holding the world in his hand. "But what would that leave us? Where would we be? Our identity would be gone. My enemy is my mirror."

Caesar nodded, looking over to his men, and then back to Reggie, "Julius Caesar was an interesting man. But we're not living in the days of old. Thousands of years ago, things were different. Desires were different. I don't know if Julius would have acted the same way, if he were alive today. I, too, know a little about the man."

Caesar took a sip of water, "My father, he was just a farmer in El Salvador. But he used to bring me these books that he found at the markets. *Books*, he would say, are pages and pages of free wisdom. This is how I learned English. Reading those old books."

And Giuseppe is in the back, pouring himself another drink, more nervous than a preacher on a school bus.

Caesar went on to tell them a story he had read. As a young man, Julius Caesar was captured, one time, by a band of pirates. They wanted a ransom for his return. The asking price was 20 talents, which was a hefty sum back then. He laughed at them, saying that a man of his nobility was worth no less than 50 talents. He even offered to pay the sum himself.

Some of the men who worked for him were sent to collect and return the ransom, while he was left alone with these violent pirates. While in their company, Caesar participated in their games, sometimes even playing a bit rough with them.

He used to joke with them that he would have them all crucified one day. All for a laugh.

They were amused by this courageous young man. In fact, the pirates practically adopted him as one of their own. Eventually, the ransom was paid, and Caesar was set free. They said their goodbyes and that was that.

Or was it?

He proceeded to the nearest port where he manned several ships, at his own expense, and then went after the pirates. He tracked them back to their hidden camp, and surprised them. And they welcomed him back. But Caesar was not as endearing as they were.

He immediately had them arrested, had his money returned, and as he had joked so many times with them . . .

"He had them crucified," Caesar said. "He was a man of his word, even if that word was taken lightly."

The message was coming across clear. The Matas weren't here to forget the past. They would never forget what had happened to Juan-Carlos, and his son. But they were here, and that was a step towards something.

The waitresses approached with several bottles of wine, setting them about the table so that everyone was served. As they filled the glasses, everyone at the table shifted uneasily in their chairs. Reggie looked down and studied his menu, not really looking at the choices so much as gathering his thoughts.

There was a sincerity in Caesar's words. He was an honest man. He was one of the few, Reggie thought, that still followed the code.

Honor on the battlefield.

Looking up, Reggie said, "Gentlemen, I recommend the *Beef Carpaccio*, with *Dauphinoise potatoes*. It's as close to heaven as we'll ever get in this world."

Caesar locked eyes with Reggie while the rest of the room, and anyone near enough to not get caught, watched them. These two men were able to call on their men for so much violence and terror. For New York, it was like watching two political adversaries staring each other down. Who would flinch first?

Giuseppe was sweating, pouring himself his sixth drink.

"*Calamaras rellenos*," Caesar said to one of the waitresses. " . . . and I'll try the *Dauphinoise potatoes*, like the gentleman recommends."

169

The waitresses went around the table as the different thugs asked their quiet questions, and ordered food they could neither pronounce, nor understand.

Hector and Felipe had the *Constantine al Finoccio* . . . with the potatoes. Ruthless, he had the *Ossobuco alla Milanese*, and the potatoes. Nino and Pepe, they both chose the *Beef Carpaccio*, but Pepe insisted that he wanted no part of the *Dauphinoise potatoes*, glaring at Ronnie King across the table as he placed his order.

Again, the waitresses scampered off. And again the table was silent and unsteady, like a bed sheet pulled so tight that if any side of it comes un-tucked, the whole thing would explode. There was a false symmetry, here. One tiny wrong move, and the whole thing would unravel.

They made small talk for the next hour as they ate, and towards the end of the meal, Reggie was ready to present his solution.

Finishing the last bits of his meat, he took a sip of smooth white wine, and wiped his face with a napkin that was as soft as woven silk. In fact, it might have been. With his thumb, Reggie played with the platinum ring on his index finger. "Caesar, I have a proposition for you and your men."

"I'm listening," Caesar said as he washed his dessert down with cold water.

"I want us to agree to a cease-fire," Reggie said, sensing all of the unsteady eyes looking at him. Even from his own side of the table he felt it. "We have both lost men that were very close to us. Men that can never be replaced. But we can have a peace between us that was never possible before."

"You mean when Juan-Carlos was alive?" Caesar said, behind eyes that betrayed nothing of his anger.

170

Reggie nodded slowly, "Yes, Caesar. A peace that Juan-Carlos would never have entertained . . . much less agreed to."

"Is that why you had him killed?" Hector asked, speaking up for the first time since they had sat down. Caesar turned to him, and Hector immediately backed down, almost shrinking in his seat.

"Things got out of hand, recently," Reggie explained delicately. "It started as an eye-for-an-eye, and you know where that goes. Pretty soon, everybody's more concerned with killing than with making our financial interest succeed. Dyin' ain't no way to make a fuckin' livin'. I never intended for it to get out of control.

"But . . . what's in the past is unchangeable. I want the violence to stop before every fed in the state has all of us in their cross-hairs. We're bringing to much heat. I'm sure you have to be feeling it, too."

"Of course," Caesar said, sitting forward in his chair, " . . . but what do you expect me to do, lay down? Let you assassinate my boss and forget it, as if it's just water under the fucking bridge? You killed his son, for Christ sakes! This is no small matter. There are soldiers, and then there are those who must never be targeted. And it was you," he said, pointing at all of the Black Royals, " . . . all of you, who started that. How can we possibly coexist?"

The proposal that Reggie presented was simple, "We split the territories up. We take a map, and we agree on every block, street corner, and building. We come up with an arrangement that will maximize all of our financial interests. And we get fuckin' paid in the process. I'm not afraid of going to war with you, Caesar. I'm just not interested in it. I'm in this for the money, plain and simple."

Pepe wiped his face, stood, and tossed his napkin on the table, as everyone turned to watch him. He snorted, "I think I need to be excused." And with that he left the large dining room.

Caesar looked at the empty seat, and the fire that was behind the eyes of his men, and then he looked across the table at the Black Royals, equally unenthusiastic about a peace agreement with the Matas. And he knew that he had to rise above his own rage, his own need for revenge, and be bigger than his emotions.

He had to do what was best for the Matas, even if it didn't necessarily seem *right*.

"I will need some time to study your proposal," Caesar said, clearing his throat. "We should meet again in the next couple of days . . . perhaps next week, to discuss this further. I can't rush into a decision like this. But I will give you this . . . I will tell all of my men that there is to be no violence between the Matas and the Black Royals until we have arrived at some final decision. I suggest that you do the same with your men."

Caesar started to turn, and then he said, "The *Dauphinoise potatoes* were a wise choice." He pursed his lips, "I need you to talk to your men . . . bridle them."

"Consider it done," Reggie said, his thumb still sliding across the ring.

Caesar stood, and immediately, his men raised from their seats. From his jacket pocket he pulled out a wallet and began removing several 100-dollar bills.

"I've got this," Reggie said, trying to stop him.

Caesar tossed a couple thousand dollars down on the table in crisp, new bills. "No . . . I insist," he said.

And with that, Caesar and his men left the room without another word.

Giuseppe took another drink, this time scotch . . . old and potent. Aged for years, just for Sunday afternoons like this.

After they were gone, Reggie looked over at his men. "Well, what do you boys think?"

"That mother fucker is cold," Ruthless said. "Real calm. Real careful." He lifted his shoulders and dropped them, his arms crossed in front of his chest. "He ain't like Juan-Carlos. He's with that new-school shit."

Ronnie, still munching on a bread stick, stood slowly up and walked around, stretching his arms out, side-to-side as he spoke. "Thing is, man, 'bout them Matas, you ain't never gonna know what the motha-fuckas' thinkin'. But . . . you know . . . they's into getting paid, just like us. Shit, we keep killin' each other, there ain't gonna be nobody left to work the streets. And, shit . . . I'm trying to live it. Ain't no point makin' all this money just to get shot."

Reggie took a deep breath and sighed. "We wait for a call, then."

"Yeah," Ruthless said, " . . . or a bullet."

TWENTY-ONE

THE CHURCH OF the Divine Cross was a small red-bricked church with white and grey trim. It had tall, multi-colored stained glass windows, with crosses that formed in the center of the dark blue, and deep yellow shards of glass. All around the church were the signs of rebuilding and renewal, all of it trying to cover up the damage that Hurricane Katrina had unleashed in her tempestuous rage. New paint over buckled wood. New doors over collapsing houses. Small, green trees next to broken, rotting grey tubes that used to be trees.

The skeletons left in Katrina's wake.

The Sunday evening service was one that everyone in the neighborhood tried to attend. There was singing and praising, hopes and tears. Silence, and somber memory of the dead, and days gone by. Inside the church, dark wooden pews were filled with faces, both old and young. And it was like a giant family, each of them sharing their pain with their neighbors, doing the best they could to rebuild something for their future. Where FEMA and Mr. Bush had fallen short, these

174

men and women and children all gathered together, their arms and hearts extended.

The warped, creaking wooden floor had its own personality just as much a member of the church as its Pastor. The laughter and murmurs of the capacity crowd quieted as Pastor Adam Edwards— formerly known as Sheriff Edwards—walked slowly between the pews, smiling here, tapping a shoulder there. He had been a force in the community for the last 40 years.

After retiring from the Sheriff's Department, he had become a pastor, doing his best to help the community any way he knew how. He gave everything he had of himself to the families, and especially their children. The *children*, he'd remind them all, they were the future of this city. They will be our mothers and fathers, our mayors and policemen.

The kids will save us all . . . or so he claimed.

The tall, black man, with just a hint of grey hair sprouting on his otherwise shaved head, smiled affectionately, taking several steps up and turning at the front, behind a glossy black podium. His charcoal-grey suit fit him snugly. He was a big man, well over six-feet, with strong, etched features. His eyes were dark brown, his chin square and stern. He was the kind of man you could easily imagine getting the answers out of a suspect who didn't want to talk.

"1 look down here at all of these faces," Pastor Edwards said slowly, his eyes making a connection to each person as he spoke vibrantly, " . . . and I see somethin' special. I see a love, floating around us all. Can you see it?"

He looked out into the first couple of rows, to a large white woman wearing a red, striped dress. "What about you, Mrs. Simmons? Can you see the love around each of us?"

She nodded.

He looked farther back, "And you . . . Mr. Davis, and your sister Clair, and her two beautiful little girls. Children of God. Can you see it?"

"Amen" they all said in unison as they looked around at each other. A few people whispered. They were like one big organism, all feeling for each other, all pulling for the person sitting next to them. Nodding their heads as he spoke, his low, mellow voice permeating the church.

He continued, his eyes accepting each and every one of them as a part of his family. And sitting in the back row, under the cover of *amen's* and *hallelujahs*, Victor nudged Voodoo on the arm. "This be the guy?"

"Yeah," Voodoo said flatly. "He's the one."

Victor and Voodoo were wearing suits, a rare fashion choice for Victor, but a necessary one. They didn't want to stick out too much. Already they were strangers in this church. And a bleach-white Russian sitting next to a muscled black man looked strange enough.

They were both wearing sunglasses, an old technique that Victor said kept people from seeing your intentions. Your motives, your desires . . . those are sitting in your eyes. And if people can't see them, you're already ahead of the game.

Victor studied Pastor Edwards as he spoke. "He talk well," he said, as a black woman, probably in her mid-40's glanced back at the unlikely pair.

"They all do," Voodoo said. "When I was a kid, Ms. Josephine brought me here to feel the *word*."

"What did it feel like?"

Voodoo shrugged, "It felt like people putting money in a basket. Like people hoping that God would solve their problems so that they wouldn't have to do it themselves. Like a God lottery or something."

"I take Chicago with the points, and I be happy every time. But this guy . . . I no give him *nothing*," Victor said, crossing his arms in front of him. "I don't like this preacher."

Again, the black woman with the curly black hair and small gold earrings turned towards them, squinting.

The service went on for about 35 more minutes, with singing, clapping, praising, the whole nine yards. Some people were crying as Pastor Edwards spoke about the sacrifices that Moses made to cleanse his people. The sacrifices that Jesus made for all of us to be given a chance. A chance at an eternal life. So much better than this one we live of floods, and famine, and pain, and torture, and war, and starvation.

Our souls, he said, could be saved if we only had the courage to submit to Him. To confess our worst sins and beg Him to take us unto Heaven. He said all these things, Pastor Edwards, and it looked as if he might cry. This big, strong, capable man, brought almost to tears by the joy of salvation.

"I don't think he be really cry," Victor snorted. "Preacher all the same. Dyengi, dyengi, dyengi."

Money, money, money.

Voodoo's lips curved up, smiling for a second. Maybe Victor was right about the glasses. And maybe it was more than that. Perhaps when people couldn't see your motives, you *could* see theirs. As if they're just looking at a two-way mirror, fixing their shirt, or picking something out of their teeth. But you're on the other side, just inches away, calmly reading everything about them.

Victor's odd-ball way of looking at things was sometimes oddly correct. He was glad that Victor had come with him, to the place where his life had started. They were as close to family as either of them had.

177

And then they became quiet again, collectively, as if they all knew that it was time to pray. And for several minutes different people in the room stood and gave thanks, or begged God for just a sparkle of hope for some sickly child, water damaged house, or impossible to repay sub-prime mortgage. Asking the Lord to help them keep their home, their wife, or their dignity, they spoke.

And everyone closed their eyes, their heads down, their thoughts . . . maybe on the person talking. Or, perhaps, drifting to themselves, and their own problems. Save us all, *but save me first.*

As the service came to a close, Pastor Edwards reminded everyone about a bake-sale for the rebuilding of the Church's religious library. Slowly, the congregation stood, turning left, shaking hands, turning right, shaking hands. Hugs here and there, as they took each other into their arms, and prayers, and thoughts.

Victor didn't say anything, but Voodoo could tell that he held these people in contempt. He knew that his comrade would have rather plucked his fingernails out, than to have stood up and asked God for help.

It was beneath him.

Victor didn't beg for anything. He did it himself. Go out in to the cold Siberian forests and see if God helps you. Victor would give you a teethy smile and say, *I don't think so.*

They both stood, along with everyone else, their eyes watching Pastor Edwards beneath their sunglasses. And as the people began to leave the church, they did, too. It wouldn't be long, now.

Keeping an eye on him, they floated out to the parking lot with the river of Christians.

"You know his car?" Voodoo asked under his breath as they smiled and nodded to people they didn't know.

Victor answered. "Da, konyechna."

Yes, of course.

As they neared their rented *Caprice Classic*, the black woman that had been staring at them during the service slowly approached, her steps nervous and unsure. And as they had opened the doors on the *Caprice*, she raised her arm slightly. Victor saw her and motioned with his head to Voodoo.

"Excuse me," she said, her voice unsteady. "You're new to the church?"

Voodoo studied her. She was thin, and delicate. All of her actions were humble. Her eyes, used to looking down, were wide and scared. A lifetime of sacrificing. She might have been a mouse in another life. An injured puppy, perhaps. Whatever the story . . . somebody had hurt her.

Abused her.

Violated her trust.

"You just move into the area?" she asked politely, braving a smile.

"Passing through," Voodoo said.

She nodded, her eyes lowering again, her hands almost trembling in front of the blue buttons on her long, black dress.

Victor narrowed his eyes behind his glasses, seeing something
about this woman that looked familiar. Something, he'd seen before. He leaned on the car for a moment, and then nodded to the woman. "You have very nice church, here."

"Thank you," she said, deciding whether or not to take a step forward . . . closer to Voodoo.

179

Victor nodded as politely as he knew how, and then got into the driver seat, closing the door behind him. Out came his lighter, out came his cigarette.

Click-snap, click-snap, as he tossed the white stick into his mouth, not lighting it. He tapped his left hand on the steering wheel, waiting for Voodoo to join him.

Looking across the rear window, he could see the Pastor getting into his *Ford Focus* with a young girl, maybe fifteen, maybe less. "Hey," Victor grunted, "on idut, seychas!"

He's going, now!

Voodoo, with his hand on the edge of the car door, his body about to enter, he said, "Look, you . . . you have a beautiful church. Wonderful people. Tell me, Candice," he said, glancing around as he lowered his voice, " . . . is that him?"

She swallowed hard, tears welling up in her eyes. She wanted to collapse. To fall to the ground and cry, and scream, and curse. She wanted to ask God why it all happened. She wanted to do all of these things. But she didn't.

She lowered her head, her shoulders rising, and then dropping down, down, down, as she sobbed. And slowly she nodded, her eyes trying to look up . . . but without the strength.

"It's not your fault," Voodoo said. "None of it was your fault." And with that he slid into the car and closed the door.

Victor wasted no time putting the car into reverse, as if he was still in New York, slamming the pedal, screeching his way backwards until he hit someone or something. Seconds later, he was tearing down the black asphalt street, hugging a pair of faded yellow stripes, as he searched for Pastor Edward's car.

"Who was she?" Victor asked, already knowing the answer.

Voodoo didn't respond for a few seconds, his mind putting the pictures in their appropriate locations. Two left turns, and a right turn later, he said, " . . . that was my mother."

"She have your face," Victor said. "But not your courage."

"She was just a little girl . . . a little girl who trusted too much."

"Now we deal with . . . pyed," Victor said, his voice growing cold and violent.

"That's right," Voodoo said. "Now we deal with pyed."

TWENTY-TWO

THEY PARKED NEAR the tree line at the *Motel 6* where Pastor Adam Edwards had entered. He and the young girl, soft and innocent, wearing a yellow dress with green piping and green slippers, had gone into room 23. Perhaps they were planning some church function?

Maybe they were getting a bunch of church-related material together?

A surprise party, even?

There might be any number of good reasons for Pastor Edwards to be alone with this young girl. But sitting in the car, sliding magazines into their pistols, neither Victor or Voodoo could think of any.

"In Russia," Victor said through his teeth, " . . . we be fuck these guys up."

"You just get the girl out of there," Voodoo said. "I need to take care of this one personally."

Click-click.

Like they'd done it a thousand times, the silencers were screwed onto the threaded barrels, locking firmly to the cold steel.

Voodoo nodded, sliding the gun into a hidden holster in his jacket. And without another word they got out of the car and headed towards the stairwell near the pool, where nobody was swimming.

They nodded politely as they walked past a cleaning lady who was wearing a set of headphones, and probably wouldn't have noticed them if they were wearing Santa Clause costumes. They passed the rooms one-by-one.

35

34

33

Inside, Caroline was sitting, her arms crossed in front of her, rocking back and forth on the bed. From the bathroom, Pastor Edwards was speaking to her.

"Now you know that God loves you, sweetheart."

"Yes, Pastor," she said, her voice as soft as a single strand of silk. Her eyes darted nervously around the room. Maybe she knew what was coming, maybe not.

"You know that I love you, just like God . . . "

"Yes, Pastor."

31

30

29

" . . . and you know that I would never have you do anything that God didn't like, right, Caroline?"

She nodded as the door to the bathroom opened slowly. Pastor Edwards was wearing a towel around his waist. Only a towel. And as he approached her, her eyes got wide and afraid. He sat down on the bed next to her. "Caroline, when you really love somebody, the way God loves somebody, you have to show your affections."

Caroline's soft hazel eyes were trembling. Her thin arms, now hugging her own body, hoping for a miracle. Not understanding what this man, this good man, was saying. Pastor Edwards was everything in the community. Everybody loved him. Surely, she could trust him. He had been the one to baptize her, even. If she couldn't trust him . . . who could she trust?

"When we love each other, like God does . . . " Pastor Edwards said barely over a whisper, " . . . we show our love by touching each other."

With every inch of Caroline's young body that his eyes took in, he felt himself growing under the towel. She was so clean, so perfect. Like the snow, before people have walked through it. Like a sweet piece of apple pie, fresh from the oven. His mouth watered with desire.

She looked up at him with such innocence, as so many girls had done before.

So trusting.

So helpless.

"Do you love me, Caroline?" he said, placing his giant hand on the back of her tiny neck, slowly rubbing the sides of her neck with his meaty fingers.

He leaned closer to her, her mouth hanging open, not knowing that this wasn't the way love worked. And then . . .

A bright flash illuminated the room as the door swung open!

"What the hell?" Pastor Edwards blurted as he squinted.

Voodoo and Victor quickly entered. Voodoo's eyes locked on Pastor Edwards, as Victor did a quick search of the motel room.

Victor barked, "Clear," and then he walked to the side of the bed, just outside of Pastor Edward's reach. The man was an intimidating figure, even half naked, wearing a robe.

Looking at the small child, one hand steady with the silenced *Glock 17*, Victor said, "Little girl, what is your name?"

Scared, shaking almost uncontrollably, she said, "Car . . . Car-o-line."

Victor smiled, "Caroline, you need to come with me. I will take you to your parents, okay?"

She didn't have the courage to look over at Pastor Edwards for permission. She got up and hugged Victor. Quickly, he led her out of the room, stopping briefly at the door and turning back.

In a flash, he spun his Glock around and fired one shot *Psst!*

Pastor Edwards yelped as he bent forward clutching his knee.

"Sorry," Victor said, as he left the room. "I couldn't resist."

The door closed quickly behind them.

Alone in the room Voodoo looked at this man, his knee bleeding uncontrollably. Doubled over, his large hands dripping the blood as it surged, the man grimaced.

"Who the fuck are you!?" Edwards yelled, no longer a man of God.

"Do you remember, Candice Jacobs?" Voodoo said carefully as he twisted his neck to the side, stretching it back and forth.

"Who . . . " Edwards said, clutching his knee as his towel came undone.

185

"Candice Jacobs," Voodoo said with no emotion in his voice. " . . . the little girl you raped 29 years ago. Just like the girl you were about to rape. Like all the girls you have been molesting the last forty years. Am I ringing any bells here?"

"I don't know who the fuck you think you are," Edwards said between breaths, " . . . but I've got friends. This is my town! Your fuckin' dead. I'm Adam Edwards. I'm—"

"I know who you are, you piece of shit. You're a predator. A monster," Voodoo said.

And without another word, Voodoo spun, lifting his right leg and bringing his shin down across Edwards' neck, sending the man crumbling to the ground.

Before Edwards could react, Voodoo was standing over him with his silenced *Glock*.

His hands trying to cover and protect his face, Edwards screamed, "Who are you?"

"I'm just a messenger. And your time on this earth is finished. I hope God forgives you. Because . . . I don't."

Psst-psst, psst.

Two to the chest, one to the head, just under the nose. Edwards was just a pile of warm meat now. No longer would he rob young girls of their dignity and innocence.

He scooped up the spent shell casings, sliding them into his pocket before he left the room.

As they walked away, the plastic 'Do Not Disturb' sign was dangling on the outside of the door. Nobody would bother Pastor Adam Edwards for several hours.

The man so many people in the community loved.

Their guiding light.

Their pillar of hope.

A serial rapist,

Voodoo's father.

TWENTY-THREE

IT WAS DARK when they arrived back at Ms. Josephine's old house. And as creepy as it had looked during the day, it was a whole new league of spooky, at night. The moon's beams of bluish-white light that managed to sneak through the trees left long, contorted shadows across the rough ground. Each stretched shadow looking like its own ghost, slowly bending and leaning with the wind, as if they were watching them drive down the rough path.

"This place is like scary movie," Victor said, *click-snapping* his lighter.

He and Voodoo had taken the little girl back to the church, with specific instruction that she didn't see the 'police officers' that stormed in and dealt with Pastor Edwards. That would probably only give them a couple of hours before people started asking questions.

But there was nothing they could do.

No evidence.

And once the story of what Pastor Edwards was doing leaked out people would be doing their best to cover-up the

188

black cloud that would surely follow him, and the people he had hurt.

Before they left town, probably forever, they needed to see Ms. Josephine one last time. And so they pulled up to her old house, skidding as the rising dust made the car's headlights into bright white lasers.

As they carefully walked across the porch, taking slow, deliberate steps, Ms. Josephine called to them, "I had a feeling it was you two boys."

Victor and Voodoo traded curious glances as they passed through the threshold of the big, black door. Creaking its way open,
they saw the candles from before, smaller, melted, dying.

"Ms. Josephine," Voodoo said, seeing her sitting up on the couch, her hands in her lap. Her eyes were baggy as if she hadn't slept in 50 years.

"I was waitin' for you two to come back here. I had a dream about you last night. That you . . . that you *fixed* things with that man. That horrible, awful man," and then she started to cough again.

Like the slowly burning candles, close to their bitter end, she was not long for this world.

They walked closer to her, pulling chairs covered in soft red fabric nearer to the couch. They sat quietly, just comforting her

"I'm sorry I didn't come to see you," Voodoo said, his voice soft and full of emotion. It was the only time Victor had ever heard him speak like this. "I wanted to . . . but," he shrugged, his shoulders lowering beneath his chin, his eyes looking sadly down. He wasn't wearing his glasses. The candles flickered in his black eyes, making it look like his eyes were on fire.

189

She smiled, putting a trembling hand on his knee, "It doesn't matter now, baby. You did . . . " she coughed several more times, her eyes squinting more with each cough.

She steadied herself, " . . . you did what you had to do. I knew when I looked at you, that first moment when your momma brought you here. I knew." She closed her eyes, bringing the memories back. "You were something special. Sent from some other place. You never belonged here, child. Anyone who ever met you knew you were a different spirit. You needed to find yourself."

She looked over at Victor, " . . . and when I saw you come along, well . . . I knew that you would turn him into a man. Into the man he was destined to be."

Voodoo glanced briefly at Victor, and then at this beautiful woman who was more a mother to him than anyone else in the world. She taught him to look past the world we see, and find out for himself, that there was more to life, than what we can touch and smell. That there are things that we can't see, that are around us, all the time. That we all have purpose in this life. She taught him all of these things. And for that he could never repay her.

"Is there anything I can get for you?" he said, his voice almost a whisper as he spoke.

Victor looked down, not wanting to watch this. Not even knowing this woman, but loving her. Feeling as if they, too, shared some kind of unexplainable connection. This was hurting him, and he tried to swallow away the ache. Make the pain just disappear. But it wouldn't. He wished there was something he could say that would make her alright again. But those words were beyond him. Beyond anybody

"I sorry," he said, " . . . I sorry."

Wheezing with each breath, she still smiled. Fighting, minute after minute, she still seemed happy. Content. Calm.

She cleared her throat, "I love you, Ty. My little Voodoo child. Always have. Always will. And after we all gone from this place, we'll all sit down, on that other side, and just have ourselves a big laugh. All this worry over nothin'."

Voodoo took several breaths, choosing his words carefully, "Ms. Josephine . . . I've done things. Bad things. I've . . . "

"Aw shush, now," she said, dismissing his words with a wave of her hand. And then her eyes widened, animated like if she was 25-years-old again.

"Listen, the both of you, cause this is important. This place . . . all of this," she said opening her arms up to the world, ". . . it ain't nothin' but an illusion. We're all just here to learn lessons. We're just ghosts. We walk around, we pick things up and look at them. Maybe we learn from the things we see, maybe not. But it's about the journey we take. The tryin'."

"Every step you take is a new lesson you gonna learn. Each person you meet, that's another picture you gonna take with you when you leave this dream."

She took both of their hands in hers, all of them connected to her energy, feeling a warmth that they couldn't possibly describe to anyone that wasn't there. It was her love.

"You follow a code in your time here," she ordered them. "And it don't matter what that code is, as long as you stay true to yourself. Even the scorpions and the snakes follow their own code. We may think they dangerous, but that's only cause we don't understand them. Just cause other people don't agree with your way, that doesn't mean nothin'. As long as you stay true to yourself . . . that's all that matters."

191

And then she sat back, still holding on to their hands. "Ty, do you remember how I wanted my funeral to be? Do you still remember?"

"Yes, Ma'am."

"And will you still honor that?"

"I . . . " Voodoo tried to answer, but his voice was choked. His eyes blinking over and over, trying not to cry.

"When I cross over, I don't want it to be cold," she told them. "I want to have the ferryman smile his big old smile, kiss me on the cheek, and take me to that other place. And I want you two to be the last pictures I take with me.

Voodoo leaned in and wrapped her up in his arms, holding her, feeling her love one last time. And he could feel her tears forming warm little spots on his shirt, near his neck. Warm little puddles of love and pain and life and struggle.

"Okay, baby," she said, clearing her throat as she squeezed him with all the strength she could muster. She sighed, "It's time for me to go."

And so they sat there, the three of them, in complete silence. The candles, one by one, flickering out. Nothing but gentle lines of smoke lifting and dancing their way upwards into the darkness.

She closed her eyes and laid her head back, and in that deep, solemn silence, she passed away. That one last slow breath . . . gone.

Victor and Voodoo sat there, holding her hands, neither of them wanting to speak. No words would suffice.

Finally, Voodoo took several long breaths, cleared his throat, and raised his head to look at Victor . . . his only family left in this world. His only real family.

"Let's go."

Victor nodded, and they stood slowly up. He squinted his eyes, an idea suddenly coming to him. "Hold on," he said as he fished some quarters out of his pocket. Delicately he extended his arm, his palm open, showing Voodoo the quarters. "For the Ferryman."

Voodoo nodded, taking the quarters and slowly placing them on her eyes.

Then, without another word, they went about the task of preparing the house. It only took a few minutes, and they were standing on the front patio, pulling the heavy black door shut.

There was a distinct, gas odor coming from inside, as they both nodded to each other.

Voodoo wrapped his knuckles against the door one last time, turning to Victor, "Light it."

And with that he bent down, using his *Zippo* that he never actually seemed to light a cigarette with, and set the porch ablaze. The fire caught quickly, and within minutes the entire place was a two-story ball of reddish-orange flames.

The shadows danced around them as they pulled off, and in the rearview mirror, they watched as the old Victorian mansion collapsed in on itself, sending Ms. Josephine to the other side, just the way she had wanted. Any past that was Voodoo's early life, was now gone, burnt ashes rising into the cool night sky, dissipating into the blackness above.

"Let's go home," Victor said.

"Yeah," Voodoo said.

And without another word, they headed to the airport.

TWENTY-FOUR

NEW YORK
A FEW NIGHTS LATER . . .

AS RUTHLESS DROVE his black *Range Rover* down Washington Avenue he rolled the window halfway down, letting the calm fall wind
blow against his face. The New York sky was pitch dark, moonless, with just a few shining stars breaking through the scattered clouds.

20 minutes earlier, Ruthless had gotten an emergency call. After hearing Nino's good news, he quickly got out of bed with Joy and one of her white girlfriends, gotten dressed, and rushed out of their suite at the Hilton.

With Ruthless, business always came first. Even before sex.

Just a block away from the 48th Police Precinct, Ruthless pulled up and parked behind a dark grey *Ford Excursion*. He saw one of his men standing on the front steps, smoking a blunt. Ruthless got out of his truck, his eyes darting around cautiously, and shut the door.

He was wearing a black and brown leather *Pelle Pelle* jacket, faded blue baggy jeans, and black ankle-high

Timberland boots. When he approached the man on the steps they nodded, and shook hands.

The man blew out a puff of smoke, sniffed and said, "Nino and Jamal got 'em both inside. They been waiting for you." The man looked at the blunt, smiled to himself. "Yeah, they waitin'."

Ruthless grinned, slapped the guy on the shoulder and said, "Keep an eye out for the cops."

"Don't worry, I got this," the man said as he sat down and finished smoking.

When Ruthless walked into the house he noticed how well decorated the place was. Wall to wall carpet, large fresh-water fish tank, a hanging gold chandelier with large glass crystals that sparkled like giant diamonds, a white leather sectional, a huge plasma television.

The place screamed money.

Ruthless glanced around, shaking his head at the expensive furniture, and exquisite artwork. As he was inspecting the place, he heard some noises coming from upstairs and headed for the stairs.

Walking slowly up the stairs, his hand sliding along a curving oak railing, he felt for his pistol. With the flip of his thumb, the catch released and he pulled out the *H&K USP 9mm*. From the other side off his jacket he removed the long, black silencer and slowly threaded it onto the end of the barrel. He liked the weight of the pistol in his hand. It felt efficient, balanced . . . permanent. So quiet it almost didn't seem fair

He had been waiting for this day to come for almost two years. It would be the day of payback and revenge. When Ruthless walked into the bedroom where all of the noises were emanating, he saw Nino and Jamal standing over the two tied-up naked bodies. All soft skin and silver duct tape and sweat.

Then man looked to be badly beaten, his face fat and swollen as if a baseball player had used his head for batting practice.

The girl tied to him, his attractive brown-skinned wife, was still fresh and untouched. With absolutely no idea what was about to happen.

They were lying on a large king-sized bed with their hands tied behind their backs, and their mouths taped shut. The couple wore the masks of complete fear and horror on their faces.

"We spotted them on Fordom Road. Then we followed them to this place," Nino said, feeling pretty good about himself. His eyes did a quick circle of the room, "Nice, huh?"

Ruthless nodded his head, and then stared at the couple for a moment, thinking of exactly how to proceed. He walked slowly over to the bed and sat down beside the terrified man, his eyes dilated as big as saucers. The whites of his eyes were bloodshot, and his cheeks and brow were so puffed and swollen that he could barely see. Behind the mountain of inflated skin, two little blue marbles nervously danced back and forth.

Ruthless squinted, looking at the man's tiny eyes and grinned. "Kevin . . . you must be one of the dumbest mother-fuckers in the world. Or, either the craziest!"

"Retarded," Nino added.

The man shook and quivered, squirming around on the bed to get as far away from Ruthless as he could, but he hardly moved. His wife, she just sat there, taking short little breaths as she imagined the awful things that were about to happen. She didn't have a clue. Neither of them had ever been this frightened, not in their entire lives.

"Nigga," Ruthless said, "you get one of my top men thirty years in the feds, and ain't have enough sense to stay away from New York? That don't make no fuckin' sense to me. And you supposed to be smart. Maybe you *is* retarded."

Nino and Jamal both stood back laughing.

"You fucked me, you little ratty-assed bitch!" Ruthless said as he backhanded the naked man across the bed.

Slap!

Ruthless stood glancing back and forth between Kevin and his naked wife. Ideas were forming in his twisted mind.

"Let me think," Ruthless said as he pulled of his jacket and tossed it to Nino, the pistol still in his hand. "How can I do to you what you've done to me? How can I get a sense of satisfaction, some kind of compensation? Does anyone know? Kevin," he yelled, " . . . you got any ideas?"

Ruthless walked over to Nino and handed him the pistol, all of them laughing. All of them knowing exactly where this was heading.

He looked across the room, and on a night-table beside the bed there was an off-white phone with a clock-radio built in. A smile slowly formed on Ruthless' stoic face.

He walked across the room, slowly unbuttoning his shirt and laying it down on the soft, grey carpet. Menacing and scary with his clothes on, now that his muscled chest was showing, the woman began to sob, uncontrollably. He was a monster.

Without talking he separated the two, leaving Kevin on the left side of the large bed, and his wife on the right side.

He rolled her onto her stomach, and slowly untapped her hands leaving dark marks where the tape had been on her wrists.

"See, Kevin," Ruthless said, grabbing the woman by her thin waist and pulling her to the edge of the bed so that just her legs were hanging over. "You took something from me. Stole it. And then you ran to the fuckin' feds. So I'm gonna take something from you. While you sit there and watch."

Ruthless, his hands still on the woman's hips, used his knee to spread her legs apart as she started to cry all over the blue satin comforter. He glanced over at Nino who was nodding slowly, happy to enjoy front row seats at this show.

Ruthless placed one of his hands in the small of the woman's back, pressing her thin chest down onto the bed. She tried to wiggle and free herself, but it was pointless. And finally, it seemed as if she just gave up, locking eyes with her husband. Hoping for a miracle.

Kevin shrimped forward as if he was going to help his wife, but Nino yelled, "Hey . . . Kevin!" And Kevin turned to see the silenced pistol pointing at him from the edge of the bed.

Inside that wet, silver tape, Kevin was mumbling every word he could think of that might make his wife know how sorry he was. But she couldn't hear any of it. Her arms hugging her chest, her hands covering her face.

Maybe it would all just go away.

Some terrible nightmare that would suddenly end.

Ruthless, his jeans now unzipped, used his free hand to pull himself free of his boxers, and pressed the tip of his dick softly against the sides of the woman's small round ass. "You fucked my man, Kevin. Now I'm gonna fuck your wife. Hell, maybe she'll like it."

And with that he thrust himself deep inside of her, as she screamed under the tape. Deeper and deeper, each time his hips pressed forward, as if he was stabbing her to death. Each powerful press of his hips more violent then the last, as if he was trying to cut her in half. Break her into two pieces.

The woman's hands reached out, grabbing and tearing at the shiny blue fabric while Ruthless continued to pound harder and harder. Her entire body was shaking back and forth, the whole bed rocking as if there was an earthquake.

He felt himself coming close, so he stopped, pulled himself out of her, and noticed some warm blood smeared around his hips.

He looked up with a cryptic smile on his face, and then forced himself into her ass. And suddenly, her body tensed as he ripped and tore his way into her. Like forcing a baseball bat into the delicate shaft of a small fragile flower.

Sparks and pain and blackness flashed before her eyes as she lost consciousness. And her body went completely slack, so that Ruthless was more or less fucking an inanimate object. A piece of warm meat. But not a person.

A hot, wet . . . thing.

As he felt himself getting closer to coming, he reached forward, grabbing around her neck, and lifted her head up so that Kevin could watch her body bounce up and down like dead weight. He pushed as far into her ass as he could, and then, slid his arm around her neck.

Gritting his teeth, he lifted her neck close to his face, and then broke her neck with a quick motion.

Snap!

Several cracks and pops, and she started to gurgle, her face muscles contorted as blood started to pour out of her nose and mouth with the escaping of the last breath.

"Ooh . . . yeah," he said, his eyes closed tightly as he took slow breaths while he came deep inside of her. He enjoyed the pulsing orgasm for several seconds.

"That's the best part, Kevin . . . when they die. Their whole body tenses up, and you ain't got no choice but to cum all up in that bitch."

Kevin was different. Like a zombie the blood drained from his face as he rocked back and forth. He was beyond crying, now. Growing closer and closer to shock each and every second.

Ruthless let the dead woman's naked body fall to the bed in a heap. He pulled out of her and wiped himself off on the comforter, slowly pulling his boxers and pants back up.

"Now . . . " he said as he buttoned his pants, "you know what it feels like to get something you love taken away from you. Trust me," he smiled, " . . . that was the best dick that skinny bitch ever felt."

Ruthless walked back around the bed, picking up his shirt along the way. Nino still had the pistol trained on Kevin. Jamal was watching the hallway door, just in case anyone decided to stop by.

Ruthless went over and grabbed the phone-clock-radio from the night-stand and raised it over his head. His eyes narrowed as his teeth started to show, like a hungry animal getting ready to attack.

"I called you over and over, you ratty mother-fucker. Was your phone broken? Let's see," Ruthless said, and then he brought the bottom of the phone down across Kevin's face, opening a deep gash in his nose and cheek.

The bell inside the phone made a muffled ring sound as the phone smashed down again and again, as if somebody was calling from some place beyond.

Ding!

"Does the fucking phone work, Kevin? Huh? I can't hear you mother-fucker!"

Again, Ruthless brought the phone down, using it like a hammer. Each time cutting and chopping at Kevin's face. And now, it was nothing more than open, gushing meat and muscle. With each hit, more skin was removed . . . more bone and muscle exposed.

Ding! Ding . . . ding!

Kevin's eyes rolled back in his head as he curled into the fetal position on the bed, shaking, and pissing all over himself.

And still, Ruthless did not stop. Even as the phone broke apart, he continued to hit.

And hit.

And hit.

And then, realizing he was wearing himself out on a dead body, he stopped to catch his wind, shaking his dread-locks away from his face. He took several long deep breaths, dropping what was left of the phone between the two dead bodies and turning to Nino.

"Think I went too far?" he asked as he sucked the cool climate-controlled air into his lungs.

"If anything," Nino said, "you was too easy on the guy."

Ruthless laughed as he backed away from the bed, looking at the mess he caused. "We got to burn this bitch to the ground."

Nino nodded. "Take off, Ruthless . . . me and Jamal gonna take care of this mess."

Ruthless buttoned up his shirt, still staring at the bed and the carnage he had created. As he took back his pistol and jacket, he whiffed the air a couple of times, the mixture of death and sex and rage thick in the air.

Nodding to the bodies, "Yeah . . . maybe I did let him off too easy."

TWENTY-FIVE

EVERY TIME THAT Voodoo came to Victor's house he saw something. And almost always, in stark contrast to the clean, modern furnishings in his house, that new something he saw was designed for violence. He lived far enough outside of New York City that he could bring his work home with him.

He lived in a nice, quiet suburban neighborhood where people drove *Volvos*, had 401(k) retirement accounts, grey hair, ugly golfing pants, and names like *Jim* and *Betty*. A retirement neighborhood where the neighbors waved to that successful young oil man they thought he was.

Victor figured that '*Oil man*' sounded better than '*Russian gangster specialized in contract killings and worldwide arms dealing*'.

Victor met him at the front door, wearing just a pair of *Adidas* track pants, a pair of old brown slippers, and a sparkling watch with more diamonds on it than the crown jewels. It was so heavy it seemed to pull his left arm lower than the right. Victor looked ghostly white, as usual, with a

203

cigarette sitting behind his right ear as if he might need it at any moment. In right hand, his trusty *Zippo*.

"I be have something to show you," Victor said as they entered house. Before closing the door, he peeked his head left and right, just to make sure that nobody was paying him any *extra* attention.

"Nobody followed me," Voodoo said.

"Yeah," Victor answered skeptically. "Well . . . it's better be paranoid, than be dead." He shut the door and triple locked it. Sliding on by, he seemed as if his slippers never left the floor. "Come."

"I've been doing my prep on the Reggie job," Voodoo explained. "I'm going to have to get close. I'll need some heavy gear, but quiet."

Standing in the middle of a lavishly furnished living room, light colored greys and off-whites for the English-styled furniture, Victor shook his watch. He brought the iced-out *Cartier* to his face, squinting. He tapped it several times with his fingers, frowning. " . . . what time you have?"

Voodoo glanced at his black-faced *Movado*, "Nine forty-five, give or take."

Frustrated, Victor shook his head and then crossed his arms over his pale, thin chest. At the top of his chest, near his shoulders, and on both sides, he had nautical stars tattooed in thick bluish-black ink. And on each arm, on the inside of each biceps he had small, crudely drawn executioners.

Most people wouldn't think much about the tattoos, but in Russia their meaning was clear: The stars represented his rank and status as an accomplished criminal, and member of organized crime. They signified that he hadn't been a rat, or a snitch. The executioners symbolized the act of killing. This

204

kind of ink told anyone in the know that he would accept contracts to take human life . . . without question.

In fact, in Russia, he couldn't refuse a contract. It's part of the *Code of Thieves*. In eastern bloc countries, being a Criminal is a status symbol. A position of respect and authority; admiration, even. These tattoos also signified that he had been inside a Russian prison . . . and lived to not tell the story.

"I have fifty-thousand dollar watch that don't tell time correctly." He shrugged. "Anyway, I have some new toys."

Victor nodded towards a large grey sofa with powder blue throw pillows. As he walked to the right side of the sofa and reached down, Voodoo said, "This place doesn't seem like you."

Victor glanced back as his hands touched a hidden button under the sofa, "I like to make oil paintings, too. Now what you think?"

Voodoo smiled as an audible *thump-click* sounded, the cushions on the sofa lifting up where they would normally be sitting. It was a hidden compartment, and inside it was an odd wooden crate, with red Russian print on the sides.

Victor raised his eyebrows several times, reaching his hands down and knocking his knuckles against the crate. Nodding proudly he said, "I wait six month for the order . . . I know guy in Croatia. He be live in Zagreb. He know old Russian Colonel who escaped from Afghanistan with lots of very nice equipment. I buy from him every now and then. Very expensive, but very nice."

Victor felt around beside the crate for a small black crowbar to pry up the edges of the wooden crate. The box squeaked as the top inched its way open. Victor's hand pushed aside the foam packing beads, and turned to see Voodoo's reaction.

Voodoo stepped in closer, his eyes doing a double-take. "Whoa!"

Victor smiled proudly.

"How in the hell did you get that past customs?" Voodoo asked, astonished.

The Russian winked, his grey eyes narrow and sinister, "I Victor. I be get anything from a banana to a battle ship. I can get you . . . right now," he said, like a used-car salesman giving his pitch to some young kid with money in his pocket. " . . . T-seventy-two Russian Tank. Full reactive armor. One-hundred twenty-five millimeter main cannon."

His eyes lit up, "But . . . that's not all. It also have V-twelve, multi-fuel engine, with eight-hundred and forty horse power. Did I mention that the main cannon has a two-thousand yard range, with laser range finder and night-vision targeting system?"

Victor put his arm around Voodoo's shoulders, "And, just in case you find yourself in the middle of Nuclear war . . . it also have nuclear, biological, radiological shield, so that you don't have babies born with two heads and flippers."

Voodoo smiled at the pitch, "And how much could you get me into one of those for? I mean . . . your best *drive-it-off-the-lot-right-now* offer. What are we talking about?"

Victor squinted, his brain calculating. Gears turning. Mice running. "You a shrewd negotiator. But . . . for you, because you my best friend . . . I be get you the Commander's model, plus title, tax, and license, for . . . ah . . . one-hundred-and-five thousand dollars." And then as an afterthought he added, "You have to pay for shipping, of course."

"Of course," Voodoo said, kneeling over the crate. "Tell me about this little puppy. What's the range?"

"Close to three-thousand meters," Victor said as he ran his finger along the cold black tube. "In good weather . . . two miles. And it will track the target at five-hundred fifty mile-per-hour."

"Can you get more?"

Victor grinned, his bleach white teeth showing barely under his thin lips. "I got two more," he said, motioning his head towards the wall, where a picture of Red Square hung in a large polished-silver frame. Under the picture was some kind of proverb that probably only made sense if you were raised in Moscow, bred on vodka and potatoes.

"Victor," Voodoo said as he stood slowly, " . . . you constantly amaze me."

Victor nodded, still focused on the grainy image of Red Square, in Moscow. To most Russians, it was an almost holy place. The Tomb of Vladimir Illich Lenin—a great hero among Russians. Victor probably spent a good portion of time standing quietly, in the middle of his living room, just staring at that grainy, black-and-white picture.

"You miss it?" Voodoo asked as he stood beside Victor

In a soft tone, Victor answered, "Russia be very different, now. The Russia I knew, back when we were Soviet Union, it all change. Where I grow up in Serov," he said, turning his head slightly, " . . . this is east side of Ural mountains, very quiet place. Everything be different. But, you know . . . *that* Russia," he said, pointing at the picture with the crowbar, " . . . that Russia be gone now. It's all colors and capitalism and bla-bla-bla."

207

"Why don't you go back and visit?" Voodoo said. "When all of this work is finished. It'd do you some good to get away. A vacation."

Victor looked at him as if he was crazy, "We just had a vacation to New Orleans."

"That was a working vacation," Voodoo pointed out. Victor dismissed the idea, turning and heading into another room. "Come on . . . I got more stuff to show you."

Voodoo glanced at the picture for a few seconds more, nodded to himself, and then followed Victor out of the living room. *People*, he thought, *are much more complex than they look.*

TWENTY-SIX

DAN GONZALEZ WALKED back and forth in the empty visiting room, waiting for the guards to bring in Alex Karsh. A lot of things were spiraling around inside of his mind, and he had a gut feeling that Alex just might be able to shed a little light. He knew that the mercenary was still reluctant to talk to a federal agent, but each time they met he got to understand the man a bit more.

A loud, almost metallic, voice beamed over the intercom, "The inmate is in the corridor."

Dan walked over to a circular table, and sat down in his white plastic chair. He scooted in and reached for a large envelope full of photographs. But this time, they were not snap-shots of the dead. They were different shots of members of the Black Royals, and the Matas, coming and going from a restaurant in New York, called *Cipriani*.

They had been taken by an undercover narcotics officer who had been posing as a Valet guy, parking cars that were worth more money than he would probably make working for the next 10 years. *Bentleys, Ferraris, McLaren Mercedes*, and more.

The undercover officer had even pulled prints off several of the expensive luxury cars. Because of the dubious nature of such tactics, none of the information gained would be admissible in a court of law, but then . . . missions like this were designed for the sole purpose of gathering intelligence.

To know your enemy.

After a series of loud thumps, four guards frog-marched Alex Karsh into the visiting room.

"Cuffs and shackles," Dan said, making a little twisting gesture with his wrist holding an invisible key.

"He's dangerous," a tall, skinny, white guard said.

Dan continued to stare at the guard, not feeling as though he needed to repeat himself.

"Alright," the guard said reluctantly. "It's on you, then." And they removed the cuffs, shackles, and belly chain, mumbling to themselves about how *fucking stupid* lawyers are.

"Nice one, boys," Alex said with a polite smile.

"Good luck with your appeal, Karsh," the guard said sarcastically as they left the visiting room.

"What was that all about?" Dan asked as he took the photographs out of the envelope.

Alex shook his head, "These guys think that people who are on appeal are dreamers, wasting their time at the law library, fighting a case they'll never win. Jail-house lawyers, you know. They're probably right."

"They think you're on appeal?"

"Dan," Alex explained as if he was talking to a child, lowering his voice, ". . . if I'm not on my appeal, then that means I'm in here telling you something I shouldn't be. As in, snitching, or ratting. And in a place like this . . . rats don't live very long. They'll stab you so many times you'll look like swiss cheese with tomato sauce pouring out."

Dan nodded, realizing just how dangerous a maximum security facility really was. It's easy to lose touch, to forget, when you're on the other side of the fence.

"Don't worry, Alex. I won't get you jammed up. I'm just a good old lawyer, trying my best to get my client back on the street."

Alex smiled, "Right, then. What have you got for me?"

"Pictures," Dan said as he slid the first stack across the table. They were all pictures of the Matas, from Caesar, all the way on down.

Alex took them, one by one, studying the different faces. "These guys still alive?"

"Yeah, they're all alive and kicking. Well, kicking and shooting. That's the problem. You recognize any of them?"

Alex flipped slowly through the photos, squinting, shaking his head. "No luck, mate. Sorry." He slid the pile back across the table. Caesar's flat, two-dimensional image was on top, making him look like some fashion model dressed in a nice suit with sunglasses and long, dark hair.

Dan nodded, sighed, and then sent a second stack across the table. This time they were pictures of the Black Royals. Alex went through the glossy photographs one after the next.

Again, he shrugged, pursing his lips together as his cheeks filled with air. Blowing out, he said, "No, mate. Nothing."

Alex placed his hands on the table, steepling his fingers. "These guys is all locals, Dan. You know where I worked. None of these guys ever worked in central Africa. You know that I'd never come in contact with any of these bloaks."

211

Dan rubbed his tired eyes, and then his temples, making little circles with his fingers. He took a deep breath and slowly exhaled. His face looked worn.

Beat.

Grasping at straws.

And that was exactly how he wanted to look. He sighed, and put his hands on a third pile of pictures, sliding them across the table with a deliberately painstaking motion. He had a *whatever* expression on his face, as if he didn't really care anymore.

Thinking this was pointless, Alex grabbed the next stack. These were neither Black Royals, nor the El Salvadorian Matas. The faces in this pile were all pale-white, with cold, dead eyes. They were all from the CIA's files on the Russian Syndicate. But Dan didn't say any of this. He just leaned back in his chair, balancing on the back two legs. Waiting.

Alex thumbed his way from one face to the next, studying them closely. Perhaps a little closer than he had studied the other pictures. He was looking for somebody in particular. Each time he came to another picture, he would pick it up, look at the man's eyes, then say, "No," and flip the picture over to make a second pile.

Dan watched Alex's face for any reaction. He watched his hands and fingers, his neck, and his nose, for any hint of recognition.

"No . . . "Alex said, flipping another picture.

"No. "

Flip.

"No. "

Flip.

And then he came to a picture that held his attention for a couple of seconds. Maybe a few seconds too many. Alex's eyes darted up, noticing Dan curiously observing him, and then back to the photo of the Russian mobster.

"No," he said quickly, flipping over the photo, face down into the '*seen*' pile.

But Alex *did* know the face. It was Nickolai Chyorni. The head of the Russian Syndicate in the United States. Perhaps the leader of the most dangerous criminal organization on the East Coast. Oh, yeah . . . he and Alex had a *long* history.

"Sorry, Dan," Alex finally said, sliding the last pile of photos across the table.

"Nothing at all, huh?" Dan said, not pressing too hard, but just enough.

Alex crossed his arms, a sign of defensiveness, and said, "Nothing."

Dan's fingers tapped lightly on the stack of pictures as if he was playing a small piano. "Those guys in that last batch," he said almost as an afterthought, as if it wasn't too important, "not that it makes any difference to you, but . . . they all live in New York. They have a building in Brighton Beach."

Alex nodded, and Dan could see the blood starting to simmer in his veins. Alex tried to shrug it off, but it was too forced a gesture to be genuine.

It's hard to hide hate. Especially from a trained interrogator.

Dan reached into his shirt pocket and pulled out a white business card, tossing it across the table. Alex picked it up, studying the black print.

"If you ever need to get in touch with me . . . " Dan said, just above a whisper, " . . . under the radar. That's the number. Let it ring three times, then hang-up. Call back three minutes later."

Alex studied the card, then Dan, then the card, again. He couldn't believe what he was hearing.

"Well," Dan said, as he gathered the pictures and stood up, stretching his back. "If you think of anything . . . don't hesitate to call. And, hey . . . good luck with your appeal."

Alex nodded almost imperceptibly, sitting in his plastic chair, staring at this business card, as Dan made his way to the far side of the visiting room.

"You guys finished?" the loud voice boomed.

Dan nodded, then turned back to Alex and waved, wiggling his thumb and pinkie fingers, mouthing the words, *'Call me'.*

A few minutes later Dan found himself outside the visiting room, desperately looking for a cigarette. He needed something to relax him, even though he hadn't smoked in over a week.

Looking around, he asked one of the guards, who shrugged noncommittally and went back to his paperwork. Dan walked out the Visitor's exit, and walked out into the brisk wind, squinting as his eyes adjusted to the sun.

Almost immediately, a tall, skinny Lieutenant, by the name of Lt. Brandon, followed Dan out. The same man who had walked Alex into the Visiting room earlier extended a pack of *Marlboro lights*. He shook the pack, rattling the cigarettes to get Dan's attention.

Dan turned, "Your a life saver." He shrugged, "I'm trying to quit, but it's impossible."

214

"We ain't gonna live forever," Lt. Brandon said as he fished for a lighter. "Might as well get the most out of life while we're here."

"Good point," Dan said as they lit up. "Good point, indeed."

TWENTY-SEVEN

INSIDE A SMALL HOUSE, ON 179TH STREET...

HECTOR, PEPE, AND Felipe stood around listening as Caesar explained to them that he was calling off the contracted hit on Reggie King.

Caesar stood up from his chair and walked around the room as he spoke. "This thing is about making money. Now is the time to start moving away from war, and towards our real focus . . . money. It's all about making money. That's all it's ever really been about, just that we all kind of lost our direction."

"But what about Juan-Carlos? We can't just let them get away with that!" Pepe barked.

Caesar walked over to Pepe and looked down into his wide angry eyes. "Pepe, I respect your loyalty to Juan-Carlos, but he is gone, now. I am here to see to it that what is best for the Matas is made to happen. And if we continue to keep this war with the Royals raging, no one will win. One of my inside sources has already told me that the feds have formed some kind of special task-force out of New York, and they're out to take both sides down."

Caesar put his hand on Pepe's shoulder, turning his attention to the others, "In the last month, over twelve men and women were killed because of this war. Now the Black Royals have made us an offer, and I've agreed to except it. I don't want you to think that I rushed this decision. And I value each of your opinions on any issue I consider. But this decision has been made. Case closed."

Caesar watched as Pepe dropped his head in frustration. He then let go of his shoulder, and turned, walking towards Hector. "Call the Russian and tell him that we want the hit on Reggie suspended . . . at least for the meantime. ASAP., Hector."

"I'll take care of it, today," Hector said.

Caesar looked around at everyone inside the small, tense, room. "If anyone has anything to say, please speak now."

No one said a word. They already knew what the decision was, and that it wouldn't change.

"Okay, then," Caesar said, "everyone can go back to work. Pepe, I need you and Felipe to go over to the Melbrook projects and do a *pick-up*."

Caesar turned back to Hector, "I need you to make sure that all of our drug houses are supplied and ready for distribution."

Hector nodded.

"And don't forget to call the Russian," Caesar reminded.

They all watched as Caesar grabbed his jacket and walked over towards the door. In a slow, quiet line, they followed behind him.

When Caesar walked out of the house, three of his men were standing guard around the front door, with another few around the sides of the small house. Loaded pistols were underneath each of their t-shirts, and they looked poised for violence.

As the group of Matas made their way outside, they stood around watching while Caesar walked over to a tinted black *Mercedes Benz*.

"I'm going over to Juan-Carlos' house to check on Carmen. Then I'm going to Philly to take care of some business."

Without another word, he climbed into the back of the *Mercedes* and gave instructions to the driver as he closed the back door.

Still, nobody talked.

Once the car had started to pull off, down the street, Pepe turned to Hector and said, "I still don't agree with Caesar's decision. Those niggers killed our boss and his son."

" . . . and Maria," Felipe added.

Hector knew that Pepe was still very upset with Caesar for calling off the hit on Reggie King. But there was nothing that anyone could do about it. Caesar had made up his mind, and no one would dare challenge him.

"Pepe, you have to get over it," Hector said softly. "Juan-Carlos is dead and Caesar is our new boss. His choices are final. So . . . just leave it alone. They'll be a time for revenge. Just not right now."

Hector watched as Pepe angrily turned and stalked away, with Felipe right on his heels. They climbed into a grey *Toyota Camry* and sped off down the street.

Hector turned and made his way to a black *Escalade*. The other guards climbed in with him. They had to make sure the drug houses were supplied, and he had to call Victor, and call-off the contract.

218

}}}

Inside one of the Black Royals' stash houses, everyone was seated at a large brown table looking at Reggie as he talked on his cell phone.

"Yeah, uh-hu . . . don't worry about that. You have my word," he said, nodding as he spoke.

After closing up his cell phone, he looked around the table at his men. Each one of them with anticipation, and curiosity etched into their faces.

"That was Caesar," Reggie said to the men. "He called me to say that the Matas have agreed to our offer of a truce. The war is over." There was a fair amount of excitement in his voice.

Some of the faces were cautious, and skeptical, as if this might be too good to be true. Others were empty, not caring one way or the other. Ruthless was in that second group. If he had it his way, every single Mata would be killed.

"It's time to get back to the business of stacking money," Reggie said slowly. It was as if a heavy weight had been taken off of his shoulders. "Both sides have lost a lot of good men. From this moment on, our war is no longer with the Matas. Now, with a bit of luck, we can concentrate on the only things that really matter. Paper, and power. Everything else is a waste of time."

Nino and Jamal both stood up from their seats and walked over to the two large green duffel bags that were laying in the corner of the room.

They each grabbed a bag, and by the way it strained them, the bags must have been quite heavy.

They each found a spot on the table, lifting the bags up, and slowly emptied them of their contents as everyone else in the room stared.

Stacks of money wrapped in thick rubber bands rolled out across the glossy topped table. It was more than two-million dollars, all of it from drug profits. It was the weekly pull from the Patterson, Mitchells, Edenwald, and Forest projects. The Black Royals' top four drug operations.

"This is what it's all about, gentlemen," Reggie said, picking up one of the stacks of money and raising it to his nose.

He took a long, deliberate whiff of the stack of cash, closing his eyes as if it was a fine wine. When his eyes opened, a satisfied look softened his face, "Money . . . dead presidents! There ain't nothing sweeter than that smell."

The men smiled, a few of them laughing.

"Where's Ronnie at?" Ruthless asked as he reached down grabbed a money counting machine that was sitting under his chair.

"He called me early this morning and said that he had some business to take care of," Reggie said with a grin. "I'll see him later tonight."

Jamal stood up, a strange look of confusion on his face, "Hey, Reggie . . . don't you have a birthday coming up soon?"

Reggie smiled, half embarrassed, "Thanks for reminding me. Yes. In a couple of days."

"Well," Jamal offered, "how about we celebrate it like we did last year? I got a friend that can get us the entire VIP section at that new Manhattan nightclub . . . Mars Twenty-one Twelve."

Reggie considered it for a while as he played with the money stack. "What the hell. Why not? Since the war with the Matas is over with, now, I think it might be good for us to get out and have a little fun." He looked over at Jamal, tossing the cash back down into the mountain of green. "Hook it up."

Ruthless placed a stack of bills inside the money counting machine, listening as the pleasing sound of 20-dollar bills flipping by flooded the room.

"We still have to be cautious," he said. "Ain't no guarantees in this shit. I'm gonna make sure that some of our men are hangin' in and out of the club . . . just to keep things safe."

"Better to be safe than sorry," Reggie said to himself, nodding.

"That's fine. You do that, Ruthless. I want this to be a nice party. A celebration of the end of the bloodshed."

Jamal had a sinister grin on his face, "Oh, yeah . . . we gonna celebrate. We gonna do it up right."

Everyone sat around nodding their heads in agreement. This is what it was all about.

$$\} \} \}$$

NEW ROCHELLE . . .

Hearing the sound of the doorbell, Carmen rushed down the stairs fixing her robe. When she reached the front door, she looked out the small peep-hole, and was surprised to see Caesar standing there, waiting patiently. She put her hand to her chest, feeling her heart racing. She took several deep, slow breaths, and then opened the door.

"Caesar, what brings you over here?"

He smiled, as they hugged each other. "I haven't seen you in a while," he said, stepping inside the house, "and I just wanted to come by and make sure you were doing okay." He studied her, "You know . . . after what happened."

"I'm doing as fine as I can," she said, her face lowering. "But, honestly, I miss my husband and step-son so much that it kills me just to think about them not being here. I keep expecting them to just walk in, like nothing happened. Like all of this was a horrible dream," she said as her eyes welled up with tears.

She wiped her face. "Since their deaths . . . I've been a nervous wreck. I mean . . . " She shrugged, tears rolling down her cheeks again.

Caesar saw the hurt and torture in her eyes, and he knew how much the pain could hurt. Even though Carmen was young enough to be Juan-Carlo's daughter, he had never once doubted her love for the man. He reached out and gave her another hug, wrapping her tightly in his arms.

Carmen laid her head on his chest, as the tears fell down from her eyes.

"Everything will be alright," he assured her. "You know that if you ever need me . . . I'm here for you. You're like my little sister. Like family. You will always be close to all of us."

"Thank you, Caesar. Thank you so much."

"So, do you plan on staying in this big house, all by yourself? I figured, with all of the memories . . . "

"No, I was thinking about selling it. And maybe moving out of New York and starting over again, somewhere new," Carmen said, as she backed away, wiping her eyes with her hands. She swallowed several times, taking a breath and trying to smile.

"Well, whatever you decide to do, you'll have my full support. You're young and beautiful, and you still have a lot of good years ahead of you," he said with a gentle, caring smile. "Just keep me posted on whatever you decide."

"I will, Caesar. Thank you."

They hugged each other again, and Caesar turned and headed back out the door. She started to slowly close the door behind him, waving at him, watching carefully as he headed to his car.

As he pulled away, she shut and locked the door, turned around and leaned back against the door as she sighed.

She made her way up the stairs, sweat forming on her brow. *That was close*, she thought. *Too close*.

Moments later she made her way to the master bedroom, opening the door slowly.

Ronnie King was standing flat against the far wall, crouched down, aiming his loaded 9mm in the general area of the bedroom door.

"You can put that up," she said. "He's gone." She took her robe off, laying it across the arm of a chair.

Ronnie walked slowly over to the bed and sat his gun down on the night stand.

"Now can we get back to where we were before we were disturbed," she said, climbing on top of his body.

Ronnie spun Carmen around and laid her on her back. "I believe that I was on top, and you was moaning and calling out me and God's name," he said, as they started kissing.

TWENTY-EIGHT

ALL OF THE lights were off in Voodoo's apartment. There was a single, vanilla candle burning slowly on the glass kitchen table. It sent just the hint of light into Voodoo's bedroom, where he and Angie were quietly laying.

They were both completely naked, only a thin black sheet covering their bodies. Angie crawled slowly towards Voodoo, trying desperately to figure out what was going on inside his head. Her hand traced circles on his stomach while he laid back, staring up at the darkness.

" . . . Where did you go on your business trip?" she asked.

He hadn't told her much . . . ever. But he was especially vague about he and Victor's recent excursion to Louisiana. Sometimes he even felt like talking to her. Not in any conventional *girlfriend* or *boyfriend* sense, but just to be polite. He kept people at bay for a reason: if you let people get close to you, they'll hurt you. Whether it's intentional or accidental. People hurt the ones they care about. He knew that lesson well enough, learning it through his early life experiences.

He liked the way things were. He didn't see any reason to change the nature of their relationship. Victor always told him '*Your friends be money. If you have lots of money, you have lots of friends.*' And Victor was right. This was a material world. And it was something he had always strived for . . . financial independence.

He would never allow himself to be in and out of the streets the way his mother had been.

So he had chosen this life for himself, and he was comfortable with the rules he had to live by. His *Code*, as Ms. Josephine had said. And being close to a girl, that was a dangerous proposition. The arrangement he had with Angie was perfect. It was satisfying to both of them. And there was nothing they couldn't both walk away from. At least, that's how it had been.

But in life . . . things change.

She did have some qualities that he liked in a woman. Angie was really attractive, and very soft and feminine, the way he would want a girl to be. She was very quiet, almost like a cat. She could sit, all alone, in front of a mirror, doing the simplest of things and enjoy herself.

Sometimes, he liked to just sit back and watch her do her girlish things. She intrigued him. And despite his best efforts, he found himself thinking about her, every now and then.

But then, she was another person who could get in his way . . . cause him to hesitate. And that was something he simply could not afford. The bottom line was: Contract Killers don't have attachments.

Her hands still sliding around his belly button, she asked him, "Do you get board doing all of your insurance stuff?" She stared into the relative darkness, only barely being able to see the outline of his head, wondering if he was looking at her, or whether he was even awake. He had the ability to be so cold and distant, like some animal that doesn't trust people.

The same things that she liked about him, also scared her. There was something more to him. Something she couldn't put her finger on. A primal quality.

Barely above a whisper, he said, "I don't necessarily think that what a person does for a living speaks completely about their personality."

In the darkness she smiled, bringing herself closer to him, her chest leaned up against his hips, she kissed the side of his hip. "So, I guess you don't like your job, then?"

"That's not what I meant."

Her kisses got closer to the inside of his leg, her right hand gently massaging deep inside his thigh, toying with him. The only sounds were of her lips touching his skin. Each kiss closer than the last.

"How do you feel about me?" she wondered as she slowly climbed on top of him, tossing the soft sheet to the side.

"What do you mean?" Voodoo asked.

Slowly, inch by inch, she lowered herself down, taking him deep into her warm, wet body.

"I mean, how do you *feel* about me?"

In the darkness, with only the two of them breathing deeply, she could feel his throbbing pulse inside of her, as if they had become one. She rocked her hips ever so slightly back and forth, hands spread out on his chest.

" . . . that's . . . a . . . a difficult question . . . to answer," he said, swallowing between words.

His hands reached up, cupping her breasts, as she lifted her body up and down. Her movements were so gentle and slow, that he found himself paralyzed by her body.

"I don't judge you . . . ooh . . . " she started to say, between quiet moans. " . . . because you are . . . aaah . . . an insurance salesman."

Voodoo found it difficult to have this conversation right at this moment. This was not a discussion he wanted to have, anyway. Not because he feared being mean to her, or hurting her feelings. But because he didn't really know what he was feeling.

When he had left for New Orleans with Victor, he thought that he basically had things figured out. He would put his history to bed, and that would be that. But when he was down there, in that strange town, with its strange customs and mysticism, he caught himself rethinking things he thought were a certainty. And, to his dismay, he found himself thinking of her. Of Angie.

She stopped rocking back and forth, and lowered her hips all the way down, taking him completely inside of her. She then leaned forward until they were chest to chest, their body's touching in every possible way.

She leaned her head in, kissing him on the neck. Kissing him on the cheek. And even though they had never, ever, kissed each other for real, she whispered to him, "I like you Ty. I think about you."

Her lips were hovering over his, just inches away. He could feel her warm breath, smell the cinnamon gum she always chewed. He couldn't see her face, but he knew it well enough by now.

"I don't . . . "

"What?" she said, wanting to know once and for all, what he was thinking.

" . . . I don't think this is the best time for this."

"You want me to leave?" she said, backing her head away from him.

"No," he said, suddenly reaching up, arching his back, and rolling them over so that he was on top of her. "I don't think that this is the time to talk about you liking me or me liking you." He pushed slowly into her, her legs resting on his shoulders.

She reached out, her hands wrapping the outsides of his legs, feeling every inch of him sending quivers throughout her body. "You said you liked me!"

"No," he said as he thrust over and over, each time feeling every part of her body devouring him. " . . . I said . . . this . . . isn't . . . a good . . . time . . . to talk about . . . any of that."

But she heard what she wanted to hear, and Voodoo knew it. Angie knew, in that way that women just *know* things, that some part of him liked her. Some tiny, hidden away place, that he might never admit to . . . *that* part of him liked her. And it was enough to send her into the most incredible place she had ever been.

The moans became louder and longer. Her body shaking as though there was an earthquake rumbling inside of them. Her body and his, they fit perfectly, as if they were designed at the same factory. Meant to be sold together as a pair.

Every time he pulled his hips away and entered her again, she felt herself falling farther down a point of no return. And faster and faster he went, until she couldn't hold back any longer.

And at the exact same moment, they both came together. He inside of her, as a flash waved through his body like lightening. She, around him, the most wonderful feeling of orgasm changing the world she thought she knew.

And neither of them could speak. Not even a word. Not a sound. They both laid there, the electricity surging between them, both of their bodies pulsing . . . thundering. And so they stayed inside each other, as one, for several minutes, just letting the vibrations ebb and flow through them.

Breathing heavily, Voodoo was covered in sweat, and before he could consider what he was doing, he found himself leaning in and kissing her delicately on the lips, then quickly backing away, realizing he had more than a business relationship with her. He awkwardly backed away, heading for the bathroom.

He needed cold water to splash on his face. He needed to take a shower. He needed to prepare for the Reggie job. He needed to do anything accept talk to her about *them*.

She laid there silent, so happy she couldn't put it into words. It was alike all the Christmas's and birthdays and perfect wonderful gifts she could have ever asked for . . . but more. And no moment in her life, up to that point, could even hold a candle to what had just happened. He kissed her. He did it without thinking. It didn't matter what he said, now.

She knew.

There was hope.

And for Angie, a glimmer of hope was all she needed to make everything worth the effort. And there were no words for what she felt.

So she sat there as he walked into the bathroom and shut the door. She heard the faucet turn on, then off. Then the quiet hum of the shower. And as she sat there, smiling and sweating and her heart feeling like it was about to jump out of her chest, she heard her phone chirping away in her purse.

She took several breaths, wiping the sweat from her eyes as she sat up. Almost dizzy, she scooted to the edge of the bed and made her way into the living room where her purse was. She could see the blue glow strobing inside her brown leather bag as she grabbed it.

"Hello?" she said softly, pulling the cell phone to her cheek.

"Girl, it's Joy. Where you at?"

"I'm with Ty," she whispered.

"Oh, God," Joy said, . . . I can hear you smiling."

"Shut up," Angie said. And yeah, she was smiling.

"Look, there's a party at Mars Twenty-one Twelve."

"When?"

"Tomorrow night," Joy said. "And *we're* going."

"I don't know," Angie said, sitting on the edge of the couch, the candle light illuminating her naked body.

"Don't know? Shit girl, we goin'! So don't even trip."

"Fine, whatever. We'll go to the party. I'll see you later."

"I'll see ya," Joy said, " . . . and hey?"

"What?"

"Make sure you get your money from that nig—"

"Okay, Joy," Angie interrupted, " . . . byyyyyye." Angie disconnected the call.

She tossed the phone back into her purse and scampered back into the bedroom, crawling back into his bed, waiting for him to come back.

She was infected by him.

She was in love.

TWENTY-NINE

THE BLACK *MERCEDES Benz* pulled up and parked in front of a small row house on 3rd and Lehigh Avenue. Sitting in the back seat, Caesar saw there were two, huge Spanish men, standing around talking quietly. Both men were low-ranking members of the Matas. Suddenly they both noticed him, and snapped to action, rushing over and opening back door.

When Caesar stepped outside the car, the first man greeted him with a hug, and the customary kiss on both sides of the face. The other man approached, and showed the same respect for Caesar. They both knew that the new boss rarely showed up, and when he did . . . he was treated like royalty.

"Con permiso, Senor," one of the men said. "Pedro is waiting inside."

Both men watched as Caesar turned, nodded, and walked up to the door. When he stepped inside the house, one of them turned and said, "I wonder what brings the boss down to Philly? The violence, maybe?"

The other guard cocked his head to the side, his eyebrow raised curiously, "I don't know, but whatever it is . . . it must be really important."

When Caesar walked into the house, two more men were sitting in the living room, on a sofa, discussing something. And immediately upon seeing him, they rushed to his side, greeting him with the utmost respect. Caesar could make you very rich . . . or very dead.

Caesar studied one of the men and said, "Tito, leave us alone for a moment. I have some things to discuss with Pedro."

"Sure, Boss," Tito said as he headed towards the door, "I'll be right outside."

As soon as he left, shutting the door behind him, Caesar and Pedro walked slowly over to the sofa and sat down. Caesar crossed his leg and stared out towards the window.

Pedro Ramirez was one of Caesar's top Lieutenants, and the leader of the Philly Matas. He was also Caesar's first cousin.

"So what brings you to Philly, cuz? Did you get the money I sent over?"

"Yes, Pedro. I got the money a few days ago. But . . . that's not the reason I'm here," Caesar said, his tone very serious.

"Then what is it?" Pedro asked curiously.

"Right now, New York is very hot! Since the death of Juan-Carlos, things have gotten a lot worse. I recently found out that there's a special task-force assigned to taking out the Matas, and our rivals, the Black Royals.

"Is that why you called the truce with the Black Royals?" Pedro wondered.

Caesar ran his fingers through his hair, blowing out a slow breath. "That is one of the reasons. I know that our war with the Black Royals will continue to make matters worse . . ."

"And that will make the Fed's job easier," Pedro added. "They'll focus on destroying all of us. Both sides."

"Exactly," Caesar said, his face looking tired.

"So . . . what do you have planned?"

Caesar looked Pedro straight into his curious eyes and said, "In the next month or so, I'll be concentrating more on moving everything out of New York. Maybe here, to Philly. I'm not sure, yet. Even though our war with the Royals in over with, our battle with the feds will continue. And Like I said, New York City is just too hot right now!"

"Caesar, you're the boss. Whatever you decide, I'm okay with it. You always have my support, a hundred percent. We have lost lots of good men to long prison sentences . . . and to the grave. I think that it would be a good move for you and our brothers in the New York Matas to come join us here in Philly."

"Well," Caesar said, "it won't be for a few months . . . until I've figured everything out. Maybe we'll just come until the heat passes by."

Caesar shrugged, crossing his arms in front of his chest, "It's good to disappear sometimes. Especially when all the eyes are focused on you."

Caesar reached over and squeezed Pedro's shoulder a few times. "Yeah."

Slowly they stood from the sofa, taking stock of each other. They had shared some hard times together.

"Whatever you decide . . . " Pedro said.

"I'll keep you posted, and let you know what I decide."

233

Pedro smiled, "You just be safe out there in New York. I wouldn't want anything to happen to you, Caesar. Being the boss is different than anything else. Everything comes down on you. You are our voice." He looked down, shaking his head from side to side, " . . . what a headache."

"Don't worry about me. I'll be fine," Caesar said. "Now that our little war with the Black Royals has come to an end I can concentrate more on making our futures. Dinero."

Pedro lowered his voice, "Do you . . . actually . . . trust them? The blacks?"

"No," Caesar said as they walked towards the door, "but if the violence had continued at the level it was going, we were all going to lose. We made a temporary agreement."

Pedro nodded his head. "Just be careful, Caesar. A truce or not, those niggers will always be our enemies." Pedro wrapped his cousin up in a hug, "If anything was to happen to you, I would make sure that I personally killed each and every person responsible."

When they walked outside, Tito and the guards were standing around talking. After saying his goodbye's, Caesar walked over to the car and got inside. Then he rolled down the window and said, "Matadores por Vida!"

"Matadores por Vida!" they barked in unison.

They waved to him as the window raised, and the *Mercedes* pulled away.

} } }

LEWISBURG MAXIMUM-SECURITY PRISON . . .

Everything was about the numbers to Alex Karsh. There is no problem so big, that with the efficient and accurate use of mathematics, it could not be overcome. Every time he took a trip to the visiting room, he counted his steps. He memorized patterns in the guard's activities.

He looked for mistakes, and lapses in security. He looked at cracks in the walls and flooring that might hint at structural problems, or water damage.

He measured the size and depth of the bolts that were used to keep every piece of furniture and window framing in place. He calculated the time it would take to scale walls, fences, and rooftops.

He looked for weakness in the staff. People he might be able to seduce, or turn. He looked for the kinds of indicators that would tell him who the staff members were who were most likely to be *bought* or persuaded to look the other way.

Every day was filled with mathematics and possibilities. An angle.

He had been in seven different prisons during his life, before he had been kidnapped to the United States.

Two had been in South Africa.

One in the Congo.

Twice in the same prison in Rwanda.

Once in Kenya.

And one time, for two weeks, in Germany.

And in every one of those prisons, he found a way to escape. His formula was simple: *Do the correct math, and kill anyone who gets in the way of your escape plan.*

In Africa, many of the United Nation's security forces didn't even bother to arrest him, on several occasions, knowing that it was just an exercise in futility because he would just *'Hop the Fence.'* In fact, that's where he got the nickname, *The Wolf.* An animal who could just disappear.

It was a game to Alex. He knew he was going to find a way out. The only questions was: How long would it take?

And so, while other inmates were writing letters to the girls who would eventually leave them, Alex would study the architecture. While the other prisoners were feeling sorry for themselves, looking at smuggled-in pornography, or involving themselves with gang-related activities . . . Mr. Karsh was plotting.

The reason that Alex had been placed in the Florence ADX (Super-max) in the first place was that anywhere else, they would lose him.

Everyone at the State Department knew this. Special Agent Dan Gonzales knew this.

And that's exactly why Alex walked around with a smile on his face. If he could see the sunlight . . . then he could get to it.

THIRTY

FRONT DOOR of the trendy nightclub was divided into two parts: the regular entrance, and the VIP entrance. The two sides were divided by large, chrome stanchions, with black velvet ropes making a boundary between the two.

On each side there were several large, muscular door guys with crisp black suits, smooth shaven heads, and small radio earpieces that hooked behind their ears and ran down into their suits. Mars 2112 was the kind of place where only *pretty* people get to go.

If you weren't somebody special, you would have to take your chances with the public entrance. But good luck with that. If you weren't an attractive female, or surrounded by attractive females, your chances of getting in were remote at best.

Most likely, the door guy would look at your driver's license, shake his head, tell you that he thought it wasn't really *you*. If you argued, he'd just have some of the local police—that they paid 50 bucks-an-hour—ask you to leave.

Voodoo, wearing a pair of faded jeans, with a leather jacket, and a baseball cap turned backwards, walked casually

237

up to the entrance. He stood patiently, with a large wooden box in his hands. It was marked *'Patron Silver Tequila'*.

There were several models, and some producer from *FOX*, flirting their way into the club. Behind the door guys, was a large sign for *'Hot 97'*, the local hip-hop station that supplied the club with one of their DJ's for the night.

After each attractive woman was chatted-up sufficiently by the door guys they were sent into the club. The squirmy producer guy shook one of the door guys' hands, giving him a wad of hundreds that would have probably been a down payment on a nice house.

Voodoo, waiting with the wooden shipping crate in his arms, peeked out the side of his tinted glasses, "Hey, I got deliveries to make!"

One of the door guys looked him up and down, "Who's this for?" He searched a metal clipboard with several printed names on it, shaking his head. "I don't see anything . . . "

"Look," Voodoo said, "this is Patron Silver-Label Tequila. It's for some private party in the VIP section. It's already been paid for, but if you want me to leave—"

The door guy realized that it was for Reggie King's party, and instantly his demeanor changed. He held up his hands, "Hey, I'm sorry, I didn't . . . just . . . just let me have the box and I'll take it on back."

"No way, man," Voodoo said. "I gotta see this one all the way to the bar. I need signatures and all sorts of shit."

"Okay," the door guy said. "Let this guy through," he yelled to the other door guys He turned, pointing, "Head in, go right. VIP section is over on the left, up a flight of stairs."

"On the left, flight of stairs," Voodoo repeated frustrated, as if he was pressed for time. "Got it"

Two minutes later he was surrounded by pulsing music and beautiful people. Everyone in the club looked like they modeled for somebody, or starred in some big movie. There were actors and rappers and singers and porn stars.

The lights—suspended high above the dance floor—were almost hypnotic as they blinked and fluttered. Green and blue lasers shot back and forth around the club as if there was some futuristic battle going on. But the only battle here was to get close to the ladies because they were hot, and sexy, and all over the place.

Voodoo made his way to the stairs that led to the VIP section, and another security guy nodded, unhooked a velvet rope and let him head up.

Across the club, unbeknownst to Voodoo, Angie and Joy were at the bar, wearing skin-tight dresses that left nothing to the imagination. A bartender made his way quickly over to them, "The gentlemen over there," he said, pointing across the bar counter, "wanted me to send you two lovely ladies a couple drinks."

Joy and Angie leaned over the bar, looking at the men. They were young and attractive, probably in the entertainment industry. Joy leaned closer to the bartender, "What kind of drinks did they order us?"

She turned and winked at Angie, whispering, "This is how you can tell if they're worth the effort."

"They told me to get the two of you each a shot of *Hennessey*, and to inform you that if you would like, they've got a fresh bottle of *Cristal* waiting to be shared."

Joy and Angie smiled. Joy nodded, "Tell them . . . tell them to have our glasses waiting."

The bartender smiled and slid their *Hennessey's* forward, heading back down the busy bar to do his part in this upscale mating ritual.

"Girl," Joy said to Angie, "I told you we was gonna have some fun, tonight. Make you forget all about that, whatever his name is."

Angie shook her head, "His name is Ty."

"Whatever," Joy said slamming the drink. "Let's go drink some Cristal."

Angie's eyes widened sarcastically, "Wow, can we?!"

At the top of the stairs, Voodoo met another security guy. Again, a velvet rope was opened and he was sent in the direction of the VIP section's bar.

Nobody, not one single security guard, or doorguy, had thought to check the box. Voodoo had expected they would. That's why his silenced pistols were duct-taped to the bottom of the box, where both of his hands were.

"Over here!" a well dressed bartender said, raising his arm. He had obviously been informed by the door guys that some delivery guy was on his way up with a box full of expensive liquor.

As Voodoo entered the VIP area he instantly noticed that there were only two men, and about five or six women that looked like high-end call girls. Well, that would make sense if it was this guy's birthday party.

"Jamal," Reggie said, laying back on a couch as three girls slithered around him like snakes on ecstasy. Two of the girls were wearing just their *Victoria's Secret* bras, rubbing and grinding all over Reggie as he lifted his hand, "Grab me some Hypnotic, we're empty over here."

"I got you, I got you," the tall, slim Jamal said, not wearing a shirt as he sauntered around.

Voodoo could tell that they had been dressed nice, at least, when they entered. But with each passing song, and each new drink, they lost more and more of their clothes . . . and so did the girls.

All around them were small screens going from one hit song to the next. Nelly, Missy Elliot, Eve, 50-cent. And the thump of the music was as powerful as the scent of exotic perfume that surrounded all of them. The whole VIP area was dark.

Voodoo imagined this might be the kind of place he'd like to come, if he was into that kind of thing.

He approached the bar, the bartender nodding, with a polite smile on his face. "Just put them on the counter, here. I'll sign for them."

"Sure," Voodoo said, lifting the box towards the black counter top.

He set just the corner of the box up on the bar, noticing a tall shirtless man to his left. On the man's right shoulder was a thick black tattoo of the letters 'B.R'.

Voodoo gripped both pistols, Victor's voice echoing in his mind.

"Reggie is primary target, but anyone else . . . do what you want. No problem if you hit other peoples."

Voodoo took one quick breath and shoved the box across the bar, pulling the guns free as the crate of *Patron* headed off the other side, falling towards the floor.

In the same motion the pistols were spinning with him, hitting Jamal in the face with each barrel. He fell to the ground like a bag of old potatoes.

Instantly Voodoo was making a straight line for Reggie King, who still hadn't realized there was trouble. Behind him the box of Tequila crashed to the ground, the bartender yelling something frantic.

Reggie looked up, his eyes growing three times larger. The girls around him started to open their mouths, but saw both of the silenced *Glock 17's* pointing at them.

"What the fuck is this?" Reggie said, his face growing tight and angry. He was going to try and intimidate Voodoo.

Voodoo steadied the silencers at Reggie's body, and then suddenly the man grabbed-up one of the girls—a thin Hispanic girl wearing only a short green skirt without a shirt on.

She held her hands in front of her face, her elbows pressing against her breasts, as if she could block the bullets.

Voodoo fired three quick bursts with each pistol.

Psst-psst-psst, with both the right and left guns!

The girl's hands grasped for her stomach and chest as she slumped forward and fell off to the side, collapsing to the floor. Beneath her, Reggie's clenched hands locked with his fingers curled and bent.

As the girl fell away from him, he didn't move. He could only stare.

The bullets—Teflon-coated *'cookie-cutters'*—had passed right through her like hot knives through soft butter. He had six of them lodged in his chest, and it had taken away his ability to speak. All he could do was watch as this mysterious assassin backed away the gun barrels moving around the room at all of the potential targets.

All Reggie could do was bleed internally as Voodoo pointed the gun at the bartender who was almost in shock from the violence.

And all that Reggie could muster was just the slightest hint of a moan. Nothing more than a whimper, as his heart stopped, eyes fading to blackness as the life leaked out of him. Slowly his head slumped forward, blood and spit dripping onto his muscled bare chest.

All of this happened in less than 15 seconds. In the amount of time it takes to light a match, and watch it blow out . . . it was all over.

And in less than 25 seconds, Voodoo was heading back down the stairs, nodding as if nothing was out of order.

As if there wasn't a dead crime boss slumped over on a soft leather couch.

As if there weren't six holes through a brown skinned call-girl, that perfectly matched the holes in Reggie King's chest.

A copy of a copy

Voodoo knew he had a good 30 or 40 seconds before anyone was aware of what had happened. The bartender in the VIP would wake up in a couple of minutes with a nasty headache. The other callgirls, they knew well enough that when things like this happen, they didn't *see* anything.

And Jamal, well . . . he had been given a lead headache. They would be scraping his grey matter from the carpet for the next six months.

Voodoo's hands were seemingly resting in his jacket pockets, but the bottoms of the pockets were cut out so that he could hold and fire both pistols before anyone could react. He made his way past the security guard at the bottom of the stairs nodding as the man let him through.

Across the club Joy and Angie were being chatted up by two young entertainment lawyers, in town for some special CD release. They had the idea of getting Joy and Angie to be their late night sexual snack. Joy and Angie were having a good time, laughing and flirting, when Angle happened to glance over and see a man who kind of looked like Ty, passing from the VIP stairway.

Surely it couldn't be him . . . could it?

Slowly lowering her glass of champagne, she squinted across the club, through the crowd of famous and infamous people.

"I think that's Ty. Coming from the VIP section," she said, putting her glass down on a small, circular table.

"What you say, girl?" Joy said, laughing as Nino and Ruthless danced their way through the crowd, over to the girls.

" . . . I think," Angie said as she started walking towards the front of the club, " . . . that was Ty."

"You drunk, girl?" Joy asked as Nino came up behind her with a bottle of *Cristal*.

"I'll be right back," Angie yelled as she zigged and zagged her way through the bouncing and gyrating crowd.

Voodoo strolled past the door guys, still with his cap on. Still wearing his tinted glasses. Just some delivery guy. Another anonymous face among all of the other beautiful, recognizable people. A guy nobody would pay attention to.

In a place as trendy as Mars 2112, nobody would remember a some guy carrying a box of tequila.

Hidden in plain sight.

Voodoo turned right, his eyes still tracking back and forth, looking for any sign of trouble. He walked past the door guys, not saying a word. A nod here, a shrug there; that was it. The door guys were all so busy with a group of underwear models that they didn't even see him leave.

And like a ghost . . . he was gone.

Angie walked quickly to the door, looking for him. If it was him? With all of the people and excitement at the front door, it was impossible to find some guy that might just be the guy she's fallen for. In a dark club. Through the lasers and the smoke, and the flashing lights.

Frustrated, with Ty on her mind, Angie turned around and walked back into the club where it suddenly seemed much brighter. The overhead lights, the ones turned on at the end of the night, they were on. The music had stopped, and people were staring and pointing towards the VIP section, upstairs.

Two of Joy's friends—Ruthless and Nino, the guys who had invited them to the party—were running up the stairs, taking them three at a time.

Angie looked over at Joy, who was walking towards her. She lifted her hands, shrugging curiously, "What happened?"

All of the smiles and laughter were gone from Joy's face. "You know Sheri . . . she just came out of the VIP, where they were doing a private party with Reggie King."

"The gangster guy?" Angie said.

"Yeah," Joy said, lowering her voice. "She told Ruthless that something had just happened to Reggie and Monica. Something really bad. And then she passed out, and hit her head on a chair."

"Oh God, is she okay?"

"I don't know," Joy said. "But something must have freaked her out."

Suddenly, Ruthless came running down the stairs, as the two security guards started talking urgently into their radios.

"Shut the fucking club down, now!" Ruthless yelled. "Nobody gets out of here until I see 'em!"

The DJ's got on the intercom and said that there was an accident, and that they should all just sit down and relax for a couple of minutes until everything could be sorted out. But that's usually the point where people start asking questions.

Especially when gangsters start running around, giving orders.

Nino came down the stairs a few minutes later and found Joy and Angie in the corner. "Hey, look, some bad shit just went down."

"What's going on?" Joy asked him, her eyes scared.

He took a deep breath, looking around, as he lowered his voice to just above a whisper, "Reggie and Jamal just got killed and a girl too . . . "

"Oh my God," Angie said, her fingers covering her mouth. "Do you know who the girl was?"

"Spanish girl," Nino said, his face looking pale and sick.

Joy reached in to hug him, but Nino pushed her away. "There was blood fucking everywhere. Whoever this dude was, he . . ." but he couldn't finish the thought.

Joy's eyes narrowed, slowly turning to meet Angie's. "Hey, didn't you say your trick was coming down from VIP?"

"What?"

"That john you always talkin' about. You said he was comin' from the VIP?"

"No," Angie said, shaking her head, "it wasn't him. I just thought it looked like him for a second. But it wasn't him."

Nino's eyes widened, "You saw somebody coming from upstairs?" He lurched forward, grabbing Angie by both arms.

"No," she said, feeling his fingers digging into her thin arms, "It was somebody else, I don't—"

Nino shook her, "Listen, Bitch . . . if you saw the motha-fucka that did this, or might have done this shit, you better open your goddamn mouth!"

Angie started to cry, "Joy, what's going on?"

"These people are serious, Angie," Joy said coldly. "You better tell him everything you know."

246

"But 1 . . . 1 don't know anything," Angie pleaded. "It was just some guy I saw, across the club. I didn't even get a good look at the—"

And then a powerful voice thundered behind her. "You better start remembering everything you can," Ruthless said as he grabbed her by the neck and spun her around. "Cause that might be the man who killed my boss."

Angie felt her heart beat in her neck, where Ruthless' large hand was crimped down like heavy vice-grips.

THIRTY-ONE

CAESAR'S HAND REACHED for his cell phone on by the forth ring. Still half asleep, he brought the phone to his face.

"Que?" Caesar said, groggily.

"I thought we had a fuckin' truce! What the fuck was that about?" Ronnie King yelled into the phone. His voice was quivering,
on the verge of total rage.

Caesar sat up, not understanding what was going on. "Who is this?"

"This is Ronnie King, Caesar. And I guess we at war?"

"Espera, espera!" Caesar said as he rubbed his eyes.
Wait, wait!

Caesar cleared his throat, "I don't have any idea what you are talking about. Where is Reggie? I need to talk to him."

"Reggie's dead! Somebody just shot him at Mars Twenty-one Twelve. They killed Reggie, Jamal, and a prostitute. And the shit was professional, Caesar. This wasn't no accidental shooting."

Caesar reached over and clicked on a small lamp on his nightstand. "Reggie is dead? It didn't come from us," he

248

explained. "Why would we make a truce with the Black Royals and then violate it the next day?"

"That's what I want to know," Ronnie barked. "This sounds like some kind of fuckin' *trick* play."

Caesar stood up and started to pace around his room. He had specifically ordered Hector to call off the hit. And there was no way that Hector would have ignored that order. No, something else was going on here.

"Look," Caesar said, his free hand scratching his forehead, "Let me . . . 1 want to get my men together and make sure none of us had anything to do with it. It could have been dirty cops, or other competitors, I don't know. But I promise you, if any of my men are responsible, I will deliver them to you personally."

Ronnie didn't answer immediately. And in that pause a thousand things were running through both of their minds. "You've got until I bury my brother to figure this out. I don't hear from you . . . all bets is off."

"You have my word, Ronnie. One way or another," Caesar assured him, "I'll get to the bottom of this."

"Yeah," Ronnie said, "you do that."

"Ronnie . . . I want you to know that I respected your brother. He is a good man."

"Was . . . " Ronnie reminded. "He *was* a good man. Get back with me, Caesar. Sooner than later!"

And then the line went dead.

Caesar called Hector's cell phone, and waited as it rang.

"Caesar," Hector said excitedly, "have you heard about Reggie King?"

"Yes, Hector . . . I have," Caesar said, controlling his tone. "I am going to ask you a question and I want you to answer me very clearly and honestly. Did you call off the contract on Reggie King? I need to know, regardless of the answer."

"I assure you, boss," Hector said carefully, "that I called Victor and told him the job was off. He told me that was fine. He even said that he would credit the first payment towards a future job."

Caesar considered their options. "Alright, Hector. We need to make sure that we had absolutely nothing to do with this. They're looking for an excuse to go to war. And I'm not so much worried about that, but about the exposure it will bring us. We can't fight the Black Royals *and* the feds. But it may be out of our hands. His brother, Ronnie . . . he was not in the best of spirits. As you might imagine."

"Yes, boss," Hector agreed. "I'll call Pepe and Felipe and make sure that nothing happened. But I promise you, I called off that hit."

Caesar sat back down on his bed, a platinum cross hanging from a thin chain around his neck. His fingers played with the cross, staring at the small, form of Jesus being crucified.

"Caesar?" Hector asked.

"Yes, I'm here. I was just considering some things. I want you to talk to the Russian, and then get back with me . . . immediately."

"Si, Jeffe. Si."

$$ \} \} \} $$

VICTOR'S PLACE . . .

Victor's eyes were squinting, trying to focus on some small circuitry he was soldering. He was sitting at a small table,

250

with a bright, white light shining down on the small wires he was working with. All over the table were small tools for cutting and crimping wires. And as he leaned in to attach a small green wire to the circuit board, he heard his iPhone start to sing the Russian national anthem.

"Suka!" he said, letting go of the wire and replacing the soldering gun in its housing. He cursed under his breath as he stood up and slid over to the couch where the phone was singing. He noticed Hector Fernandez' number on the caller ID. He had expected the call, but not so soon. "Hyelloa?"

"Victor, this is Hector."

"You be up very late, tonight," Victor said as he turned around to his television and watched late-night *CNN Headline news*. It was a rerun of *Larry King Live*.

"Victor, we have a problem," Hector said, speaking slowly as if Victor didn't understand English at all. As if he was a third-grader.

"Problem? Tell me problem."

"The problem is that I told you to call of the job we had discussed," Hector explained.

"Yeah, so what? You cancelled job," Victor shrugged. "What is problem? I tell you I be credit your money. I no give back initial deposit. I use for future, you know this."

"Somebody just killed Reggie King, *that's* the problem."

"Yeah, I know about this."

"You know already?"

"Of course I know," Victor snorted. "Different client ask for same job as you. I don't know why. Not my business."

Hector was quiet. He was considering his words very carefully, "Victor . . . you're telling me that somebody *else* had Reggie hit?"

251

"Yes, yes. Different people. I be like middle-man for many people. I simple businessman. You a client, they a client."

"Okay," Hector said frantically. "Uh . . . I'll get back with you later. Thanks Victor."

"No problem. Think of it as free hit for you. Like birthday gift."

"I'll call you," Hector said as he hung up.

Victor shrugged, glanced at the television, and walked back over to his circuit board.

} } }

" . . . that's exactly what Victor said, Jeffe," Hector explained to Caesar just moments after he had hung up with the Russian.

The lights in Caesar's house were on now, as people started moving around. Men with guns were walking around, checking to make sure they would not be surprised by an attack from the Black Royals.

"I don't like any of this," Caesar said. "Somebody is playing games with all of us."

"You want me to call Victor again, and ask him about his client?"

"No . . . " Caesar said, "I want you to bring him to me. I want to talk to him, face-to-face, and see if he can explain things sufficiently. If he is responsible, we need to know about it, now. I can't call Ronnie King and tell him that somebody else took the job that we had originally contracted, and then cancelled. That would be the beginning of another war."

"I'll get Victor, then."

"Sooner than later, Hector. And take Pepe and Felipe with you." And then Caesar ended the call and closed his eyes. They were in a real tight spot, now.

"Esta segura, Caesar," one of his bodyguards said as he walked past the living room.

It's safe, Caesar.

Caesar nodded slowly, turned, and headed back to his bedroom. He needed to get a couple hours of sleep if it was at all possible. Something told him that things were about to get very hectic.

THIRTY-TWO

LEWISBURG MAXIMUM-SECURITY PRISON
4:13 AM. SATURDAY MORNING . . .

ALEX KARSH MADE his way over the second of the three high-fences. Even though the facility was known as the '*Wall*', he was escaping near the front of the prison, by the Receiving and Discharge area . . . where there are only two fences.

To get past the razor-sharp, coiled concertina wire, he used shoe laces that pulled the wire just far enough for him to throw the heavy green wool blanket—that was cut into a poncho—over the top of the fence.

To keep himself from falling when he tied the wire back, he had fashioned one of his belts with a hook that would let him rest on the fence, digging in with his feet. He wasn't worried about the electronic sensors because it had been storming for the last couple of days, and the security system was probably getting tons of false positives.

In the cold and wet weather, the roving patrol trucks would pass by only every four to five minutes. And he would be past this fence in less than a minute.

Quickly he worked his way over the fence, grabbing the wool blanket and ripping the shoe laces off of the concertina wire as he climbed down and flattened out on his stomach.

One more fence and he was free.

As he waited for the rovers to pass, he wondered why so many doors had *accidentally* been left unlocked? Why there hadn't been any alarms yet?

Either the guards were super forgetful, or something else was going on. But, as they say, 'Chance favors the prepared mind.' He had been waiting for an opportunity to disappear, and it had come his way. Bad weather was perfect for him. The mess that storms cause creates the perfect cover.

The white rover truck drove slowly by, the guard inside probably changing radio stations as he inspected another false reading on the fence. And without even stopping, the truck drove past.

A trick that Alex had learned while in South Africa was that black-and-white cameras—the kind normally used for security purposes—have bad problems with fences. The fence turns into a mess of static, and if a person moves casually slow, he can be right in front of the camera and not show up.

With color cameras, the trick is to let the bad weather help you. But this prison was old. Most likely, the fence cameras were far enough away that it wouldn't matter what quality they were. The constant rain was screwing everything up.

Quickly, he started up the last fence. Climbing to the edge of the wire, hooking himself in, and leaning back while he fished two more shoelaces out of his pocket. It took him less than 10 seconds to tie each side. Then he tossed over the wool blanket, grabbing behind his shoulders and tossing it up, over his head, so that it laid across the top of the fence.

Unhook, climb over, re-hook, grab the wool blanket/poncho, pull the laces off the wire, and that was that.

He was out into the tree line leaving nothing but wet squishes in his wake. The soles of his shoes were wrapped with newspaper so that they wouldn't leave any discernible tracks . . . at least, none that the dogs would be able to work with. The rain would wash away any traces of Alex Karsh.

Years from now he would be another myth. A prison legend that people talk about when they refer to where they did their time. There would be no manhunt for Alex Karsh. No press conferences, or search parties. No US Marshalls running around in circles looking for him.

Because, Alex Karsh didn't exist.

He was just a number . . . nothing more.

} } }

LIEUTENANT'S OFFICE
5:00 AM. 'COUNT-TIME'...

Lieutenant Brandon had decided to work a double shift, filling in for one of the other guards. This shift between midnight and 8 am. was referred to as the *graveyard shift.* Normally a lieutenant wouldn't be walking around in the units, doing a count. That was menial work, reserved for officers, not higher ranking Lieutenants or Captains.

But Lt. Brandon didn't mind. Besides, it got him out of that stuffy office.

He made his way to D-unit, walking by each cell, tapping his flashlight against the door if at least some part of the prisoner's body was not showing. He did the count with another officer, who was walking right behind him. As he approached cell D-19, he stopped, looking into the cell, and talking, as the guard behind him hesitated.

"Hey . . . " Lt. Brandon said, beating on the door. "Don't sleep in the nude. We have female guards here. Put some fucking clothes on," he barked, turning to Officer Sheryl Johnston.

She laughed quietly, added the prisoner to her count, and continued on past the Lieutenant.

Lt. Brandon looked back in the empty room, "Wait till you get back to your own country before you try any more of that striptease shit!"

20 minutes later Lt. Brandon was back in his office, pulling his cell phone out. He dialed the number on a small business card and waited for three rings. Hung up. Then called back 90 seconds later.

The familiar voice answered, "Law office."

"Do you guys handle divorce cases?"

"What kind of divorce?"

"She left me," Lt. Brandon said with a sad smile. "That, that . . . *bitch* up and left me."

"You're sure she's gone? Absolutely positive?"

"Gone like a bird," Lt. Brandon said as he leaned back and put his boots up on the desk.

"When will your kids realize she's gone?"

"Bout two hours, I'd say."

"I'll take care of everything," Special Agent Dan Gonzalez assured him.

"Make sure you get me a damn good settlement," the lieutenant said, " . . . because I'm not sure I can go on working in a job like this. You know . . . separation anxiety, and all that."

"You'll be just fine." And then the line went dead.

In two hours they would conduct another count, and at that point they would discover that the inmate in cell D-19 had somehow escaped.

Then he would get yelled at for being the duty officer. Then he'd get reprimanded. And then, a couple months later, he would resign, saying that there was a cloud over his head from the mysterious escape of an even more mysterious prisoner.

And then he would retire to some small, warm country where people didn't speak any English, and their government didn't extradite.

$$\} \} \}$$

THE OTHER SIDE OF THE FENCE . . .

Alex watched from behind a parked semi-trailer, waiting for the perfect car to drive by. And he didn't have to wait too long. A green *Honda Accord* pulled in to get gas at the pump near the street.

It was far enough away from the snack-shop that the person driving would be out for a while. He only had a few more minutes of darkness left to maneuver.

And so he did what he did best . . . disappear

$$\} \} \}$$

7 MINUTES LATER . . .

Peter Reddien, a young Biology major, working on his post-graduate studies, had driven about five miles when he got the shock of his life. The voice behind him was chillingly calm and haunting. "If you make *any* noise, or do anything *crazy*, I'll shoot you in the head."

When Alex had his attention he continued, "*Slowly*, I want you to take out your wallet and place it in the passenger's seat."

Peter didn't say a word. His long, bony arms pulled out his brown, worn wallet and tossed it gently to the side, his body shaking the whole time.

"Pull the car to the side of the road, slowly," Alex instructed. "Use your turn signal, check your blind spot. Nothing stupid."

Peter nervously checked his rearview mirror, and slowly brought the *Accord* to the shoulder. After the car stopped, the kid put his hands on the steering wheel, much like he would if this was a traffic stop.

"Now, I want you to open your door and get out of the car, walking around to the passenger side."

Peter nodded, slowly unbuckling his seatbelt.

"And," Alex added, "try not to get hit by traffic as you do so."

A minute later Alex was sitting in the driver's seat, looking through the kid's wallet. There was $127.00, a driver's license, and several credit cards.

Alex glanced at the scared kid, standing like an idiot outside the passenger door. Anyone in their right mind would have taken off running. *College kids*, Alex laughed to himself. Socially inept. He rolled down the passenger window, handing the wallet back to the kid with all of the credit cards, and a 20-dollar bill. He glanced down at the license.

"Listen . . . Peter George Reddien, of One Twenty-nine Glossy Meadow Drive," he looked up, " . . . I'm going to take your car, and a hundred bucks, and your driver's license. When I'm done with it, I'll park it at a shopping center and you'll get it back. The hundred bucks, that's a gift you just gave to a guy in need. A big, mean, black guy . . . the one who stole your car. You got a cell phone?"

"Yes, sir," Peter replied unsteadily, not sure what was going to happen next.

"Call yourself a taxi, and don't report your car stolen until tonight. If you do, I know where you live."

"I won't, sir. I won't," Peter answered quickly. Nothing like this had ever happened to him before. In a strange way, it was almost an adventure for him.

"Peter," Alex said curiously, "what do you do for a living?"

"I'm a post-grad student."

"Huh?" Alex said. "You get *paid* for that?"

"I have a grant."

"I don't know about all that. Well, just consider this a life lesson." And with that he shifted the car into drive, and sped away.

Peter watched as his car headed off into the bluish darkness, the sun just starting to make the sky brighter than black. It's not often that you get carjacked by a South African assassin. Especially one wearing prison khakis

}}}

VICTOR'S PLACE
8:00 AM . . .

Victor rolled over, grabbing his iPhone without looking to see who it was, "Da?"

Yes?

"Victor, it's Hector."

"Hyelloa, Hector," Victor said, rolling over so that he was blinking his eyes toward the ceiling, " . . . what I can do for you?"

"We wanted to thank you for the job . . . last night."

"It's no problem," Victor said, coughing the taste of vodka in his throat. "No cost to you."

"We're very appreciative of that," Hector said pleasantly. "We have decided to use your services again."

"This job be urgent, or what?" Victor asked, wondering if he would be able to sleep for a couple more hours.

"It's kind of urgent, yes. Could we meet later to discuss it?"

"Yeah," Victor said, glancing at his diamond encrusted *Cartier* watch that still couldn't hold the time. Frustrated, he looked at the clock on the phone. "You like hamburger?"

"Sure," Hector said.

"Okay, we be meet at Carl's, near the bridge, in Brooklyn."

"What time?"

"Ah," Victor rubbed his forehead, " . . . eleven-thirty."

"Victor," Hector said. "I'll see you then."

"Okay," Victor said as he disconnected the call and closed his eyes. In this town, killing was a growth industry.

THIRTY-THREE

VOODOO WALKED AROUND to the back of the car, popping the trunk, as his eyes scanned the area. They had crossed the line. But then, so had he.

He could hear Victor's words echoing in the back of his head as if the Russian was right there talking to him. He'd say, *don't ever get close to nobody. Don't make attachments that people can use against you. Don't love nobody, and they can't be used as leverage.*

But Voodoo had made the mistake of getting too close to her. Close to Angie. He didn't know exactly what they were . . . but it was more than a client/customer relationship. She was different. She was innocent. And he would not allow her to become a casualty of his business.

So now, it was time to fix things. He was wearing baggy black fatigue pants, with several pockets. His tight black *Under-Armor* t-shirt clung to his body so that it wouldn't get snagged on anything. He reached into the trunk and pulled out a large, thick, bullet-proof vest.

As he slid his arms into the vest he began checking the pockets to make sure everything was packed. Magazines for the *H&K Mp-5SD* were on the left, and magazines for the *Sig-Saur P-228* 9mm were on the right.

The *Heckler and Koch* machine-gun was fitted with a long silencer that would spit out Teflon-coated 9mm. bullets at just above a whisper. In fact, the weapon is commonly referred to as the '*Hush-puppy*.'

He slung the *Mp-5SD* over his shoulder, and then grabbed the *P-228* and slid it into a thigh holster on his right leg. He had over ten magazines for each weapon. More than 400 rounds of high-grade, Teflon-coated death.

In each magazine, he loaded a tracer as the second-to-last round, so that he would see a glowing red shot to let him know it was time to change magazines. He didn't want to be surprised with an empty weapon in the middle of a firefight.

And he was expecting a big one.

Also dangling from the vest were two smoke grenades, and two flash grenades. In an enclosed space, like those he would be fighting in, the flash bangs would put most people right on their ass, unable to defend themselves.

This was a rescue mission, but that didn't mean that he was going to let anyone walk out of there if they were involved. They had crossed the line when they kidnapped Angie. A line they would only get to see in flashes, as he made his way to her. Anyone in his way was a target.

Plain and simple.

Anyone with a gun was fair game.

He grabbed a black bag and unzipped it, pulling out a pair of night-vision goggles. He slid the harness over his head, but raised the goggles up until the lights went out. The last thing he grabbed was a large pair of wire cutters.

Just in case.

Closing the trunk, he walked a short distance to the small fenced in area where the power meters were. The tiny bolt lock keeping the gate closed was popped quickly and he walked inside, studying the different posts. There were several meter boxes, sticking out of the ground, about 4 feet high.

There were dogs barking somewhere nearby, as if this was some third-world country. He could also hear the sound of rap music playing off in the distance, probably from one of the apartments in the complex.

And the smell . . . well, it was a mixture of oil, and poverty.

He used his wire cutters to snip the security tabs on the different meter boxes. And then, with a quick motion, he pulled the meter boxes strait out, gauges and all. Three simple pulls and everything except the lonely dogs, was silent. It was like somebody unplugged everything, all at once.

No more rap music.

No televisions.

Just dogs barking, people wondering what was going on.

Leaving the caged area, he jogged towards the Mitchells Housing Projects building, preparing himself mentally for 20 flights of stairs, and the gun toting Black Royals that would try and stop him.

He noticed that several sets of emergency flood lights had turned on, near each of the exits. But everything else was off.

No elevators.

No air conditioners.

Voodoo made his way to an open door, near a stairwell. A thin, black woman with a baby in her arms walked outside, wondering what happened to the power. People were starting to yell. She stopped suddenly when she saw Voodoo.

"Where did they take the girl?" Voodoo asked quietly.

"What girl, what do you mean?" the frightened woman replied, shielding her child from this strange, armed man.

"The Black Royals . . . where are they? I won't ask again."

"You a cop?" she asked carefully, her eyes looking at all of his guns.

"No. "

" . . . you . . . you gonna kill 'em?" she asked, not bothered by prospect of those drug dealers getting a little of their own medicine.

"Yes," Voodoo said coldly.

"Eighteenth floor, they got the whole thing locked down," she said.

"Go inside, get into your bathtub, and stay down. Lock the door," Voodoo said as he headed up the stairs.

She backed into her house and slammed the door quickly, locking it.

}}}

ON THE 18TH FLOOR . . .

"This ain't normal!" Nino shouted.

"No shit," Ruthless yelled back. "He's here. It's just one nigga, so we shouldn't have too much trouble."

Men were running to each window, with *AK-47s* and shotguns.

"Anyone who sees anything needs to tell me first!" Ruthless yelled as he walked over to Angie. "You're boyfriend is coming to save you, bitch. After I kill his bitch ass, I might just take some time to be alone with you."

Angie sat in the corner of the apartment, hugging her knees with her arms. Her eyes were swollen from crying, her mascara leaving two bluish black lines down her cheeks. She couldn't say anything. She didn't know what to think.

Ty, the man she had fallen in love with, was an insurance salesman. Not some psycho hitman. Ruthless didn't know what he was talking about. None of them did.

She still remembered a few hours earlier, when Joy had gone through her phone, finding a number with the name 'TY' beside it in the directory. Her friend . . . or at least, who she *thought* was her friend, had given the phone to Ruthless and told him *that* was who he was looking for.

Angie had begged her, "How do you know anything about him? He had nothing to do with any of this." But none of that mattered to Ruthless and his goons.

They had put a pistol between her legs, pushing it deep inside of her as they all laughed, until she could no longer speak.

And she hadn't uttered a word since.

Ruthless had dialed the number and told Ty that he had better come over to the Mitchells Projects, and they would work out a deal for Angie's life. After Ruthless hung up her phone he smiled, telling his friends that they were going to get the man who killed Reggie first, and later . . . they'd fuck his hooker girlfriend.

"Don't worry, bitch," Ruthless said chillingly, checking to make sure his pistols were loaded. "I'm gonna treat you like my own girl. I'm a fuck you till you bleed."

Still, she showed no reaction, her hands and feet tied with wire.

Nino found several men walking down the hallway on the 18th floor, "Hey, I need you to stay in two's, head down the stairs and see what's up. That dude is on his way. And if he is who we think . . . he dangerous!"

"We got this," one of the Black Royals said, as the men headed away. Nino was sweating, looking around at the other men. They had ten well armed soldiers. Not even Rambo would be able to get past that.

Right?

}}}

Voodoo had the the *Mp-5SD* level with his night-vision goggles. His scope had an Infra-red beam, so that he could see where his bullets were going, but only through the goggles. To him, the whole complex was bright and green, with shades of grey. To everybody else . . . blackness.

His entire body was like that of a tiger, perfectly balanced and quick as he ascended the stairs. Each time he made a turn he slowed down, showing none of his body, as the barrel passed around every possible nook and cranny where a target might be lurking. The people he was hunting, they weren't human to him . . . just targets.

No different than a video game. Score enough points, and he would get to save the girl.

About five stories up, he heard footsteps several floors above him, trying to be quiet as they made their way down the steps.

Some men were whispering nearby.

}}}

AK-47s at the ready, the four men, walking in pairs, made their way down the stairwell from the 7th floor to the 6th. Their voices were echoing and vibrating all around them. Occasionally they would hear some curious resident stick their head into the stairwell, wondering aloud what was going on.

The man in the lead, Jerome, motioned with his hand, loud whispering, "He down here . . . " and he pointed with his gun barrel. "We need to stay together."

"Man," another guy said, holding a shotgun to his shoulder, "if we stay together, he's gonna get all of us at the same time."

"Let's kill this nigga, man," Jerome said, walking down the next flight of stairs. The barrel of his *AK-47* was shaking slightly. He was used to being the hunter . . . not the other way around.

They continued slowly, down to the 6th floor, and then down to the 5th. Still nothing. He had to be within the next couple of floors.

Strangely, the emergency lights were off from the 6th floor, on down.

"Ain't no fuckin' light in here!" one of the men said worrisomely.

}}}

Voodoo waited behind the door at the 6th floor until the men had passed. He watched as the man—a bright shade of green in his goggles—followed his friends down the next flight of stairs.

He crouched near the edge of the stairs, steadying his *Mp-5SD*. A bright white spot illuminated the back of the unknowing target. He fired a quick burst of three!

Pss-pss-psst!

The man fell forward, crashing into one of his partners.

"What the fuck?" one of the men yelled as his hommie fell lifelessly down the stairs. As he turned and squinted, another silent burst found his chest.

Pss-pss-psst!

He fell backwards, pulling the trigger of his *AK-47* just long enough for a quick burst of rounds to fire. The bullets ricocheted off of the concrete wall before the gun fell to the floor.

"He's above us!" Jerome yelled, and as he turned the corner he pulled the trigger, unloading a barrage of 7.62 rounds, that bounced and exploded off of everything.

When the magazine was empty, he ducked down, ordering the other man to go by. "He's up there!"

The other man ran by, opening up with his shotgun.

Boom! Boom! Boooomm!!

"Come on mother-fucker!" he yelled, as he flattened himself against the left side wall, breathing hard.

Jerome was struggling to put another magazine into the gun. The combination of darkness, ear-shattering noise, and his nerves didn't mix well. "Where's he at?"

But he didn't hear an answer.

Two bodies were off to his right—Black Royals who had been alive less than a minute ago.

"Yo, man . . . where's he at?"

Still no answer.

Voodoo put the bright white dot on Jerome's upper lip, just below the nose. One single, shot splattered his brain out across the stairwell, dropping the gangster instantly. Like pulling the building's meter box, a shot above the teeth . . . it turns off the power.

Forever.

Quickly, Voodoo went to the bodies one-by-one, putting a silent head shot into each of them. He turned, and headed up towards the 18th floor. The element of surprise was gone, now. And within minutes the police would be storming the building.

He figured he had two minutes to kill.

}}}

The instant that Nino heard the gunshots in the stairwell, he knew trouble was coming. Part of him felt sure that his men had killed the assassin. But another part of him, it said that violence was on its way up.

Nino ran down the hallway, shouting at the two men guarding the door to 18F, "If somebody come through that door without announcing who they are . . . shoot 'em!"

"No problem," one of the guards said, holding an *AR-15* at his waist. "Ain't nobody gettin' through this door."

Nino jogged back down the hall, trying to figure out how a single man could get past them. He kneeled down, giving himself a good angle on the stairwell door. If he came through that door, they'd have him.

Any second now.

}}}

At the 19th floor, Voodoo took a few seconds to slow his breathing down. He didn't want to get surprised by any more lurking men. It was going to be difficult enough already. He carefully walked back down to the 18th floor.

He expected five to ten more men. All of them with machine guns. He reminded himself to stay off of the walls. *Bullets like walls.* Victor taught him that, because of the combination of bendable metal, and the shock wave that surrounds a bullet as it travels, bullets have a tendency to travel down walls.

In the dark, in a firefight, many people often get shot, clinging to walls.

He made his way to the door that he knew they would be watching. He let the *Mp-5SD* hang as he freed up a flash grenade, pulling the pin, and holding the grenade in his right hand.

With his left, he reached for the bottom corner of the door. Slowly, he tested to see if it was open.

It was.

He counted to himself . . . 3 . . . 2 . . . and with one motion he opened the door no more than 6 inches, and tossed in the flash grenade.

Seeing the door open, both Nino and the other men opened fire at the door.

Quickly Voodoo ran halfway up the stairs so that he could fire down on any attackers.

Ba-booooom!

The whole 18th floor rattled

Neither Nino, nor the guards were prepared for what came after the door had popped open and closed. The deafening explosion and the bright white flash put them all on their backs as the concussion reverberated through the hallway.

It felt like being hit in the head with a shovel. And after their eyes had adjusted to the darkness, the flash had made them all blind.

Blind and deaf . . . like helpless little mice.

And the cat was coming.

Voodoo waited until the grenade had enough time to do its work and then he raced through the door, looking for targets.

He fired two more bursts at a guy on the ground with a gun laying next to him. The man moaned as the bullets tore through his body.

Then another burst at his partner. He then ducked and turned, seeing a man crawling, blood coming out of his mouth, pouring onto the floor. In the goggles, the blood looked black and thick.

Voodoo ran up to the man, kicking him powerfully in the ribs. The man fell over, grabbing his stomach in the fetal position.

"The girl," Voodoo hissed. "Where?"

Nino heard a distorted voice, not being able to see anything. It was like some demon was talking to him.

The voice got louder, "Angie . . . what apartment is she in? I won't ask you again."

But Nino couldn't answer the demon. His brain was all mixed-up. All he saw was the grenade exploding, and now . . . nothing but bright white with silver sparkles. As if he was staring at the sun and couldn't close his eyes.

Voodoo shrugged.

Psst!

Nino's body flattened lifeless and dead on the cold floor.

He made his way over to the apartment where the two men were bleeding all over the place. They were moaning, gurgling for air.

Psst-psst!

Two quick head shots quieted them down.

He noticed a bright reddish flash as he fired the second head shot. In a practiced motion, he dropped the magazine from his *Mp-5SD*, and slapped a new one into place.

He took three breaths and then kicked at the door, just beside the knob. The door fell open and he dived into the room, rolling forward, trying to cover as much space as possible. Anyone in the room would shoot at the door, and he wouldn't be there.

But there wasn't anyone in the room. Only the muffled sound of somebody trying to yell from a back room.

♩ ♩ ♩

Ruthless had picked Angie up by the neck, his free hand holding a pistol to her head.

"I'm in here, mother-fucker! You want this bitch alive you better put all your shit down. Otherwise, I'ma put her brains all over the carpet!"

The only light in the room came from outside, from other buildings, and street lights, and the moon. And Ruthless watched as the dark figure crept into the room, his voice low and eerie.

"Let her go, and you get to live," Voodoo said, looking at the large man standing behind Angie, holding a pistol to her head. He needed to get the man thinking about him, and not about shooting Angie.

"Put your guns on the floor, or I kill her right now," Ruthless said, rage boiling in his eyes. His whole body shaking with anger.

"I have a message from Reggie King," Voodoo said, watching Angie's shiny green tears. The little light coming in the room seemed bright in the goggles.

Suddenly, Ruthless lost his train of thought, "What did you say?" He tightened his finger around the trigger, his mind telling him to shoot at the shadow in the darkness.

"Reggie wanted me to give you a message," Voodoo said as he fired between Angie's shoulder and head, sending a round into the big man's neck.

Ruthless pulled the trigger as the strange feeling sent him falling backwards, crashing into the window, then falling to the floor. His shot narrowly missed Angie's face, the bullet going through the bedroom wall.

Angie tried to scream, but still, she couldn't talk. She couldn't see what was in the shadows, but she remembered that same voice in the darkness of Ty's apartment.

He rushed to her, pulling out his cutters, and freeing her arms and legs. Without a word he grabbed her, looking back at Ruthless as the big man clutched at his throat.

"Reggie says he'll see you on the other side," Voodoo said cryptically.

The flashing red and blue lights of the police vehicles approaching reflected through the apartment as Voodoo ran, basically dragging Angie behind him.

"Hurry!" he barked as he entered the hallway.

They made their way into the stairwell, and down the stairs in a couple of minutes. Angie felt like it was all some horrible nightmare. Some dream that she couldn't awaken

274

from. But still . . . she could not speak. Her mind had disconnected.

At the bottom of the stairs, Voodoo pressed Angie against the wall as he checked right and left. He turned to her, "We don't have much time. Keep up."

And with that he rocketed out of the doorway, towards a pair of double doors. Once outside they saw people all around, some in pajamas, others half dressed with their kids. There were people everywhere, and they saw Voodoo and Angie. Some of them started to point at them as the police cars raced closer. There were flashes of red and blue all around the projects. There was no way he would make it to his car.

Too late.

He quickly changed course, running the other way, around the back of the projects, in another direction. There didn't seem to be any police cars near a small construction site that he decided to cut through.

Still, he was basically pulling, and Angie was basically being dragged. Somehow, though, she kept her feet underneath her.

At the other side of the construction site he pulled off his goggles, hooking them to a clip on his vest. He turned and grabbed both of Angie's shoulders, looking at her directly in those beautiful, scared eyes.

"This is my fault, Angie. I'm sorry."

She just stared at him, tears starting to well up in her eyes. She wanted to talk.

To scream.

To kiss him.

To hit him.

But she couldn't find the right answer.

"I got you into this, I'll get you out of it. Just bear with me for a few more minutes . . . alright?"

She nodded, almost imperceptibly, and he smiled. And it might of been the first smile she had seen from him. He leaned in and kissed her on the forehead.

"Okay," he said, his eyes darting around as he got his bearings, " . . . we need to keep moving."

"Freeze!" a voice with a thick Brooklyn accent barked. "Put your hands where I can see um!"

The police officer shined a flashlight on them, "What the fuck?!"

The cop moved closer, his hand steady with a *Glock 17*. On his radio, another officer was asking if he'd found anything behind the construction site.

The cop got closer, "Don't even think about reaching for that pistol there," and then his jaw dropped, " . . . Ty?"

This cop, Officer Anthony Ferretti, was Ty's neighbor.

"Anthony?" Voodoo said.

Anthony lowered his pistol, putting it back in the holster. "What the fuck are you two doing out here?"

"You need to trust me, Anthony," Voodoo said.

"Were you a part of all that?" Anthony said, waving his flashlight at the housing project filled with dead bodies.

"They kidnapped her, Anthony. They didn't leave me any choice."

Over his police radio a voice asked, "Officer Ferretti . . . you got anything?"

Anthony swallowed, shutting his flashlight off. He reached up and toggled his radio, leaning into the microphone on his breast pocket, " . . . No . . . nothin' here. I been through every inch of this place. They musta gone the other way . . . over."

276

" . . . keep looking."

"Roger that," Anthony nodded slowly, his eyes looking at the scared, bruised girl beside Ty. He remembered her from Ty's apartment.

"Those bastards hurt you, sweetheart?" Anthony asked, his voice soft. She nodded and then began to cry. Her body deciding enough was enough, she slumped over and started to fall, as Voodoo caught her.

"There's a used-car lot," Anthony said, "about a half mile that way." He pointed with his flash light. "I'll pick you up in a half-hour."

And without another word, he turned and walked back towards the housing projects.

THIRTY-FOUR

INSIDE CARMEN'S LAVISH condo she and Ronnie laid in bed after having just finished their third round of untamed sex. Their naked bodies were covered in beads of warm sweat, and Carmen's legs were still trembling form the powerful orgasm she had experienced.

They were two people that were deeply in lust with each other. And when they were together, nothing else mattered in the world.

Carmen was laying across Ronnie's chest while he ran his fingers slowly through her long black hair. The only light inside the bedroom was the flickering yellow coming from the three scented candles situated throughout the room. They filled the air with a deep tropical scent.

The bed had a CD-player and two small speakers built inside it. And Carmen and Ronnie laid back, enjoying the lovely voice of Whitney Houston flowing out of them.

The chirping sound of Ronnie's cell phone snapped them both out of their peaceful relaxation. For a moment he thought about not answering it. But as it continued to ring, he hesitantly reached over to the nightstand and grabbed it

First he checked the caller-ID, seeing who it was that was disturbing him. When he saw Ruthless' name on the small screen he quickly answered, "Ruthless, what's up?"

"Yo, Ronnie. This me, Meechie," a voice said into the phone.

Ronnie didn't understand as he sat up, "What? Where's Ruthless?"

"I . . . I think he's dead!" Meechie mumbled.

"What?" Ronnie shouted as he jumped up out of the bed.

Carmen sat up in bed with a frightened look on her face. She hadn't heard Ronnie this animated since they had found out about Reggie. And now something else?

"Ronnie, man . . . shit over at the Michells Project is crazy! Cops is all over the place. Somebody turned all the lights off and the next thing you know, seven or eight of our men are all scattered throughout the building. They all dead. It's like some horror movie. A bloodbath, man!"

"Slow down, Meechie. Take a breath."

"Whoever is responsible for this . . . he had to be a professional."

"And . . . and Ruthless is one of the dead?" Ronnie muttered.

"I think so," Meechie answered pensively. "The paramedics were carrying bodies in every direction. The cops got the whole projects taped off. I don't think nobody survived."

"What happened to the girl?"

"Ain't seen her either, she's probably one of the dead bodies covered with a sheet," Meechie answered delicately.

Ronnie sat back down on the bed and put his head down. His confused mind was racing with thoughts. He was scared. More scared than he had ever been in his entire life. All of the men who he looked up to. Who he considered invincible. Larger than life. They were gone.

They were all dead.

In less than 48 hours, his brother Reggie, and half of his crew had been wiped out by somebody. His mind couldn't absorb it.

"Ronnie . . . yo, Ronnie?"

"Yeah, Meechie . . . what's up?"

"I think you should skip town until all of this shit calm down. Who knows, maybe the person responsible for all of this is coming for you next. They got Reggie and Ruthless.

Ronnie thought about what Meechie had said, looking over at Carmen. He hadn't seen her like this before. She looked worried, now.

"Yeah," Ronnie replied, "you probably right. I'll call you back later," he said closing his cell phone.

Carmen scooted across the bed towards him, "What happened?"

Ronnie's arms dropped to his sides, his shoulders slumping as he sat. "Somebody just killed all of our men over at the Mitchells Projects."

He turned to her, "That was one of my men on the phone and he said that whoever did it might be coming for me, next."

Carmen reached out and hugged him, as the tears welled-up and started falling down her soft brown cheeks.

Ronnie looked into her watery eyes and said, "Carmen . . . do you love me?"

She nodded, swallowing hard, "Yes! Yes, baby! I love you more than anything in this world." And she wasn't just saying it. She was being honest, her words more true than she had been in so long.

"Then I want you to hurry-up and get dressed. Pack up some of your belongings, cause we outta here."

"Where are we going?" Carmen asked as she got out of the bed.

"Somewhere that no one can find us," Ronnie said as he reached down on the floor and grabbed his jeans.

30 minutes later, Ronnie and Carmen were walking out the front door of her apartment building. Each of them were carrying a large suitcase. They placed the cases on the back seat of Ronnie's brand new *Range Rover*, then got inside quickly.

As Ronnie pulled off down the street, nervousness was pulsing through both of their bodies, making it hard to concentrate on anything but escape. The killer could be anywhere . . . anyone.

His loaded 9mm. was underneath his white t-shirt, ready to be used without any hesitation.

As he headed towards the Bronx he still couldn't believe the bad news. How could everything change so fast?

40 minutes later, Ronnie pulled up and parked in front of a small house near 150th and Courtland Avenue. Carmen watched as Ronnie got out of the truck and rushed into the house. Moments later, Ronnie jogged out of the house, carrying a large green duffel bag, glancing nervously in every direction.

He opened the back door and tossed the bag next to the two suitcases. After closing the door, he rushed back around and got behind the wheel.

Seconds later they were speeding off down the street. Something very strange was going on, and whatever it was . . . he didn't want to be around to become another one of its victims.

} } }

Voodoo sat beside Angie, watching her watching him. He no longer had his vest and his guns and grenades. He was just wearing black cargo pants with a white t-shirt. He pulled out a large envelope and handed it to her.

Without speaking she took it, glanced at him through her dazed eyes, and then back down at the envelope.

Voodoo glanced around, seeing if anyone was paying them any interest. They were at a small diner, inside the airport. At least there, they could be sure that nobody else had guns.

She carefully opened the envelope and reached inside. The first thing she felt was a thick wad of cash. She pulled it up just to the edge of the envelope, seeing the yellow and white band with *$10,000* marked on it. It was a brick of 100-dollar bills. She looked up at Ty, her eyes asking, *why?*

"Think of it as a severance package," Voodoo said. "Seeing as your out of a job, now."

She let go of the money and found a smaller, blue envelope. She removed it, opening it carefully. Her eyes studied it for a moment.

It was a first-class, one-way ticket to San Diego, California . . . where her mother lived. She looked at Ty, now curious as to how he knew about her family.

Voodoo seemed to hear the question in her gaze. "I *Googled* you." He looked around, taking a quick sip of

282

lukewarm coffee. He lowered his voice, "You need to get out of here. And don't come back . . . ever."

She dropped the ticket down into the envelope and grabbed for the last item . . . a cell phone. She picked it up and set it on the table in front of her plate of uneaten scrambled eggs.

Voodoo yawned, not having slept in what felt like weeks. "It's yours. But don't use it. It's an emergency phone."

A woman's voice came over the intercom, "Attention all passengers of flight eight-sixteen, Service from JFK to LAX, we will begin passenger boarding now at gate . . . "

"That's you," Voodoo said, dropping a 20-dollar bill on the table for the meal and sliding out of the booth.

Angie put the cell phone into her purse, along with the stack of money, and grabbed the ticket. Without a word she stood, up and they both walked quietly to her gate.

As they approached, people were lined up, waiting with their tickets in hand. Outside the large glass windows she could see a giant plane of silver and blue and white. It was so big it was intimidating.

They made their way to the small check-in desk and she numbly handed her ticket to the flight attendant. The woman robotically punched in some numbers on her computer, smiled her plastic smile, and handed Angie back a stamped ticket.

"You may board whenever you wish," she said, as if she'd said it a million times.

Slowly, they approached the ramp, and just before she entered the passageway to the plane, she turned back to him. She stepped in, and wrapped him up in a hug.

And whispering into his ear as she clutched him tightly, she said, "I love you, Ty. Whoever you are. I love you."

He could feel the tears making his t-shirt warm and wet near his neck.

"Will I ever see you again?" she asked so quietly that he more felt the words, than actually hearing them.

"I'll call you," Voodoo said softly, not wanting to let go of her. Feeling as though, for the first time, he would be losing something if she got on that plane. But then, if she stayed, he might put her in more danger.

"You don't sell insurance, do you?" she said as she gazed into his eyes.

He had a slight grin on his face, "You know what I like best about you, Angie?"

She swallowed, shaking her head, *no*.

"You don't ask too many questions."

And with that said, he kissed her.

On the lips.

And he meant it

He then backed away, turned her around by the shoulders, and slapped her once lightly on the ass, as he motioned for her to go.

She squinted her eyes playfully at him, wiping away the last of her tears.

He turned away, not daring to look back. And left the gate. *It's strange, too,* he thought. That the things in life you don't think about, suddenly become so important in that exact moment when you're walking away from them.

This girl who he had been with for months, without giving a second thought as she walked out of his door on so many nights, was now tearing at his soul as she walked out of his life.

What a cruel thing love is.

THIRTY-FIVE

VICTOR WAITED QUIETLY inside the dark garage, waiting for the El Salvadorians to return. He wasn't so much waiting by choice. His wrists and ankles were heavily duct-taped to the sides and of a thick wooden chair. He had been surprised by the boldness with which Hector had acted.

It had started the minute their meeting had begun. Victor had been expecting a new assignment. He had figured that after Reggie King, the Matas would want Ronnie taken out. They had a credit of $200,000. Usually, that kind of money burns a hole in peoples' pockets. Especially when those people are fighting over turf during a drug war.

Hector had started the conversation by thanking him for having Reggie King disposed of. He then asked who the contractor had been.

To which Victor had replied, without looking up from his plate full of bacon and potatoes, "I don't know who is client."

"You don't know," Hector said, " . . . or you won't tell me?"

Still chewing, still balancing an unlit cigarette in his mouth, Victor answered, "What is difference?"

285

Hector had turned three shades of red before the Russian had even glanced in his direction. Finally, when he did look up at the number two man in the Matas drug organization, Victor could see he was upset.

"Why you be so angry?"

Through clenched teeth, and a tensed jaw, Hector explained, "Listen Victor . . . I have to be able to prove that we didn't order that hit. And I can't do that without your client's name."

Victor had shrugged, "I can't help you. Client con-fi-denti-al-ity! In my business, this is very important."

Hector then sat back, lifted his right hand, just a bit, four dangerous looking brown-skinned men approached their table. They made it clear that they would need to pursue this line of questioning further, but that this wasn't the best location to do so.

"You're coming with us gringo, or we'll kill every person in here," were the exact words they had used.

And by the way the guy kind of spit as he talked, stroking a pistol that was tucked just inside his jacket . . . Victor knew he was probably telling the truth. He figured that there was no point in everyone dying. Not quite fair to have a bunch of innocent people suffer for Victor's dealings.

Victor was a lot of things: A mercenary, an assassin, a gangster, and a sub-contractor of murder. But he still had a code. He, and he alone would deal with these men.

And after being shoved in the back of a boxy American SUV, a hood thrown quickly over his head, he ended up an hour later in this garage.

Taped to a chair

Waiting for somebody to ask him more questions after a healthy dose of pain and suffering.

When he had been in the Russian army, they had done extensive training in interrogation—both sides of the table. And one thing he knew for certain was that they would be back to question him more 'thoroughly.' Now it was just them letting him wonder. The anticipation of torture is much worse than the actual torture itself.

Once people start pulling off fingernails and hammering railroad spikes into your kneecaps . . . well, the body tends to start shutting down pretty quick.

So Victor sat quietly, taped to his chair, sitting in this dark garage, waiting for pain. He wished he could have kept that cigarette, now. He regretted not lighting-up, in the event that he would never get another chance.

He regretted not finishing that plate full of bacon and potatoes. And he regretted not having finished off that bottle of *Stolichnaya* Vodka the night before. Those are the kinds of things he was thinking when he heard footsteps and muffled talking outside the garage.

He squinted as the door opened, the light as bright as the sun shining in on him. Two little words were all he heard as the men entered the garage, "Es el."

It's him.

"El estaba solo?" Caesar asked suspiciously.

He was alone?

"Si, Jeffe," Hector replied.

Yes, Boss.

"Ponga la luz," Caesar instructed.

Turn on the light.

Victor's eyes started to adjust as the garage's interior light was turned on. There were four men around him, a few of which he recognized from the diner when they had grabbed him. Hector and another man were standing directly in front of him. They were all very well dressed, as if they had just been down to the New York Stock Exchange for a visit.

Nice tailored suits.

Shiny shoes.

Silk shirts.

Matching ties

Victor, always the charming one, said, "You dress very nice."

The man calling the shots gave him a half smile, his eyes looking the Russian up and down. He looked over at Hector and nodded.

Then Hector handed him a small plastic bag. The man took it, reached inside and grabbed Victor's iPhone. After studying it for a moment, his eyes raised, observing Victor carefully. "This is yours?"

Victor shrugged noncommittally.

The man set the phone on the ground and reached back into the bag, pulling out a shiny *Zippo* lighter with some engravings on it. The strange markings were in Russian, the words unrecognizable to Caesar.

"What does it say?"

"Read it too me," Victor said smugly, "I'll explain it to you."

And that was immediately followed by a hard slap across the face from behind, nearly knocking the Russian and his chair over to the cold concrete floor.

"My name is Caesar. I am the person who will determine whether you live or die. I alone will make the decision based on how well you convince me that you are telling the truth."

"If you want be know what lighter says," Victor said, as if he was disinterested in all of this silliness. Unfazed by the slap, he added, " . . . 1 promise I'll tell you."

288

Which brought another slap, this time from the other side. It sent him rocking to the right.

When his chair settled Victor opened his eyes, "*Whoa*! That is like shot of good Russian Wodka. And save me lots of money, too!"

Caesar raised his hand, stopping Pepe from hitting the Russian again. He had a grin on his face.

"What should I call you?" Caesar asked, walking closer to Victor.

"Victor Pavlovich," the Russian said proudly. "But you can just call me Doctor Pavlovich."

"I'm impressed," Caesar said with a smile. "I didn't know you were a doctor."

"I not doctor," Victor said. "And you're not gangster. But I like how this sound."

"Mr. Pavlovich," Caesar started, "my man here tells me that you have done several jobs for us in the past. All of it very top notch. Very clean and efficient."

"Your man is far too kind," Victor said. "I just do what I can. You know, American capitalism."

Caesar nodded. "Well, you have been a professional up to this point. But now we are in a bind, you see. I need to know who ordered the hit on Reggie King."

"You did."

Caesar sighed, "Yes, but then we called it off. I want to know who the *other* client was." He held his hands up before Victor had a chance to answer, "I already know that you told Hector that you could not give us the name. Client *confidentiality*, or whatever it was you said."

"Confidentiality," Victor echoed. "Yes."

And I would normally respect that. But this is a very different situation. All I need is a name, and then you walk out of here and lead a long, happy life. I'll even let you keep our down payment. One name for two-hundred thousand dollars. Now isn't that the very meaning of capitalism?"

"I need cigarette," Victor said, almost as if he was closing the deal.

Caesar's eyebrows furled, his expression clearly surprised. He was not used to being talked to like this. Caesar got his answers, and he got his way. But, being that Caesar needed the name, and in a show of good will, he nodded to Hector who quickly produced a cigarette from a pack.

Hector gently placed the cigarette in Victor's mouth and lit it with the *Zippo*. As he did so Victor read the engraved writing:

Yob Tvoio Mat

Victor took a few deep pulls from the cigarette, letting smoke pour out of his nose and mouth very slowly, rising up toward the light. This was all just how it should be. He wouldn't want to be tortured if all the elements weren't there. The smoke filled room. The ruthless gangsters.

The veiled threats.

The chair.

The duct tape.

All of it was perfect.

Victor had known that eventually, in his line of work, this day would come. Live by the sword . . . die by the sword.

"Now, Mr. Pavlovich," Caesar said carefully, intoning as he spoke that a wrong answer would bring about consequences, " . . . now you need to tell me who your client was, and all of this will be finished."

Victor sucked several more times, large grayish-white clouds of smoke rolling and folding in the air around them. "If I tell then they be kill me."

"If you don't tell us," Caesar said sharply, "than I will kill you."

"Either way," Victor said, not looking the least bit scared, " . . . I be dead." He shrugged disinterestedly, "Dead is dead."

Caesar realized that to continue questioning him like this would not produce results. He nodded to Hector.

Hector had an evil smile on his face as he looked over at the smaller, angry looking man in a powder-blue silk button-up shirt. "Pepe, would you like to help me convince Victor to give us a name?"

"Gladly," Pepe said as he walked around from behind Victor, so that he was looking directly at him. His eyes looked the Russian up and down several times, as if he was measuring him for something.

"I buy my clothes at Footlocker," Victor said. "Very comfortable."

Pepe nodded and walked across the room grabbing something from a dark corner. It looked like a club, or a bat, in the darkness. But as he returned it was clear that it was a machete, sharpened on both sides. The blade looked jagged and spotted where blood had been crudely wiped away.

Pepe held it in his right hand, pointing at Victor, the tip of the blade nearly poking Victor's chest. "I don't really care if you answer any of my questions. This part, here," he said, wiggling the machete in Victor's face, " . . . this is just for my enjoyment. And, you know, it ain't nothing personal, because I'm glad that you had that nigger killed."

Pepe bit down on his tongue a few times, "But, business is business, right?"

And then Pepe suddenly dropped the blade down on Victor's left thigh, cutting several inches into the flesh. Blood immediately started to pour out of the wound, the blade still inside the thigh muscle. Pepe leaned in, his eyes locked on Victor's.

But Victor did not scream. He gritted his teeth and grunted as if he was lifting a large heavy box. His eyes squinted, his face starting to sweat. But he did not yell. The pain was tearing through his body, hot and sharp from the rusted blade.

Victor tried to regain his composure as the searing pain raced through leg, up his back, and into his neck. He took long, deliberate breaths.

Pepe slowly twisted the blade back and forth in the Russian's leg as he talked. "Don't pass out on me puto. I want you to enjoy this as much as me."

With each word, Pepe's wrist changed direction. And with each new direction of the blade, more tearing muscle and flesh.

More blood.

More sweat.

Pepe smiled and then lifted the blade, pulling it from Victor's leg, "You're going to have to use a walking stick from now on." He shrugged, "There's really nothing we can do to fix that." He turned to Caesar.

Caesar approached Victor again, "Give us a name, and we take you to a hospital, right now."

"You don't want to end up in a wheelchair," Pepe said snidely.

Somehow, Victor managed a slight smile, "Why I need hospital? Don't you remember . . . I doctor. And besides, wheelchair is nice. That way, I be relax all day."

Caesar shook his head sadly, nodding to Pepe.

Suddenly, the machete blade chopped down into Victor's right thigh, so deep now that it stopped at the bone.

Victor's face tensed, his eyes shutting as every muscle in his body seemed to lock. Again he groaned . . . but nothing else. He would not allow these men the luxury of hearing him yell.

There was a horrible popping sound as the tendons in Victor's right leg broke free, causing his thigh muscles to curl up near his hip and knee. Warm blood ran freely down Victor's shins and feet, puddling on the floor around his chair.

"You're going to bleed out, puto," Pepe said. "Hold on," he added as he walked over to the corner and got a roll of duct tape. He sauntered back as if he was listening to Salsa music that nobody else could hear.

Pepe leaned in again as he started to run the tape around Victor's upper thighs. "I don't want you to pass out or loose so much blood that you go into shock. That would cheat us all of our fun."

Victor realized that he was going to die, no matter what he said. And he needed to make a call.

"Okay, okay," Victor relented. " . . . I be . . . call him . . . for . . . you."

Pepe backed away, looking over at Caesar as he spun the blade around in his hand.

"Just give me a name," Caesar said. He told him that he would take it from there.

Victor explained to them that he could reach him on the phone, only. But that he would turn over the call to Caesar so that they could discuss the problem.

Caesar told Hector to give him the phone. And carefully, Hector walked it over to Victor.

"What's the number," Hector asked, looking down at the full-color screen.

"Give me free hand," Victor said between breaths.

"Why?"

"It have finger recognition," Victor explained.

Hector touched the screen and saw a blue box come up, with a timer counting down from 35 seconds. He glanced up at Caesar for approval.

Caesar nodded.

Pepe used the machete to cut at the tape so that Victor's right hand was free.

Victor slowly freed his arm and pressed down on the pad, unlocking the phone's security program. He lifted the phone to his face, squinting between the sweat that was burning his eyes. He touched a couple of buttons quickly as the room stared at him.

"You guys should do weddings," Victor said as he touched several numbers into the phone. A yellow box in the corner lit-up the symbol 'GPS'. Then he pressed a few more, and the phone began to ring.

♩♩♩

Voodoo felt his phone vibrating in his pocket. He pulled it out as he made his way across the kitchen, to the living room. He glanced at it, instantly knowing it was Victor.

"Victor, what's up?"

"Kak dila, moy druk?" Victor said, his voice very weak.
How's it going my friend?
"Fine . . . what's wrong?" Voodoo asked.
"Ou minya yest problyemi."
I have problems.

Voodoo realized that he was speaking Russian to let him know that he was in danger. He also heard a beeping sound on his phone telling him Victor's exact location as the GPS indicator came on.

He reached for a note pad, and started scribbling the location.

"Shto eta?" Voodoo said.
What is it?

$$\}\}\}$$

Victor's eyes watered as he talked. "Fspomnayesh kvadrat-krasni?"
Remember Red-square?
"Da," Voodoo answered.
Yes.
"Ya budu umirat seychas, moy brat," Victor said eerily, as if he didn't have much time left.
I will die now, my brother.
"Ya znaio shto ya bubu dyelat," Voodoo said firmly.
I know what I will do.
"Ubivayesh . . . fcyo!" Victor barked as he hung up.
Kill . . . everyone!

He looked up at Caesar, as his fingers toggled a few more keys. He then held it out, "They want to speak to you."

"The Russians?" Caesar asked as he reached for the phone.

Victor shrugged. "It's not my problem, now."

Caesar put the phone to his ear, "Hello?" He didn't hear anything. "Hello?"

He brought the phone down from his ear, looking at the screen. He saw a Russian flag waving in the wind, taking up the entire screen. And in the middle of the screen were the same words that were engraved on the *Zippo*.

Yob Tvoio Mat

"What is this?" Caesar said angrily. "There's nobody on line. Is this your idea of a game?"

Victor smiled proudly, knowing it might be his last words on this earth. "There is old saying in Russia. Yob Tvoio Mat. It mean . . . I'd fuck your mother!"

And then he reached down with his hand, cupping some of his own warm blood as he raised his red fingers to his face. He wiped the blood slowly across his face, leaving four lines of deep red across his cheeks and nose.

Caesar tossed the phone to Hector and then crossed his arms. "You Russians are all the same. Arrogant. You think you have everything figured out. You think this country is just a playground, and everyone in it is here for your amusement."

Victor snorted, "And who are you? Wanna-be Mexican from piss-ant little country. All you do is shoot guns and make babies. All you good for is to clean my pool. Fuck you!"

Caesar's rage was no longer hidden. He was so mad that the muscles in his chin were shaking. His eyes quivering. And what made it worse was that everyone in the room was standing with their mouths hanging open. Nobody speaks to a Mata like that. And especially not to their boss.

Caesar's eyes narrowed viciously, "Pepe . . . cut this piece of shit into a million pieces."

As Caesar turned and headed toward the door, Victor called to him, "Hey Caesar . . . you know where your name come from?"

Caesar turned, not answering, and looked at the thin, bleeding Russian, still as brave as ever.

"Your, name come from Czar," Victor said. "Which is like king in Russia. Read your history . . . all kings die in the end."

Caesar turned around and walked out.

And then the rest of them left the garage so that Victor and Pepe could be alone.

THIRTY-SIX

VOODOO RACED DOWN the small streets that led to Victor's house. This was a nice neighborhood. The kind of place that hitmen and assassins weren't supposed to live. But then, this was the kind of place where Victor fit in perfectly. He was the kind of guy who people couldn't help but to like. He had been like a brother to Voodoo.

A mentor.

He had never once asked for anything from Voodoo except his loyalty. And they had a pact between them: Whichever one of them died first, the other would seek revenge.

No questions asked.

Voodoo pulled his black *Maserati* onto Victor's street, driving slowly to see if anyone was watching the house. He circled the block twice, moving in each direction, to be completely sure.

Finally, satisfied that it was safe, he pulled into the driveway and stopped the car. He sat for a moment, thinking about all of this. He knew where Victor had been, thanks to the GPS locating system that was linked to their phones.

By now, most likely, his friend was long dead. And it probably wasn't an easy death, either. Knowing Victor's mouth, he probably experienced a rare kind of tormenting and violence. Victor's last moments on this earth were likely filled with agonizing pain, and hysterical laughter. That's just the way he was.

Voodoo knew that Victor could look death in the face and smile because he had a surprise in store for his tormentors.

And so, following his pact with his Russian brother, he would kill them.

All of them.

He would kill anyone involved. And anyone even close to them. He would kill anyone who even looked funny at him.

After he walked into the house, he smelled the place. Cigarette smoke and new carpet, and cabbage. Victor loved cabbage.

Voodoo found himself in the living room, staring straight ahead at the large picture of Red-Square. " . . . *remember Red-Square* . . . " Victor had said.

Voodoo walked slowly forward, studying the picture. Delicately he outstretched his hand and knocked it against the glass in the frame. The picture rattled a bit, as if there was space behind it.

Carefully he reached up and removed the picture. Behind it was a small, grey panel. He set down the painting and felt around the edges of the panel. A piece of the panel slid to the side to reveal a keypad that was labeled with Russian letters.

"You sly devil," Voodoo said to himself as he studied the panel. He knew what the code was without even thinking. Slowly he keyed in, 'Y-O-B-T-V-O-I-O-M-A-T'

"I'd fuck your mother, "Voodoo laughed as he finished typing.

Victor used to say that all the time. He used to say it was just a slang phrase in Russia. But from the way Victor was around the ladies . . . it was probably more true than not.

A few strange noises sounded behind the wall as Voodoo backed away. Then the entire wall lowered down into the floor behind the couch.

Voodoo's eyes widened, "You clever bastard."

There were shelves full of weapons—Sniper rifles, machine guns, grenades, knives, pistols, silencers, and every kind of specialty bullet he could imagine.

This was one of those collections that Federal Agents make their careers by busting. And these weren't the kind of weapons that you would find at *Walmart*, or even at your local gun show. These were weapons designed for warfare.

For the hunting and killing of humans.

Voodoo quickly did his estimation of the army he would encounter. He figured at least ten men. But they might be expecting him, so he'd need a rifle to take targets from a distance.

His eyes locked on a *Barret Light-50*. It could take targets nearly two miles away. That ought to be fine. He removed the rifle from the shelf and set it on the soft grey carpet behind him.

He gathered up a pair of *H&K USP* 9mm pistols with silencers, several magazines, and set them down near the *Barret*.

Voodoo then considered what his room-clearing weapon would be. Normally the tool for the job was the *H&K Mp-5* submachine gun. It was small, light, easy to shoot, and never had any problems. The *Mp-5* also shot 9mm, which was good because he could carry the same ammunition for his primary weapon and his secondary pistols.

There were so many choices, but in the end, his gut instinct was the *Mp-5*. He grabbed the version with the retractable stock, several magazines, and a green laser sight. He set it all behind him.

Then, thinking about Victor and the way he probably died, he stared down at the couch. He nodded. *Yeah*, he thought, *this is what Victor would have wanted.*

He reached down and toggled the button on the side of the couch, the cushions popping up to reveal the wooden crate.

The black metal crowbar was still sitting on the crate as he kneeled down, using it to pry open the top of the crate.

Again, his eyes studied the blackish-green tube. In Russian, written in yellow writing, were firing instructions on the side of the hand-grip. But it was as simple as a disposable camera.

The *SA-7b Grail*, surface-to-air, Man Portable Air-defense System (*Man-PAD*). This particular Russian missile was an infra-red guided system that could track targets a mile away, and chase them down faster than the top speed of any civilian airplane.

Just point and shoot!

This, he thought, might come in handy if things got sideways. He carefully took the *SA-7* and set it near the other weapons. He then gathered up several hundred rounds of ammunition and started loading magazines.

35 minutes later all of his gear was loaded and ready, placed carefully inside a large black dive-bag. He grabbed a *Spectrafoam* shirt to go under his assault vest. It wouldn't stop any heavy rounds, but as far as pistols, he would be able to take a couple of hits before he went down.

He folded the couch back shut, and grabbed several grenades from the shelves before closing up the wall-safe.

He suited up in a grey *Nomex* flight suit, similar to what race car drivers and fighter pilots wear. Then he slid on a climbing harness, tightening it to his waist.

Voodoo carted all of his gear to the front door and then carefully studied the front yard, and adjacent houses, to see if there were any new vehicles. Satisfied that it was safe, he unlocked the door and headed to his *Maserati*.

Quickly he popped the trunk and set the large black bag inside, careful that nothing unintentional could occur. He would hate to hit a bump and accidentally launch a surface-to-air missile inside the car.

He closed the trunk and made his way back to Victor's house. The place seemed darker, sadder, now that he was gone. Voodoo felt that frog in his throat. That emptiness of knowing that he was alone, again.

"Goodbye, Victor Pavlovich," he whispered as he backed out of the door.

It was time to go and do what he did best. He was like an artist, summoned to paint one last masterpiece. And this time there were no hostages to rescue.

Nobody to save.

He didn't have to be careful who he hit.

Anyone in his way . . . was a target.

THIRTY-SEVEN

VOODOO BROUGHT THE *Maserati* to a stop, a few hundred feet from the main highway. He had copies of the maps he had printed off of the internet, showing the exact location where Victor had last been. And from the satellite pictures, the house was a classy affair. It didn't take much to pinpoint the location, and then get information about the house. The Internet has just about everything, if you know where to look.

Voodoo's research, along with a little side cash, led him to the blueprints of the house. The owner of the property was listed as Juan-Carlos Gutierrez. It had been built within the last ten years, in a kind of art Deco style.

From the floor plans it looked like a lot of big, rectangular, open rooms throughout. Lots of high, stepped ceilings, and a large, fully landscaped lot surrounding the masterpiece. It screamed famous actor, or drug dealer. Nobody else would be able to live in a place like that. It was the kind of house that captured the essence of Hollywood glamour, but without the headache of actually being in L.A.

Voodoo glanced at his watch, realizing that to wait for the sun to set would take too long. He needed to start his assault soon, before his targets left their nest.

His car was parked in a thick mat of medium-sized trees. He was far enough from the main road that nobody would be able to see him. He got out of the car, went quickly to the trunk and opened it.

The *Barret Light-50* was his first choice of tools. He carefully removed it, along with several, lead-lined bags. He wasted no time walking back through the trees, and finding a spot where he could look down on the house.

He laid the weapon out, using a large piece of plastic to keep his equipment off of the ground. He gently settled down onto his stomach, and pulled out a small spiral notebook. It had all sorts of adjustments for every possible type of shooting scenario. He checked the temperature, measured the windage, and took a distance measure.

53 degrees Fahrenheit.

5 to 8 mile-per-hour wind, coming from his left side.

The front gate of the property was just at 1830 meters. And the house was another 260 meters beyond that.

He flipped a few pages, matching the windage and temperature. He made the adjustments on the scope. He flipped a few more pages, and found the appropriate elevation adjustments.

He then settled behind the scope, slowly dialing the elevation knob to its correct mark. The house came into focus. And the blueprints and Internet pictures did not do it justice.

The place was incredible.

It looked like it could have been a modern art museum. It was an off-white, two-story mansion. Every corner being cut at sharp 90 degree angles. The hedges were short and square cut. The windows were large and rectangular, divided into small rectangular pieces by grey framing.

As he looked through the scope he could see just the hint of a swimming pool off to the left of the house, near a large pool house that had a second-floor balcony. It was the same color as the main house. Throughout the grass were long, grey concrete slabs, with thin lines of cropped grass between.

And not far from the edge of the pool, there was a flat area in the grass where a helicopter was parked.

Voodoo realized that this was probably a five-million dollar home. And as he counted the guards he gathered that they were going to put up a fight to protect it.

There were several ways he could go about this assault. He could start hitting guards, hoping to cause enough panic that everyone gathered inside the house, at some location where he would be able to corral them. The problem was that any position they took up would be a defensible one. And they would have him considerably outnumbered.

A panic might also send them running to the helicopter, which would be nice, but then he would have to hope that those responsible were actually in the helicopter. An idea came to his mind. Something Victor used to say about fighting against tanks. Stop the tank, then shoot the men as they escape.

He focused on the helicopter, aiming just under the large rotor. Without taking his eyes off of the sight picture, he slid his right hand around and unzipped the lead-lined bag. He pulled out a DU (Depleted Uranium) round, and slid it into the rifle as he pulled the bolt back.

He began to blink very quickly, as he closed the bolt. If he did this right, he could hit the helicopter, disabling it, without causing a panic. Most of the guards were scattered around the grounds, so none of them would even see the .50 caliber round hit the helicopter.

He flattened his body completely, breathing in and out, and then he tensed his trigger finger, ever so lightly.

Boom!

The bullet traveled the 2126 meters so fast that by the time the sound arrived, the rotor of the helicopter had already been removed. The blades crashed into the grass, falling around the cockpit of the helicopter loudly.

"Damn!" he said, realizing that the shot was overkill.

As the crack echoed around the space between Voodoo and the mansion, the guards suddenly became aware of something unnatural.

Voodoo quickly loaded a small magazine with five rounds in it. Well, the element of surprise was gone. But he could still even up the playing field a bit.

Chance always favored the attacker.

$$ \} \} \} $$

"What the fuck was that?" one of the guards said, turning back and looking towards the house. His eyes searched nervously, his *AR-15* strapped to his back. He fumbled frantically for the weapon.

Another guard jogged towards him, "Did you hear that?"

When the first guard looked up he saw the man ripped apart, near the upper chest. It was like his body had been hit with a bolt of invisible lightening. The man fell into pieces on the lawn as the second loud crack sounded.

The guard grabbed his *AR-15* and spun around, looking out into the surrounding trees and undeveloped land. It was the faceless hitman . . . he knew it. He ducked down as he reached for his radio. But he never got to make the call.

His head exploded as if it had been a water balloon smashed against the concrete. A mist of red and grey puffed into air as his body fell to the ground, shaking and contorting like a chicken with its head cut off.

People in the house were starting to run around, lights were being cut off, and orders were being screamed.

Inside the house Felipe ran to the window, watching as two guards near one of their *Suburban's* were chopped to bits by something powerful.

It looked like Juan-Carlos' funeral all over again. The men would be cut in half, and then a second later there would be a horrible crackling sound. It sounded like a storm. He backed away from the window, "Get away from all of the windows as quickly as you—"

Crack!

Felipe's body was separated into several pieces both by the bullet, and by the sharp pieces of glass that followed it into his body.

Hector and Caesar dropped to the ground, their men running
in every direction, flipping up tables and furniture to use as cover.

"Necesitamos a salir!" Hector yelled.

We need to leave!

Caesar's eyes darted around anxiously. "There's nowhere to go. We don't know how many of them there are."

"The helicopter, then?" Hector asked crawling towards the granite-covered bar near the back of the living room.

"See if you can get any of the men to check it out!" Caesar yelled as another crack sounded, sending one of his men cartwheeling

into the swimming pool in several pieces.

"Dios mio!" Caesar gasped.

My God!

He backed himself up to a black-bricked fireplace, pulling light brown and tan leather furniture with him. He had expected some kind of retaliation from the assassin, but certainly not this quickly. "Where is Pepe?"

"I'm up here, Caesar!" Pepe yelled from the second floor. He was on his belly, crawling towards a window to get a better look at their attacker. "He's in the trees somewhere!"

"Stay down!" Caesar yelled. "And get some men in here. He can't kill what he can't see. There's no direct window access to the back of the living room."

A cold breeze was whistling through the house, between the muffled yells of men, the sound of furniture being scrapped across the polished concrete floor, and the moaning of a man who had been shredded by pieces of flying glass when Felipe was hit.

} } }

Sprinting back to the car, Voodoo tossed the *Barret Light-50* in the trunk, grabbed his assault vest and *Mp-5*, and made his way back to the driver's seat. He needed to get through the front gate of that house in the next two or three minutes. He was about to see how this *Maserati* handled off-road.

Bouncing and bumping, he did his calculations as he dodged large trees and smaller stumps. He had taken out the engine blocks on all of their vehicles. The only way anyone was going to leave that property was on foot, or inside a body bag.

He had created such dismay and terror, that nobody would chance leaving the house. He had already hit six guards and four different vehicles. And the body parts were scattered all over the property, just close enough for the lucky ones inside the house to see the dead bodies jerk and spasm. That kind of thing will keep a person pinned down.

Voodoo heard the bottom of the car bottom out, screeching loudly several times as he made it to a cross street. He slammed the accelerator as he made his way to the long, curved driveway that led to the house's front gate.

}}}

In the house, everything was quiet. Only nervous, hysterical breathing breaking the eerie quiet that had fallen on all of them.

"Maybe they're gone . . . " Hector whispered as he crawled from the bar. Moments earlier he had shook his head after seeing the helicopter's rotor bent and twisted on the grass beside the pool.

Caesar glanced across the room. Several of his guards were sitting with their backs against the concrete walls, their guns at their chests. They were all waiting for something to happen.

"Do you think this is Ronnie and his guys?" Pepe barked. "Trying to pay us back for Reggie?"

Caesar counted his men. Hector, Pepe, Julio, and four others. Eight of them altogether.

"No," Caesar said, his voice just above a whisper. "This is the Russian's man."

"How do you know?" Hector said, his voice laden with fear. "There could be twenty men out there!"

Caesar checked the nickel-plated .45 pistol, making sure it had a full magazine, and that it was chambered. "It's the Russians. It always had been. We didn't pay attention. Who knows if they followed you back from wherever you grabbed him?"

He took a breath, "Maybe they've been hunting us. I don't know. But this is not the Royals. I'm guessing, they're probably all dead, too."

All of a sudden there was an explosion in the back, near the pool house. White clouds rose from a tiny canister, filling they yard with a thick fog that surrounded everything.

"Smoke grenade," Pepe said as he walked in a crouch across living room with two pistols pointed towards the back door.

The smoke started to pour in from every side of the house as they heard several more pops.

"It won't be long, now . . . " Caesar said, both of his hands on the .45, waiting for something to happen. There was no escape. His only chance was to bait the assassin into chasing one of his other men. The smoke, it works as cover for all of them.

Sure, they couldn't see him . . . but then, he couldn't see them either.

} } }

Voodoo found the lowest point in the wall, near a tree, and scaled it as fast and quietly as he could. Landing on the other side in a crouch, he saw the blanket of white smoke.

Perfect.

He reached to his side and pulled out a pair of thick goggles, similar to those he had used at the housing projects. But these were different. They didn't see tiny bits of light . . . they saw heat. They were thermal-imaging goggles, used by firefighters to save people in burning buildings.

What he saw were bits of grey and black, mixed in with the red, orange, yellow, and green colors of body heat. He could literally see through walls with these goggles. The only problem was that it was difficult to negotiate through a house, due to the fact that furniture and fixed objects didn't show very clearly. But he most certainly could see through the smoke.

He would just have to be careful where he stepped.

He fixed the goggles into place and scanned the yard. He brought his *Mp-5* around from his back, tightening the sling so he would have a steady shooting platform.

In little splashes of yellow and orange, he saw the bits and pieces of the men he had engaged with the sniper rifle. They were cooling, the colors of yellow and red and green, as the heated blood met the cool afternoon air.

He made his way to the side of the house, opposite the helicopter and swimming pool. He checked the closest room for signs of life. Nothing.

He lifted the goggles and noticed that the room was a bedroom. Inside was a large blue painting of an old hotel. On the wall were several small pictures of old men, and a thick, white-framed bed sat in the middle.

Of course the window was not locked. Why would it be? Certainly, these men had never expected this kind of assault on their palace. With a delicate precision he opened the window just enough to drop in another smoke grenade. He pulled the pin and rolled the canister over towards the comfortable-looking white-silk bed. He slipped back on the goggles and headed around the house.

He heard the muffled *pop!*

}}}

Everyone in the living room heard the noise, all of their heads turning at the same time.

"Somebody's in the bedrooms!" Caesar said tensely. He nodded towards a pair of guards. Reluctantly, they picked themselves up and headed towards the long hallway that led to the living quarters.

There were three bedrooms that they had to investigate. And none of them wanted any part of it. But then, it was better than waiting around to be killed.

}}}

Voodoo entered the kitchen. It was all black marble with stainless steel counter tops and brown-leather barstools. *Very nice*, he thought to himself as he slid in.

In his right hand, the steadied *Mp-5*. In his left, a flash bang was armed, the pin still dangling from his vest.

Inside the goggles he could see an accumulation of rich, warm colors in the living room area. He walked as slowly as he could, not letting his body make any noise as he neared the far side of the kitchen. He counted six outlines of bright color.

Six humans

Six targets.

With a practiced flick of the wrist, the flash-grenade was tossed into the living room as he backed away. He opened his mouth, covered his ears, and closed his eyes.

}}}

Ba-boom!
Caesar and his men felt the concussion of the blast at the same time they were blinded by the brilliant flash. It knocked them down onto the floor, grasping for their guns.

Caesar dropped his pistol, and couldn't see anything but a strange white-blue outline. He couldn't hear anything but a slight humming in his ears. Somebody had instantly taken the world away from him. All around him, he heard gunshots. Little bursts of three or four rounds, followed by gurgles or yelps, like dogs being hit by a large, truck.

Caesar could feel the life draining out of the room.

}}}

Voodoo made sure that he left each person in the room a little warmer than they had been. One by one, he fired on each of them as they stumbled around, silencing them quickly. Satisfied that he had killed all of them, he pulled off his goggles and ducked down. There should be two more entering the room at any moment.

Like clockwork, in they ran. Voodoo sprayed the hallway with 9mm rounds, dropping the two men instantly.

And then it was quiet, again. He crawled to a corner of the room so that nobody would sneak up behind him. He then put the *Mp-5* on his back, and pulled out one of the *USP 9s*. And he waited for Caesar to come to.

Caesar wiped at his eyes, hoping to get his vision back. And from the outer edges of his sight, he started to see colors and shapes. "Who are you?"

There was no answer.

Voodoo removed a small picture from one of his vest pockets. It was a picture of Caesar, taken several weeks ago, outside of some club.

"Whatever you're being paid," Caesar pleaded, " . . . 1 will triple it. You work for money, just like I do. You've already killed my men. This is a good business decision for you. I'll just disappear.

"Who killed the Russian?" a cold voice said from within the darkness.

"It was an accident," Caesar said worrisomely. "One of my men acted outside of my direction. He—"

"Go out with some dignity, Caesar," Voodoo said. "Meet this moment with courage and honor."

"I'll pay you ten times what they're paying you!" Caesar begged, turning in every direction trying to find out where the assassin was hiding.

"Can you bring Victor back to life?"

Caesar turned toward the corner, seeing a strange shadowy figure in the cloud of smoke. "Victor says *hello*."

Voodoo pulled the trigger three times, very quickly. Two to the chest, one to the upper lip. And then it all went black.

As Caesar's body dropped to the floor, he followed it, standing over him, both hands on the *USP 9*, pointing down at the dead body.

Gritting his teeth, seeing Victor smiling, Voodoo emptied the rest of the magazine into Caesar's limp body. He dropped the pistol, letting it bounce empty off of the hard floor. Taking a deep, slow breath he backed away.

It was over, now.

He turned, realizing that police would be here shortly. Especially with the smoke. He made his back through the kitchen and out into the yard where he headed for the area in the wall he had climbed earlier.

He heard a pop from behind, and something sent him hurling
to the ground. It felt like he'd been tackled by an NFL linebacker. He rolled over quickly, unsure what had happened.

"You like that, puto!" Pepe said. "You miscounted. You should have killed everyone in the room."

Pop-pop!

He fired two more rounds into Voodoo's chest. It sucked the air from his lungs as he fought for breath. With a horrible smile on his face, the short El Salvadorian walked towards him, tossing the pistol to the side.

He pulled out a large, jagged machete.

"I used this to chop up your white friend, puto," Pepe joked as he skipped forward. Almost like he was dancing, he went from side to side, slicing the air with the machete.

Voodoo fought for air, feeling the pressure of the rounds in his vest. The *Spectrafoam* had stopped the bullets, but they had still broken a few ribs. This guy needed to suffer. He needed to feel what Victor felt. But Voodoo didn't know if he had the strength to do it.

Pepe was within a few feet of him, and he started laughing maniacally, like some twisted circus clown. And he was making such a show of it that he wasn't prepared for

Voodoo to pullout the second pistol from his thigh holster, firing two quick rounds into Pepe's leg.

The little man collapsed to the ground, the machete falling into the grass.

Voodoo slowly lifted himself, steadying the pistol on the small man, as he clutched his bleeding leg. He walked over to Pepe.

"You killed the Russian?"

"Fuck you, puto!"

Voodoo smiled. "No . . . fuck you."

He fired two shots into each knee, the little man screaming at the top of his lungs.

Pop-pop!

He fired a shot into each shoulder, pinning Pepe to the ground in a growing pool of blood.

Pop!

Pop!

And then he fired two into Pepe's lower stomach.

Pop!

Pop!

"It will probably take you about fifteen minutes to bleed out," Voodoo said as he kneeled over the dying man. "Victor says *hello*. I want you to think about that for a while."

Pepe tried to say something, but all he could do was cough up blood. His vision started to fade, and the strange man was suddenly gone.

He heard sirens in the back ground.

And then yelling.

Then, finally . . . nothing.

}}}

As the police cars raced down the long, curving driveway, something streaked by, just above their roofs. It struck the house, near the living room, locking in on the warm fireplace, and sending a ball of rolling flames and debris 50 feet in every direction.

And the Matas were no more.

THIRTY-EIGHT

LATER THAT NIGHT...

OFFICER ANTHONY FERRETTI heard the knock at the door. Two sharp thumps.

"It's open!" he yelled, turning back from his couch.

Voodoo walked in slowly, "Anthony, it's me . . . Ty."

Anthony nodded to himself, not sure what was supposed to happen now. "You, ah...want a beer? I got *Bud* in the fridge."

Voodoo made his way into the living room with a large envelope. He handed it to Anthony awkwardly. "Insurance papers."

Anthony took the envelope, laying it down in his lap. He looked up at Voodoo, seeing his suit and glasses. "You goin' somewhere?"

"Yeah," Voodoo said as he sat down in a small grey reclining chair. "I need to leave for awhile.

Anthony nodded. "It have anything to do with the other night?" And then he backpedaled, realizing he might have asked too much. "I mean, you ain't gotta tell me or nothin'."

318

Voodoo leaned forward, a slight smile on his face. He hadn't slept in quite a while. "I need to clean up a mess, that's all."

"You see all that shit that happened in the Hamptons?" Anthony said, motioning towards the television.

"Looks like a mess," Voodoo said as pictures of a burning foundation streamed by on the *Fox News Channel*.

"They're calling it a gas-line explosion," Anthony said. "Buddy of mine in the forty-eighth precinct tells me it went a bit different. Says somebody waxed a bunch of El Salvadorian mobsters. News is running with the gas thing for now. But then . . . I guess they'd have to, eh?" He studied Ty's face for a reaction.

"They probably won't find much," Voodoo said. "When a place burns that hot, there isn't much evidence left. And besides, who's going to miss a bunch of murderous gangsters?"

"Yeah," Anthony agreed. "You're probably right."

Voodoo sat up, visibly wincing from some pain in his chest. Three cracked ribs are difficult to hide.

"You alright?"

"Oh, yeah," Voodoo said. "I had a . . . fender bender. This jerk hit me from behind."

Anthony nodded, slowly looking down at the envelope. "What's it look like?"

"Open it."

Anthony poured out the contents of the envelope on his lap. There were several thick, stapled stacks of paper. And then a single blue sheet of paper. The officer squinted, looked up, and said, "What's this?"

Voodoo raised his eyebrows, "I don't know, what's it say?"

319

Anthony picked it up and read, his eyes growing larger by the second. He put the paper in his lap and looked up at Voodoo. "I don't . . . what account is this?"

On the paper was a detailed description of a trust account for $175,000.

Voodoo smiled, "That's your daughter's trust fund. She can't spend it unless it's for tuition, or a medical emergency. But the way it's invested, it should be doubled before she ever has to touch it."

"But I—"

"Don't worry," Voodoo interrupted, " . . . it's not in your name. And not traceable. It's set up with a British bank. *Atlantic International.*"

"I can't accept this," Anthony said.

"It's not for you, Anthony. It's for your daughter. And it's already done."

Voodoo stood up and extended his hand.

Anthony grasped his hand firmly, shaking slowly as he nodded.

Voodoo nodded, backed away, and slowly headed for the door.

"How long you gonna be gone?"

Voodoo stopped, turning his head halfway, " . . . I don't know. Couple of months. Maybe more." And then he continued to the door.

Anthony stood, turning towards the front of his condo, "Hey, Ty . . . "

"Yeah?" Voodoo said without turning back.

"Fuck'em! I hope you got everyone of those bastards."

Voodoo nodded, paused for a moment . . . then walked out the door.

EPILOGUE

VLADIMIR WALKED TO the side of the heated pool, squinting at the bright sun that was reflecting off of the crystal clear water, and the tall buildings around them. In his left hand was a folded *New York Post*. In his right, a small, burnt *Zippo* lighter with Russian engravings on it.

Nikolai Chyorni was sitting at the edge of the pool, his feet kicking back and forth in the water. His bleach white skin looked even more pale in the bright sun. He had on a pair of green swimming trunks, and a thick chain dangling around his hairless chest.

"Vlady," Nikolai said affectionately, " . . . what have you brought for me?"

"I have journal, and also . . . something . . . souvenir piece," Vladimir said, nodding to the four armed bodyguards that were sitting at a round umbrella table, looking out over the city.

Nikolai waved him over, a fat cigar between his fingers. "Harasho, harasho."

Good, good.

321

Vladimir handed him the *Post*, and then opened his left hand showing the *Zippo*. They glanced at each other, and Nikolai took the blackened lighter as if it was something holy they had discovered on an archaeological dig.

For several minutes neither of them spoke. They just looked at the small, charred *Zippo*. Victor's lighter.

Nodding, Nikolai said, "You know, Victor used to carry this damned thing around. All the time. He never let it go. Like it was the only thing he truly cared about."

"Victor was *real* criminal," Vladimir said reverently. "Hard. Cold. *Criminal*."

"Da," Nikolai agreed. "Victor helped to make everything fall into place." He then flipped the lighter open and somehow, it was still able to light a flame. They both laughed, surprised.

Shaking his head, the Russian Syndicate Boss lifted the *Zippo* to his cigar, lighting it, and puffing a few times slowly.

"To Victor," he said.

Vladimir nodded. He pointed to an article on the cover of the *New York Post*.

Nikolai puffed on his cigar as he opened up the paper. It outlined all of the gang-related murders that had occurred in the last few weeks. It said that the *'Notorious Black Royals'* and the *'Violent El Salvadorian Matas'* had all but wiped each other out.

Nikolai started to laugh. Slowly at first, and then more and more until he started to cough. "This is why I love America. You can do anything, and put a Hollywood spin on it. And they print it in their papers. Suddenly, our little game become fact."

He set the paper down, placing Victor's lighter on top, as he stood and stretched. He turned and handed Vladimir his

Cuban cigar, stretching his arms wide as he prepared to jump into the water.

Leaning forward, he shifted his wait. He lowered his body and just as he leapt forward . . . *thump!*

Something drilled right through the top of his head, painting the pool instantly red as Nikolai's headless body fell into the water, flopping on his stomach.

The sound of the splash covered all the other noise.

Vladimir stood up, his eyes confused, "Nikolai!"

"Nikolai?"

}}}

Quickly, he pulled the barrel of the rifle away from the tiny hole that had been cut in the window. He was about 400 meters away from the building where the dead Russian crime boss was floating in a roof-top pool.

They'll never get that blood stain out of the concrete, he laughed to himself as he broke his rifle down into smaller and smaller parts. He rolled the parts up into a length of black leather, and then covered it up with a blue beach towel. He grabbed his cell phone as he got to the door of the office, listening for anyone who might be in the hallway.

Since it was the weekend, there wasn't anyone working in the office he had borrowed. Hearing nobody he let himself out and headed towards the elevator. He pressed the 'Down' button and waited.

He pressed *Send*, and in his ear he heard the phone ring three times. He then hung up and stepped into the waiting elevator. Buy the time he made it down to the parking garage, he had already made the second call . . . to the same number.

"Law office?"

"My appeal is finished," he said, heading for his rental car.

"Good, then. I hope everything works out for you."

"You're a good man," he said as he unlocked his car, throwing in the towel, and closing the door.

"You, too," Special Agent Dan Gonzalez replied. "You, too."

disconnecting the call, he reached up and adjusted the rearview mirror. "Look at you," Alex Karsh said as he studied his face. "We need to get you a tan."

And with that he started the car, and backed out.

♪ ♪ ♪

Bronx Lebanon Hospital ...

Joy raced down the hallway, passing nurses and doctors as she made her way to the Intensive Care Unit. At a desk she asked a nurse, "Rufus Jones, please. What room is Rufus Jones staying in?"

The nurse typed quickly on her computer, and looked up, "Room ICU three. Just down the hall, on the left-hand side."

Joy ran down the hall, turning to the left, finding the bed. And there he was. She looked at all of the machines, and she began to feel sick.

A young doctor startled her, "Are you alright?"

Frantic, she asked him, "Is he going to make it . . . is he gonna live?"

The doctor smiled, nodding his head, "He's a tough one. We thought he wasn't going to pull through, but . . . he just kept on fighting."

"Can I speak to him?" Joy asked, tears running down her face.

"He won't be able to talk back to you," the doctor said delicately. But he realized that it was tearing this young woman apart, so he tried to comfort her, " . . . but it would do him good to hear a friend's voice."

She nodded, slowly approaching him. She saw all of the bags of blood and medicine, and strange noises and wires. She lowered her head to his face, kissing him gently.

"You're gonna make it, Ruthless. You're gonna be just fine."

} } }

PUERTA VALLARTA, MEXICO
2 WEEKS LATER . . .

Ronnie and Carmen sat on the private beach, laughing as they drank fruity drinks with umbrellas served in large glasses. The cool blue waters of the Pacific were breaking on the white beach sand, the smell of salt and grilled shrimp and fresh life surrounding them. The palm trees kept the sun off of them, while they talked. All of the madness was behind them.

They were thousands of miles away from anything to do with New York. And it was almost as if it was all a bad dream.

A dream that had ended the minute they stepped into their private beach house, south of downtown Puerta Vallarta. He could hear the sound of music coming from the bar that serviced the luxurious beach front houses on this strip of beach.

"You want another one of . . . whatever it is we're drinking?" Carmen said, reaching across her chair to kiss him. He tasted tequila and coconut on her lips.

"I want to eat *you* up," Ronnie said seductively. He then yelled, "Two more of these, senorita!"

They watched a passing cruise ship as the sound of feet in the sand signaled their drinks were ready.

Carmen started to turn towards the waitress when she saw Ronnie's head jerk forward, his body suddenly shaking and spazing as he fell off the chair and into the sand.

"Ronnie!?" Carmen yelped as she turned and saw the man with a silenced pistol in his hand.

Voodoo stared at her for a moment, shook his head, and then fired two shots into her head. Her body flopped sideways, off of the chair, falling on top of Ronnie's dead body. The couple bled quietly into the warm sand.

Voodoo put another shot in Ronnie's head, just to make sure the job was done, and walked past them, not wearing any shoes.

He walked to the edge of the water, turned left, and continued on down the beach as he stripped the pistol into several smaller pieces, throwing them into the water as he walked.

His footsteps made wet little puddles in the light brown sand, but as the foamy water washed in and out . . . they were gone.

Message delivered.

And like a ghost . . . so was Voodoo.

Contract Killer

A Novel
By
JIMMY DASAINT & NICHOLAS BLACK

The Notorious Black Royals, led by the infamous King brothers, and the violent El Salvadorian Matas, led by the dangerous Juan-Carlos, are two rival drug gangs fighting a war to control the streets of New York City.

In the midst of the violence and chaos is a mysterious man known only as **Voodoo**—a contract killer who will determine the final outcome of this turf war.

Contract Killer is a fast-paced novel, filled with sex, murder, and mayhem. It's a story that will keep you turning the pages to the very end.

Coming soon:

Contract
Killer 2

DASAINT ENTERTAINMENT ORDER FORM
Ordering Books
Please visit www.dasaintentertainment.com to place online orders.

Or
You can fill out this form and send it to:

DaSaint Entertainment
PO Box 97
Bala Cynwyd, PA 19004

Title	Price	QTY
Black Scarface	$15.00	_____
Black Scarface II	$15.00	_____
Young Rich & Dangerous	$15.00	_____
What Every Woman Wants	$15.00	_____
The UnderWorld	$15.00	_____
A Rose Among Thorns	$15.00	_____
On Everything I Love	$15.00	_____
Money Desires and Regrets	$15.00	_____
Contract Killer	$15.00	_____
Ain't No Sunshine	$14.99	_____

Make Checks or Money Orders out to: DaSaint Entertainment

Name: _____

Address: _____

_____

City: _____ State:_____ Zip:_____

Telephone: _____

Email: _____

Add $3.50 for shipping and handling
$1.50 for each additional book
($4.95 for Expedited Shipping)

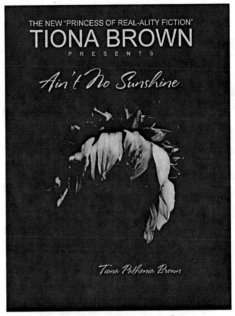

Ain't No Sunshine
A Novel By Tiona Brown

Coming soon:

Black Scarface III
The Wrath of Face